Greystoke's Confliction

Samanthya Wyatt

Love Endures

Also by

THE BROTHERS GREYSTOKE

The Daunting Greystoke (Book 1)
Greystoke Heir Apparent (Book 2)
Greystoke's Confliction (Book 3)

ONE AND ONLY COLLECTION

The Right One For Me (Book 1)
My Angel The True One (Book 2)
The Only One My Love (Book 3)

Acknowledgements

I'm so grateful to everyone who has helped to get the third book
in The Brothers Greystoke Trilogy published.
I'd like to thank my editors, my publishers, and the cover artist
who did a fantastic job. A special thank you goes to Keri at
NSP for getting me off to a rocking start, marketing my books.
Thanks to my friends' encouragement, the authors I have met,
and every person who bought my books. I sincerely hope you
enjoy reading them as much as I did creating the stories.
As always, I must recognize my husband, my main support and
source of encouragement.

Keep the Spirit!
Samanthya

Contents

Prologue

Brighton 1815

E nough of being trapped in his own guilt.

Aaron Christopher Linley Blackburn Greystoke sat in the dark, cramped space, being jostled against the unforgiving squabs as the coach navigated the rutted country roads. A hellish place he would have been content to never see again. The closer they drew to the manor, the more his guilt grew. The forbidding demon of his past, now cold and rotting in the ground, could not hold a candle to his new set of torments.

His brothers.

One he idolized. The heir. Couldn't blame Nathaniel for running off. After all, their detestable father was the one at fault. Castigating his eldest son at every instance, punishing him for nothing a 'tall. Aaron had wanted to flee with his brother. But he'd been too young at the time.

Then there was Edmund. The second son. Aaron supposed he was fortunate; although, he felt nothing of the sort. The guilt of betraying his brother weighed heavy on his chest. The three of them had come to an understanding since Nathaniel's return, but Aaron was not sure Edmund had forgiven him. How could one forgive the brother who had pitted the older two against each other?

Aaron had thought he was helping his middle brother. At least, that was his intention. Contacting the eldest seemed his only option when he found Edmund at the bottom of a bottle. And about to sell their family estate right out from under them. Nathaniel was the oldest, the rightful heir. Still, Edmund had seen it as a betrayal. And Aaron was still paying for his misstep.

He recalled the night his father passed. He stood at the foot of the master bed, cringing with ever raspy breath as he waited for his father to die. His middle brother had sent for their eldest brother, letting him know their father did not have much longer in this world. Nathaniel had come home.

"He came, Edmund. You sent for Nathaniel, and he came."

"Do not mistake our brother's arrival for anything other than what it is."

"And what is that?"

"Do you think he would have returned if I had not told him our father was dying?"

Aaron knew Nathaniel would not have come. He hated their father. Being the oldest, he had received the brunt of their father's wrath. Father showed no mercy to any of his children. But sometimes Aaron wondered if father hated his oldest. What other reason could there be for a father to treat his son thus?

"Father was not kind."

"Nor was he a dullard. Father was, however, an important man in the aristocracy."

"Did that give him the right to be cruel?"

"Did Nathaniel have the right to run away from his entitlement?"

Aaron cursed under his breath. "Entitlement. Is that what you call being beaten within an inch of his life?"

"Father got carried away, but Nathaniel was strong. It was never that bad."

"How can you say that?" Aaron shouted. It was worse than Edmund made it out to be. Their eldest brother never backed away *from their father's ire. He had saved Aaron from punishment more than once. If father had taken a stick to him, the way he had his older brother, Aaron would have whimpered and skulked away. But not Nathaniel. The more chastisement father dished out, the harder Nathaniel grew. He never cried out. He showed no emotion, other than hate.*

Father knew it. He saw it. And meted more abuse.

"He survived. We all did. Let it go, Aaron. Father will not live out the night."

Let it go? How?

Aaron gazed upon the pale white face of his father. Not much more than a skeleton, lying on the bed linen. His chest barely moved with each struggling breath. Once, he had thought the man a monster. A giant of a man, who could do anything. He could not pity the creature lying there. Whatever that made him, he simply could not do it.

It had taken a good number of months to get over that night. Not because his father died, but because his father still controlled his sons from the grave. Nathaniel left—again. Aaron thought, this time, he would never come back. It hurt, a lot, for Nathaniel had been his idol. Aaron had hero-worshiped his eldest brother, was proud and wanted to be just like him. As time went on, Nathaniel's absence created an empty place in Aaron's soul.

The carriage hit a hole in the road, nearly unseating him. He braced himself, scooted back against the squabs and crossed his arms, thinking he was prepared for the next set of bumps. He was not running, not exactly. There would be no distance far enough to escape the set of circumstances he had gotten himself into.

Edmund's angry face blazed before him. In a haze of red, his brother had thundered accusations Aaron knew he'd deserved.

He never meant to pit one brother against the other. All he had intended was for Nathaniel to come home and straighten out the mess Edmund had somehow created.

If it wasn't for those blasted megrims. Edmund was much too smart to allow himself to get caught in the clutches of a swindler. But he had. Aaron blamed himself for not noticing sooner that his brother was in trouble. It seemed reasonable that Edmund would take over running the estate since Nathaniel had rejected his inheritance. Edmund had always been the calm, rational brother, assessing a problem, then using his intellect to solve an issue, rather than using his fists. After Nathaniel took off, it'd come as no surprise when Edmund stepped into the role as if he had been born to the position, accepting the responsibilities without qualm. But then he became a recluse, hiding in his abode, never coming out in public. And when Aaron found another man accessing Greystoke Manor, their family home, he had confronted Edmund.

The showdown had not gone as he had expected. The altercation left him feeling helpless. So, he'd done the only thing he could, creating a quandary that laid him low.

The coach lurched, and the driver whistled to the team of horses. A footman opened the door and waited for Aaron to get out.

"Well, my good man. I see you have found us an inn."

The man muttered something, but Aaron was too deep in his musing to pay attention. He strode to the door, and as he was about to reach for the handle, the door opened. Another gent came out. Shouts of revelry and merriment echoed behind him. This carousing inn might be the perfect place to drink his maudlin thoughts away.

Few tables held occupants; most were empty. The rowdy bunch of drinking inhabitants took up two tables, seeming harmless enough. A man and woman sat at a corner table in the shadows, apparently sharing an evening meal. A single man sat at another, with his head propped up in his hands. And that was exactly what Aaron planned to do. Drink alone.

The wooden chair scraped the floor as he pulled it back. He dropped his hat onto the table's scarred surface, and then sat. A short man wiped his hands on his apron as he hurried over.

"Bring me ale, my good man."

"Yes, sir. Will ye be havin' supper this eve? My wife made a fine stew."

He had not eaten since his business with Anderson. He supposed he could spend the night here before heading home. It was a long ride north, and he was in no hurry to see his brother. Once again, a twinge pierced his chest. The way it did every time he thought of Edmund. Would the day ever come when thoughts of betrayal would not eat at his stomach? Perhaps if he were planning to drink himself stupid, he should have some sustenance in his belly.

He called to the man. "I will take your word for it. Bring the stew as well."

"Right away." The man went through a doorway where the most delicious smells were coming from. Yes, perhaps the food was a good idea.

Aaron guzzled the ale and ordered another. When the man brought the second ale, he also had a loaf of bread that apparently had just come from the oven. Aaron went to tear off a piece and nearly burned his fingers. He slathered butter, on the bread and his fingers, then moaned as the delicious bread melted in his mouth. "My word. Please give my compliments to your lady wife."

By the time he finished his stew, the boisterous men had gone. And he was back to thinking about his brothers, pondering what he had thoughtlessly brought about. Would his brother ever forgive him?

He had never meant for this to happen. His intention was to save his brother. Find out what plagued him. What else should he have done? Edmund would not listen. He had lost weight. He looked like the bloody devil. Aaron's worry convinced him he had to send word to Nathaniel.

Of course, Edmund saw it as treachery. Aaron had never meant to be disloyal. He had thought his brother was losing his mind and losing the family holdings as well. True, things had worked out. The three of them bonded together to get rid of the man threatening Edmund. Aaron supposed he understood Edmund's side of things. There was no other way to look at it. No matter the outcome, Aaron had gone behind Edmund's back. His brother would never forgive him. Aaron's soul was damned for hell.

If he had to dwell in this den of purgatory thriving inside his skull, he may as well drown the devils out.

He folded his linen, placed it next to his plate, and was about to call the innkeeper when the lonesome man at the next table got up, and chose to sit in the empty chair at Aaron's table. Before he could open his mouth, the man spoke.

"You got any kids?"

Lord, no.

"I am afraid not."

"Well, I do. A little girl as sweet as her mama."

Then why are you in this place instead of at home?

"She thinks I'm a good man." He sniffed.

Good God, the man is about to cry.

Most likely, the man was well into his cups. Aaron had noticed the poor sod sitting alone, but paid no attention to him after that.

"I need someone to talk to."

Aaron said the first thing that came to his mind. "Perhaps your wife?"

The older man waved his hand. "Naw. Hey, Radner. Bring me another, and one for me friend."

Aaron glanced at the glass in the man's hand.

Whisky.

No wonder the fellow was maudlin. Aaron gave a shrug. After all, had he not planned to do the same thing? He had no place to be, no one to report to, and he planned on spending the night at this inn. Having a drinking companion topped the thought of going back home.

An hour later, or three or four, Aaron had learned very little, and divulged a lot. How had he done most of the talking? Although he had learned the man's name. Colvin. Every time Aaron thought to call it a night, Colvin had sniffed and started to cry. Then he would order another drink. Now the fool was blubbering. Aaron had imprudently consumed his share of whisky and wanted to seek out his own bed.

"Come on, you ole' coot." The innkeeper was standing over Colvin. "You need to git home. My wife and me is goin' to bed."

"All right, all right. I'm a goin'." Colvin pushed out of his seat, and landed promptly on the floor.

"You want to spend the night?" the innkeeper asked.

"No, no. I've got to git home to Rebekah."

Rebekah.

Must be his daughter. He had talked about his little girl all evening.

Aaron leaned down to help the man up. Colvin was limp as a wet noodle. It was all Aaron could do to keep Colvin from falling again.

"Maybe you better take the innkeeper up on his offer and stay here tonight."

"I can't. Gotta git home to my girl. She's all alone."

What kind of man left a child alone?

Aaron glanced to the innkeeper.

"Yep. She stays home by herself."

"What about the mother?"

"Died a few years back. He comes in here a lot since then, but I ain't never seen him this bad."

Hearing that did not speak well of the innkeeper either. Both men were dolts. Aaron decided he should escort the man home. If for no other reason than to make sure his little girl was all right.

"I will help you home, Colvin. Are you able to walk?"

"Why, sure," he cackled with glee.

"Do you know where you live?" he could not help asking. Just how drunk was Colvin?

"I can show ya. Come on." Colvin turned, and Aaron waited for him to fall again, which did not happen.

Perhaps the cool wind sobered Colvin up a bit. He seemed to get his second wind once they made it outside. Aaron stepped quick to keep up with the wiry man.

"Do you have a horse?"

"Naw. Couldn't feed it if'n I did."

"You walked to the inn?"

"Sure."

I suppose that was a dumb question.

"How far is your house?"

"Just up that hill, yonder."

Aaron tugged up the collar of his coat, and followed Colvin up the hill.

As he reached the rise, he spotted a small shack with a dull light filtering through a window. He supposed the wife had left a lamp lit for her husband. But—oh yes, the wife died. Colvin had said his little girl was alone. Aaron shook his head. He would find out soon enough.

As he neared the little house, he realized it was not as small as he first thought. Nor was the dwelling as close. The vast distance would account for the mistaken judgement in size. Colvin opened the door, not bothering to be quiet, and stomped inside. Aaron removed his hat and followed. The house was empty, but neat. Everything in its place. A sofa and two chairs were in the middle of the space. A stone hearth was on one wall with a healthy fire burning, as if someone had added logs recently.

Not a sign of a woman or a child. No sound came from anywhere in the house. To the right, a framed doorway showed another room was located in back. Next to it, a staircase rose to the upper floor. He supposed a bedroom was up there for Colvin, a second for his child. If anyone was awake, they had to hear the two of them come in.

"Is your family here?" he asked Colvin.

"Awww, she's in bed."

He supposed he meant the little girl. Colvin never said how old she was. "Are you sure?"

"'Course, I'm sure. Now. Sit down and let's have a drink."

"No, thank you. I will be on my way."

The damned man began to cry, in all earnest.

"Good God, man. Do you want your daughter to wake up and see you like this?"

"Please. I need another man to talk to. I need advice."

In for a penny ...

Aaron should have kicked his own arse, but he gave a nod and allowed himself to be hustled through the doorway, to a table in a modest kitchen. Colvin grabbed a bottle out of a cabinet, and then two glasses from another. Aaron glanced around the space as he waited. The man might not be an aristocrat, but he was no pauper either. Embroidered linen lie on the surface of a small table in front of a window. A woman was definitely in attendance, if the linen and cleanliness was anything to go by. Perhaps his daughter had not been alone. Perhaps another woman had taken care of the child.

Aaron was used to staff taking care of him. He had grown up with servants, and now he had his own staff to clean his house and cook his meals. And, of course, his aunt lived with him. She made sure his home was smart and trim, everything in its proper place. The floors clean enough that one could eat off them, if one so desired. So, he knew a thing or two about how a house should be kept. This one was no exception. Someone had taken the time to be tidy. Colvin was a lucky man.

But he was blubbering again.

Good God. Aaron would stay until the man passed out.

Hopefully it would be soon.

But as it turned out, Aaron was the one who could not keep his eyes open. He could not shake the cobwebs from his mind. He thought he was standing. Someone was leading him to a ... bed? It could not be. Colvin was pickled. And for himself ... he must be dreaming.

Then ... what was happening?

And why could he not shake the fog he was floating in?

⁓ⅇⅇ⁓

Rebekah tried to go back to sleep. Knowing that her father had brought a drinking crony home set her pulse to pounding. It was bad enough he went to the tavern. But this night he dared to bring home a drunkard with him.

How could he?

Her father had taken to drinking three years ago, right after her mother died. Rebekah had only been seventeen, at an age when a young woman needed her mother. At first, he'd hid the bottles from her. She had known of his newfound pastime, but never said a word. After all, she missed her mother, too. Then he took to drinking in town.

Her parents had been close. The three of them a team, so to speak. They had done everything together. Well, pretty much everything. Papa would help her mother cook sometimes. He often helped Rebekah with her reading while mother prepared supper. He even took her, Rebekah, with him hunting for food. She held the squirrels and rabbits by the neck while he stripped the hide from their little backs. Papa believed that his child should know the true facts of life. No timid girl for his offspring, which meant no rabbits for pets. Animals were for food. Nothing went to waste. Every part of the animal was used. And what they didn't need, her father traded. He did not believe in spoiling his daughter, but they had shared some tender moments. She remembered once, he had given her a strand of beads.

Nothing foolish, Mother. Every girl deserves a bit of sparkly. And this one is for you.

Rebekah recalled the flush on her mother's face, and the endearing smile her mother gave her father. The last few years had been heartbreaking to see the sadness in her father's eyes. So, if he took a bottle or two for comfort, or spent an evening in the tavern, who was she to complain?

Crash!

But she would not stand for him bringing home his drinking companions.

She tossed the coverlet to the side and slid her feet to the cold floor. She grabbed her socks first, then after slipping them on, she grabbed her robe. Papa's company would just have to see her at her worst.

She clomped down the wooden stairs very unladylike. Mother had taught her manners, but at the moment, Rebekah did not feel hospitable. She would not allow a drunkard to tear up her home.

"What ya doing down here, girl?"

"I've come to see that you and your *friends* don't smash everything in the house."

"What ya talking about? No friends. Now go back to bed."

She glanced about. No other—then she saw a man on the floor. Passed out.

"No friends? Who is that?" She pointed to the man on the floor.

"One friend. Now, mind yer pa. Go back to bed."

"What do you plan on doing with him?"

"Not for you to worry. Now go on." He came toward her, moving his hands in a shooing direction.

"Oh, Papa. Why did you bring him to our home?" She bent down on her knees, to check to see if the man was breathing. She smoothed the hair from his face—a very handsome face. His hair was not dirty, but smooth as silk.

"Go on with ya, girl. Stop that."

Rebekah noticed his clothes. A nobleman.

A nobleman? Here with her father?

She glared up at him. "Who is this man? What have you done?"

"Not a thing. I met him in the tavern. We had a few drinks."

She was beginning to wonder if perhaps the alcohol had turned her father's mind into mush. Good Lord. A gentleman. On her floor, in her kitchen.

"Papa. If I am not mistaken, this man is an aristocrat." She glanced down, taking in the limp figure on her floor. A tall man, if she had her guess. Well dressed. Leather Hessians. This man was no pauper. She really should not leave him lying on the floor, but she had to get her father to tell her the truth. "Did you hit him?"

"What? No."

"Then how did he get on our floor?"

"Now, wait a minute, Becky." Papa called her Becky when he wanted something. Rebekah, when he was scolding her.

"Just tell me. Who is he? What did you do?"

"I'm gettin' a mite tired of you accusin' there, girl. He's a gent, true. He fell. Had too much to drink."

"You should not bring your ..." It was too late now. She heaved a sigh. "Why is he here?"

"Well ... I couldna' leave him like this in the tavern. Radner was closing up. I couldna' let him throw the man out into the muck."

She crossed her arms, folding them under her breasts. A sign that she did not believe him, which did not go unnoticed by her father. He began to squirm.

"Well, ya see, uh ... Dad blast it, girl. Let's get him off the floor."

She helped her father drag the man, carefully, over to the sofa, then heave him up. Which was not easy to do since he was of considerable size. She'd guessed correctly at his height. His legs dangled over the end of the sofa's arm.

"I'm plum tuckered out. I'm going to bed."

"Oh, no you don't. Tell me who he is."

"I can't think now, girl. Leave me be." Her father suddenly seemed more intoxicated than he had a moment ago. Most likely he was trying to put her off.

"Very well, then. Go. But do not think I will let you off so easily tomorrow morning. Friend or no. Foul head or no."

He waved a hand in her direction while heading in the opposite. He climbed the stairs, his boots clanging out every weary step.

"Now what am I to do with you," she asked the sleeping man, expecting no response. She supposed she should make him a bit more comfortable. However, there was nothing she could do about the length of the sofa. At least it was not as hard as the floor.

She glanced down taking in his awkward position. Bent at the hips, partly on his side, one leg twisted and the other bent at the knee where his boot hung down, nearly touching the floor. That had to be uncomfortable. By morning, he would have several kinks in his back and his neck, along with a pounding headache. She thought to straighten the leg, but was unsure how to go about it. Finally, she went to the end of the sofa, grabbed him by the boot and tugged.

A sound came from his mouth, making her freeze. When she heard no more, her shoulders relaxed. Next, she thought to relieve him of his boots. The darn things were heavy. She pulled and tugged, and huffed and puffed, and finally got one off. She had second thoughts of tackling the other one. Well, she could not leave the man like this. So, for a second time, she pulled and tugged. The second one came off no easier than the first. She wiped her forehead with the back of her arm. My goodness, what a chore. She gathered the footwear and placed them out of the way, by the hearth.

When she leaned over to collect a blanket from the back of the sofa, his arm moved. His hand brushed her thigh.

A jolt of electricity shot through her body. She caught her breath. Suddenly, she found herself lying on top of him.

"Mmmm ..."

Oh my. His lips vibrated against her throat. She should scream. She couldn't breathe. Nor could she move. He was hot. So hot. His hands heated everywhere he touched. Right now, they molded her back, pressed her into his muscled chest. Glory of all glories, he felt divine.

She dared a peek at his face. His eyes were heavy lidded, with barely an opening for hm to look through. Was he looking at her? Or was he still asleep?

His hand squeezed her buttock. She stiffened in shock. A corner of his mouth lifted in a slight smile.

Should she call out? Maybe if she remained immobile, he would—

Perhaps not.

She pulled back, his arms tightly locked about her. The man took liberties. She jerked from his embrace, causing him to roll to the floor.

She placed her hands on her hips as she stared down at him. The man must be completely foxed, since he did not wake. Well, he could just stay there. It would serve the bounder right.

Drat.

Even if the floor was clean, he would not be comfortable. She could not leave him on the hard floor without at least a blanket.

He mumbled something. When she turned, his hand slid up her calf.

Good Lord.

She bent down to brush his hand away. He grabbed her arm.

"Where do you think you're running off to?"

Dropping the blanket, she used both hands to right herself, but the blasted devil had more arms than an octopus. Suddenly, she was on the floor with him.

His eyes were closed, again. She screwed up her face trying to judge if he was play-acting. He mumbled again. Now was her chance to rise, but instead, she leaned closer to hear his slurred words. She felt the heat of his breath as he kissed her cheek. She froze. Not at all unpleasant, but she should not—

One hand brushed her hair, another cupped her cheek. Then he placed both hands, one on each side of her head and whispered. While she was trying to make out his words, he kissed her on the lips. She opened her mouth in shock. And he inserted his tongue.

Fire shot from her belly to her toes. She had been kissed before, but never like this. The physical contact was so intimate … The man's tongue … uh, his tongue … ummm

She forgot what she was … *oh my* …

Goose bumps broke out over her skin. He was sinfully delicious.

She did not know what was more shocking. The fact that the man had her locked in his iron grip, or that she liked being there. Her stomach felt funny, and her head giddy, as if she was the one who had been drinking. All her nerve endings were tingling.

His fingers continued their sensual assault, over her shoulders and around one side to … She gasped. His fingers lightly brushed the side of her breast. Then his full hand cupped her.

Glory be, this was intoxicating. The caress so glorious, she nearly moaned. She caught the sound just before it escaped, fearing she might wake him. Was he truly asleep? Could a man do such things and not be awake?

Nonsense. Besides, she didn't want to find out. At the moment, she was lost in the sensations rolling through her body.

And what wonderful sensations they were. As long as she pretended he slept, she could explore these new feelings without guilt.

One hand molded her back, pressing her into his chest. The other kneaded her breast, caressing the round globe as if he were cuddling a precious object. Perhaps measuring the depth and breadth to his memory.

It was mindboggling. Thrilling. He took her mouth in another kiss, slower than the first. She wondered if he felt the same tingling awareness as she. Then she was melting. Her body like goo, flowing over him in waves of heat. A hot mess of nerves and responses. An automatic reaction to every scorching touch, each sizzling caress, his sweltering heat roasting her, burning her to mindless passion.

She clutched him, not wanting to let go. Her body had a mind of its own, taking over her thoughts and actions. More. She wanted more.

He rolled, flipping their positions. His welcome weight sank over her, covering her like a warm blanket. His touch was bliss. He slowly peeled her gown from her shoulders, placing his searing lips on her skin. Hot. She was so hot. Her mind in a fog, she helped him remove her robe and gown. His eyes gleamed with appreciation. As long as he looked at her like that, she would follow him into the unknown.

He leaned down with a moan. "Beautiful." His low voice sent goosebumps over her skin; his fingers sending her into a pool of submission.

His mouth smoothed over her bare flesh, igniting flames of hunger for whatever he might give her. Whatever he might want from her.

She drowned in sensation, too far gone to care.

"I want you," he murmured.

If this was damnation ... let the fires begin.

Chapter 1

Aaron loved living in London. His town house was large and spacious, which suited his needs perfectly. But this evening, the walls were closing in, and he had no mind to sit alone and reflect on his past mistakes. Betrayal being at the top of the list. Oh, his brother had finally come around, but had he truly forgiven Aaron? At the moment, guilt was not foremost in his mind. Even his trip to Brighton—the one he barely remembered—still could not fathom how the old man had drunk him into oblivion. He was still confused over the abrupt fog that had suddenly filled his mind where he'd lost an entire night. Good God, he could not remember how he'd passed the evening. Bother all that. His friend was missing, and he could not help but feel responsible.

Aaron grabbed his hat and coat, and strode down the corridor to the front door. The afternoon held a chill. He turned up the collar of his fashionably tailored coat and ducked his head into the crisp wind. His long legs ate up the distance in short order, but then he had a purpose for his intended direction. Someone along the warehouses should know something.

Five days, and still no sign of Blade. His brothers believed Blade dead. They tried reasoning with him.

Bollocks.

What his brothers called reason, he begged to differ. Reason did not bear proof. He required proof before he would declare his friend's demise.

T'was not like Blade to disappear. Not for so many days, and without a word. Aaron hated thinking his friend had been blown to bits along with Bellingham's ship. He shuddered, which had nothing to do with the chilly wind. Unwanted thoughts ran amok in his head. A vicious circle, fathoms deep, and as dark as the latest hour of the night.

What if Bellingham had caught Blade?

Damn his brother, Edmund, for allowing Bellingham into their lives. Aaron knew the cur had been up to no good. A smuggler. Opium, no less. The man had wanted Greystoke Manor to further his illegal activities. And damned if Edmund hadn't given over to the evil blackguard. When Nathaniel had come home, he had no idea he was walking into a hornets' nest. He'd set the miscreant straight, but was shot before they could put an end to the smugglers. Nathaniel had recovered well enough, and together, Aaron and his brothers blew up the cargo in the caves. That is, Blade did. And he'd set the explosives on Bellingham's ship, sinking the vessel to the bottom of the sea with fiery thunder.

Where the hell was Blade now?

Aaron picked up his pace. Fear and anger driving him forward. Blade had been his friend for years. On one of his jaunts down to the docks, Blade had saved his hide. It smarted that Nathaniel had run, leaving Aaron and Edmund to deal with their father. Aaron rebelled. He'd taken to running off every chance he got.

Lord Greystoke was a tyrant. A nobleman with a mean streak a mile wide. Edmund, being next in line, did everything father told him to do. Like a damned puppet.

Yes, sire. Whatever you say, sire.

But Aaron was too much like Nathaniel. Silently, of course. Never aloud, and certainly not to his father. He had more sense. He'd witnessed the punishment Nathaniel had endured, and often when it had been Aaron who was the guilty party.

The smell from the docks flowed along the streets and on to the boarded sidewalks. Aaron loved the smell of the ocean. One day, he hoped to be on a ship instead of just wishing. At least, he was finally getting nearer to his goal. Even if he could not remember his night after the tavern, his trip to Brighton had been a booming success. He'd signed the documents, and now he was part owner in the Anderson Shipping Line.

A door flew open, missing him by inches. Two seagoers staggered out as shouts rumbled from the inside. Aaron stepped to the right, realizing he'd managed to avoid a collision with an already raging fight. A few more spectators wandered out, bellowing encouragement to the man of their choice while clearly making wagers. Any other time, he might join in the fun. But today, he needed answers.

When the way was clear, he stepped into the dimly lit room. With half the occupants outside, there were plenty of empty tables. Through the smoke, he searched those remaining and saw no sign of Blade. However, he recognized a few men he'd conversed with at other times when he had ventured to the London docks.

Slowly, he made his way to a table next to the far wall. A few men looked his way. Seeing nothing of interest, they turned away. A bearded man lifted his mug of ale, and glanced at Aaron over the foam. Aaron held his gaze. Mayhap the man recognized him as well. He nudged the man beside him. When the second man glanced his way, Aaron thought maybe he was not as fierce as he first believed. But then, Aaron was no fool. The men that frequented the taverns along the waterfront could be dangerous. He'd learned that disreputable men lurked everywhere. Aristocrats should not be overlooked, either.

The first man came toward him gradually. Green eyes blazed in the middle of his thickly bearded face. Aaron was glad he'd dressed in old clothing for this occasion.

"Evenin'. Mind if'n I share yer table?"

"Be my guest," Aaron replied.

The man kicked out a chair with his boot, then settled his bulk on the hard wood. "Yer lucky ya didna get caught up in the fisticuffs."

The second man, scooted a chair back and took a seat without saying a word.

"I gave them a wide berth."

"Good idea." He lifted his mug and took a hefty swallow, then wiped the foam from his beard.

A barmaid sashayed over to the table. "Hello, luv. What can I get ya?"

Aaron pointed to the mug of ale. "I'll have one of those."

She turned to the other men at the table. "You done got yers." And she swung her skirts about, heading back to the bar.

"I remember you," the bearded man said, lowering his voice.

"I was hoping you would."

The second man looked up in surprise. "What you doing down here?"

Aaron picked up right away, that these two were not as uneducated as they would have others believe. "Perhaps, I was looking for you."

His eyes got bigger.

"You lookin' for Blade?"

Every nerve in Aaron's body went on alert. He didn't ask *Blade who?* The fact that this man mentioned Blade and he knew who Aaron was spoke volumes. And he was not about to dicker around when Blade's life could be at stake. "What makes you think that?"

"I seen ya with him," the second man said.

"Basil, here, watches all the coming and goings. He's a good one to have in your camp."

Aaron leaned an elbow on the table. "You have news of Blade?" Realizing he'd given himself away, he cursed under his breath. "How do you know him?"

"He's one of us."

Aaron had no idea what the bloody hell that meant.

"What Basil is trying to tell you is that we can be trusted. We know you're a friend of Blade's."

That was yet to be seen. Or–whatever. "What do you mean he's one of you?"

"I said I remembered you, but evidently you don't remember me. My name is Pauly."

"I remember you, Pauly. You have spoken with me before. Answered a few questions for me."

"I know you're a lord. Even in those clothes, you smell of the upper class." The other man said with a sneer.

"Basil. Just 'cause our friend here is a gent, don't mean he's amiable. I hear tell there's a few bodies left in his trail. You've heard of the Greystoke brothers. What do you think they'll do to Bellingham when they find him?"

Aaron did not remember telling anyone of his status. "I too noticed your accent has changed. That doesn't matter. What news do you have of Blade?"

The tavern door opened and several men came through. Evidently the fight was over. Some grumbled, but all headed for the bar. The barmaid danced between the men, bringing his ale to their table.

"Here ya be, luv."

Aaron flipped a coin in the air, and she quickly caught it in her fingers. "That's for you." She gave him a saucy smile, before heading back to take care of the other customers.

Pauly waited to make sure no one paid attention to them before he spoke.

"There's a bloke named Bone. He and Blade were working together. On what, I don't know. I do know they were together the night a ship blew up in the harbor."

The night Blade set explosives on Bellingham's ship.

"Seadog's ship. He's a bad 'un." Basil shook his head from side to side.

"Bone is a pal to Basil," Pauly said.

"We go way back. He's a good 'un. He's the one set," Basil looked over his shoulder, then continued. "He's the one who blew up Seadog's ship."

Good God.

Captain Seadog was Bellingham's lapdog captain. Aaron hoped like hell that these two men were on his side. "How do you know that?"

"He told me."

Well. That was that.

Pauly leveled his gaze on Aaron. "Bone has been in here, and other places, looking for you."

That took Aaron back. *Bone?* Aaron could not recall ever seeing the man. "Are you sure he was looking for me?"

"Yep," Basil answered. "Said he had to tell you about Blade."

"What about him?"

Pauly spoke up. "Don't know. Wouldn't tell us nothin'. Said he had to talk to you."

"Wouldn't even tell me, and I'm his friend." Basil was clearly offended.

"Do you know where Bone is now?"

"Nay."

That's it? *Nay?* Aaron wanted to reach across the table and grab Pauly by the throat. He had a feeling if he did, he would not be awake for his next breath.

Bloody hell.

He took a moment to keep his irritation from flourishing into out-and-out rage. He had to know what happened to Blade. Time could be of the essence.

He took a deep breath. "Can you tell me how to find Bone?"

"Nay."

He wanted to shout. "Why the hell not?"

"Ifn' he don't want to be found, he won't be."

"Told us to keep an eye out fer you."

Well, thank you Basil for adding that tidbit. Getting information from these two was like milking a jackass.

"And once you found me, then what?"

"Said he'd be back."

"That's it? He'll be back?"

Both men gave a nod.

Aaron had to take another breath. Then he had to count to ten. He made it to three.

"What the bloody hell am I supposed to do now?" It took everything in him to keep his voice down. Inside, he was wound up like a tight spring.

Anger crossed Pauly's face. Basil didn't look too happy either.

"I apologize for my outburst. I'm worried about Blade. I have been looking for him all week, and I've not found one word on him. Until now. Surely, you must understand my apprehension."

"I know you're a good man. If'n we had more to tell ya, we would."

"Blade's one of us."

Yes, he'd said that. Aaron scrubbed a hand over his face. The least he could do was buy another round for these two. They came to him. Tried to help. And he knew more now than he did before entering the tavern.

Still, the unknown ate at him.

He had no idea if Blade was injured, alive or dead.

Chapter 2

T he youngest of three brothers, Aaron knew when the eldest sent a cryptic note, it really meant, *'Get your arse here now.'*

That is how he came to find himself at Greystoke Manor. Not much had changed regarding his bossy brother, but much had changed at the manor.

He handed his gloves and cloak to Nathaniel's butler. New to the manor, but seemingly loyal. Aaron had a good sense of judgement. The butler could hold his own.

Nathaniel had surprised them all, returning home and deciding to restore the house where they'd all grown up. Aaron had thought his brother would, at the very least, sell the family property. After all, Nathaniel had threatened to burn the place down a number of times. But to everyone's dismay, he not only refurbished the old mansion, he actually lived there now. With his new wife, Serena. A lovely woman. A mystery solved. Nonetheless, Nathaniel had been up to the challenge, and they were expecting their first child.

Aaron glanced to the wide staircase where generations of Greystoke portraits hung along the wall. *Good God.* Even his father's portrait hung there. He would have thought surely his brother would have torched that one. But, it seemed, as much as Nathaniel hated the man, he'd hung their father's portrait among the rest. Aaron gave a shrug of his shoulders.

As he strode down the long corridor to the main study, his boots echoed off the tall walls. *Eerie.* The sound reminded him too much of times past. When he'd hid from his father, hearing his father's footfalls echoing along the hall. He held off a shudder and marched forward. The door to the study was partially open.

He marched in. "Hello, brother. I received your summons. What has made you so anxious to desire my company?"

Nathaniel sat behind his big desk staring at a paper he held in his hand. Slowly, his gaze drifted upward and his hard eyes locked with Aaron's. Yep. He'd guessed right. This would not be a pleasant visit.

"I *summoned* you here because I hold a contract in my hand."

Well, all right. Clearly, Nathaniel did not like that Aaron had used the term *summon.* Still, how the bloody hell had Nathaniel gotten his hands on Aaron's contract?

"I would think, brother dear, that contract you hold is personal. It is my business. Not yours."

"Then why was it sent to me?"

"I have no idea," he said as he stepped to the sideboard. He took the crystal topper from the decanter and poured a generous amount of brandy into a glass. Looked like he might need it. When he turned back around, Nathaniel's eyes were dark with anger.

"Would you care to explain this?"

Aaron took a gulp from the much-needed courage swishing about in his glass, then made his way to the chair in front of Nathaniel's desk. Another reminder he would like to forget. This measured much too closely to when his father had given him a dressing down. At least Nathaniel had burned their father's hateful desk.

"Nathaniel, I do not understand your anger."

That jaw of his tightened and Aaron recognized Nathaniel's temper was about to blow.

"I did give you some warning," Aaron blurted in his own defense.

"When!"

"I mentioned to you that I was interested in ships. You asked me why I stayed here and waited for you instead of getting on with my life. You knew I took a trip to Brighton. I saw no need to tell you what I had planned. At least not until it came to completion."

His brother glanced at the paper in his hand, and then back to Aaron. "And this is what you planned?"

Why was Nathaniel so angry? He'd told Aaron not so long ago, that he should follow his own dream.

"Well, yes," Aaron answered with confusion. "The Anderson Shipping Line is in Brighton. Actually, Hardcastle contacted me."

"Hardcastle. Who is Hardcastle?"

"He runs the business on this side of the pond for Anderson. I met Mister Anderson. A likeable fellow, by the by. And what you have in your hand is the result. I still don't understand why you have a copy of my contract. And why are you so bloody angry? I hoped you might be happy for me."

Several emotions crossed Nathaniel's face, as each red shade of his skin grew darker. "I cannot believe you are making light of this. As for how I got this contract, it was addressed to the Lord of Greystoke Manor. Apparently, this man thinks I am you. Rather, you are me."

"What?"

"This," Nathaniel glanced to the paper again. "Hayes. Mister Hayes is demanding you make this right. Demanding Lord Greystoke honor his promise."

"Who the devil is Hayes?"

"The man whose name is on this contract." Nathaniel laid the document down and pressed his finger to mark a spot.

Aaron shrugged. "I don't remember him."

"You admit you signed this contract?"

Aaron didn't need to look at it. "I am of legal age. I have a mind of my own. Of course. Why would I deny it?"

"Do you also admit you ran off and left the girl?"

With the glass halfway to his lips, Aaron paused. "What girl?"

Nathaniel shook his hand in rage, the crisp paper making a crackling sound with every *swoosh*. "Your bride!"

What the bleedin' hell had gotten into his brother? "Uh, Nathaniel. I think you better calm down. Obviously, you have been at your books too long. You're not thinking straight."

Nathaniel lunged from his chair so fast, Aaron instinctively shrank back. But he quickly regained his metal.

"Now hold on!" Aaron jumped to his feet, eyeing his brother, the desk separating them. "I'm not a little boy anymore."

"You're not a man either, if you give your word and do not honor it."

Aaron's blood boiled. "Father may have been an evil bastard, but he did one thing right. He instilled our duty into each of us. You have no call to question my honor."

Again, Nathaniel shook the paper in his hand. Violently. Then he tossed it onto the desk. "Christ, Aaron," Nathaniel shouted while shoving both hands through his hair.

His brother may have scared him long ago, but now Aaron stood just as tall. He looked Nathaniel in the eye. "What are you getting so worked up over. It cannot be because I signed a contract with Anderson Shipping."

"Anderson—" Nathaniel stumbled to a halt, grabbed the parchment and all but tossed it at Aaron. "Here, brother. Is this the contract you signed?"

Some bee had stung Nathaniel's backside. There was no other explanation. Aaron picked up the paper he assumed was the contract and began reading— *Bloody hell*.

"Well?"

Aaron looked to his brother, and had difficulty finding his voice.

"Is that the contract you were bleating about?" Nathaniel shouted.

"This is a marriage contract?" Aaron managed to squeak.

"That is your signature, is it not?"

Aaron quickly scanned the document to the bottom, the words blurring into nothing. Then he saw it. A signature.

His signature!

He glanced to the top again. Shock stiffened his body. "Good God. This cannot be."

"Is that your signature?"

"It sure looks like mine."

"Did you sign that?"

"Hell, no!" He studied the signature, and the bottom fell out of his stomach. Damn, it looked like his.

"Sit down before you pass out." Nathaniel came around the desk and pushed on Aaron's shoulder. He fell into the seat he'd just lurched out of.

What the bloody hell?

"Do you know this man?"

"Who?" Aaron asked automatically, not thinking clearly.

"Hayes? His signature is next to yours."

All Aaron could do was shake his head. "No. I don't know him."

"Then how do you explain your signature, Aaron?"

"Christ," he raked a hand over his face. "I don't know."

"Hayes lives in Brighton. What did you do down there other than go to the shipping yard?"

Aaron thought back. He went to a tavern. Had a mug of ale. Met a man. "Went home with that man."

"What man?"

Good God. Had he said that out loud? "I met a man that had too much to drink. He kept rambling on about his daughter. But she was a child."

Suddenly a flash of an image lit up his skull, along with a sharp pain. A woman. With sensual eyes. And luscious lips. He shook his head. *That was just a dream.*

"You went home with this man? Then what?"

Aaron felt like a fool. He didn't know what? Now he had to explain to his brother he blacked out from drinking. Something of which he had never done. He'd seen too many others drown in their cups, gamble their wages, lose every penny they had. Some even lost their homes because they became dependent on vices. Aaron was proud that he'd never had the desire to lose his sense.

"Aaron?"

What? Oh yes. He went home with the bloke he'd met at the tavern. "Yes. I did."

"Then what?"

"Wait a minute. Let me read this." The air was beginning to circulate in the room again. He took a deep breath, and read the contract he had no memory of signing.

"I am not married. Nor did I promise to marry anyone. Bollocks, Nathaniel. I don't even remember—"

Nathaniel narrowed his eyes. "You don't remember?"

Aaron glanced to his brother, again. "The man drank me under the table. He was drunk at the tavern. At least I thought he was. He needed help getting home. Then he wanted to drink some more. He was crying, Nathaniel. I felt sorry for him."

"Why would you feel sorry for a drunkard. You said you don't remember."

Aaron shook his head. He struggled with the events of that night. "I guess the ale was stronger than I thought. Or I drank too much. I blacked out."

Nathaniel's brows rose up to his hair line. "You? You drank too much. Since when?"

"Well, that's the thing. I don't remember drinking all that much, but I did black out." Again, the vision of a beautiful woman, curves filling his hands, flashed before his eyes. Just when he thought he could see her face, the image disappeared.

Bloody hell.

"Have you suddenly started drinking to the point you black out?"

"No. I mean..." He massaged the back of his neck. No matter how hard he rubbed, the image would not reappear. "Damn it, Nathaniel. I don't know!"

Nathaniel walked around to the front of his desk. "All right, calm down."

Imagine. Nathaniel having to calm *him* down. Usually, their roles were reversed. Nathaniel had one hell of a temper.

"What is the last thing you remember?"

Aaron tried to recall his actions. "The man crying. Slumped over his cup. I remember my cup moving—all by itself. Then ... nothing."

"Do you think that is when you signed this contract?"

"Bollocks, Nathaniel. I would not—did not sign that bloody contract!"

"What about the girl you mentioned? Did you see her? Or anyone else in the house?"

"No," he said shaking his head. "No one."

Nathaniel got up, and marched back behind his desk. "If this is your signature, Aaron, this document is binding."

"I have no idea who this man is, let alone that he even has a daughter."

What was the man's name? Colvin. That's it.

"What's the name on that contract?"

Nathaniel picked up the paper and read. "Colvin Hayes."

"Yes. That's him. He'd left his daughter at home by herself. He spoke of her as a child." Even the barkeep spoke of the girl that way. Evidently, Colvin left her alone, often. "I remember wondering why the man would leave a child alone ... but what if the girl was a woman?"

Good God.

Aaron shuddered. It didn't make a damn. He was not going to marry her. "I didn't even bed the chit," he blurted.

"Let's hope not. I seriously doubt you would have been able to in your condition. However, according to this document, she is your betrothed, whether you like it or not."

"Not," he grumbled. How the hell was he to get out of this mess?

Suddenly a thought hit him. "Hayes sent that contract to you. To Lord Greystoke. He thinks I am the Greystoke heir. Simply inform him, you are the heir. He will not want a third son with no wealth."

"You have wealth."

"He doesn't need to know that."

"Mayhap if you reined in your habit of tossing coin about, he would not have gotten that idea."

"I am frugal, Nathaniel. I was not foolishly spending, nor into my cups. I simply helped a man I thought needed help."

"And got caught with your pants down."

Nathaniel may have been using a euphemism, but Aaron had the uncanny feeling he had been naked. Christ, he wished he could remember. Was it truly a dream?

Of course, it was a bloody dream.

"I do not remember a girl. Or a woman."

"You'd better. I doubt he pulled a stranger out of his hat. Whoever this woman is, she is your betrothed."

Aaron shot out of his chair. "Nathaniel. You are already married, so you can't marry her. Just tell the man he has made a mistake."

"Lord or no, heir or no, this is a contract, Aaron. With *your* signature. You must remember some part of this?"

Aaron glanced to the hated paper that would end his life as he knew it. How could he deny the bold script was not his own? "It is mine. I don't remember much. I've never been drunk out of my mind. Certainly not to the point I passed out."

He was sunk. His goose was thoroughly cooked. "Nathaniel, can't you fix this?"

"What do you think Aunt will have to say?"

"For God's sake, do not tell Aunt of this nonsense."

Nathaniel waved the document like a bloody flag. "It does not appear to be nonsense."

"I tell you someone is fabricating this story. Why in bloody hell would I sign a contract? With anyone!" he bellowed. "I am too young to be leg-shackled."

"It's not so bad, Aaron."

He jerked his gaze to Nathaniel and saw his cocky grin. How could his brother joke when Aaron's life was being threatened. "Oh sure. You're one of the lucky bastards. Serena is not fake.

She's as far from a dull-headed, social butterfly as a woman can be."

"I hope you did not just insult my wife."

"What? Of course not."

"And what of Joyanna?"

Joyanna was a blue-blood. So, Edmund also had a horseshoe up his bloody arse.

"I don't know this woman. I've never met her. No lite-skirt is going to swindle me. Nor is writing to my brother, claiming a contract that never happened, going to blackmail me."

"Aaron. How do you explain your signature?"

"Christ." Aaron dropped into a chair. "I have no idea."

He'd been having the best day of his life. His own correspondence from Anderson Shipping had arrived, so he was ready to celebrate. If he could not fix this, his life as he knew it would be over.

Devil take it.

"You could use a wife to tame your wild ways."

"Bloody hell." Aaron paced to a window, not even looking out. Suddenly he whirled about. "How old were you when you married? If not for the title, you would still be a single man. Admit it."

"We are not discussing me."

Aaron hung his head, cursing his brother under his breath. "You've grown old since taking your marriage vows."

"You will honor this contract, Aaron."

"No, I will not!"

Nathaniel glowered at him. They were nearly the same height; Nathaniel was definitely more threatening. But this was Aaron's life.

"I will go see this Mr. Hayes. He will give the truth, or by God, suffer the consequences."

"And what of the woman?"

"What about her?"

Nathaniel hiked his brow, glaring. Aaron was older now. He refused to be intimidated by his older brother.

"Hell fire, Nathanial. You cannot believe she exists." Nathaniel opened his mouth, but Aaron hurried on. "Even if she does, I will expose her father for the rotter he is. And if she is a part of his scheme, then she will suffer my wrath as well."

"Be careful. The daughter could be an innocent."

"Not if she is agreeing to this fraud."

"I'm sorry to point out that you recognized your own signature."

"Aaron slammed his fist into his opposite hand. "I can't explain it."

"Exactly my point. Until you can, you must tread carefully. You cannot go breathing fire and brimstone without knowing the facts."

"I know I did not sign that document."

"Facts, Aaron."

"Don't patronize me, brother. We were raised by the same father. I understand decorum, and I know how to take care of myself."

"Calm down. We will know soon enough. I have already sent for her."

Chapter 3

Rebekah woke with a start.

She had the same dream again. Her face aflame, she threw the covers back and slipped from the bed. What time was it? Was her father up?

Her hands covered her heated cheeks. If she did not get control of her emotions, her father would question her. She probably looked guilty as sin.

Sin.

She groaned. Yes, she had committed a very grave sin. At the time, she had not cared. Sensations swamped her. She had no control of her mind. Who knew one could completely lose one's self? Now that she had time to reflect, she knew it was wrong, and she should not have surrendered. But when the lord had kissed her, touched her, she could no more stop him—or herself—than she could have told the world to stop spinning.

"Becky? You up?"

Her heart missed a beat. Father was up and looking for her.

"I'll be right down."

"Mornings a wastin', girl. I got a letter here. Hurry up."

A letter? How long had her father been up. It could not be that late.

After the death of her mother, Rebekah's role changed. She had the duty of looking after her father. Devastated at the sudden loss of his wife, he took to drinking and ignored his role of parent. Rebekah became the head of the household, in charge of their meager budget, providing food for the table and often putting her drunken father to bed.

Here of late, things were looking up. Papa seemed to take an interest in his appearance. Not that he cared much for primping, but he drank less and even dressed in clean clothes, when the occasion called for it. At least he was not staggering about. He even helped around the house, bringing in wood for the fire, and helping with the chores. She'd prayed daily for something to shake him from his grief. Perhaps time was all he needed to crawl from the deep well in which he'd succumbed. Thankfully, he'd snapped out of it. Her dear Papa had returned to her. Seeing his spirit return had put a smile on her own face.

An ordinary girl, Rebekah had been brought up to appreciate their meager life. She dressed quickly, pinned up her hair, and slipped on her ankle boots. The air was chilly, and the wind whipped around the house. As she came down the winding stairs, she saw her father sitting in the corner at a small table he used as a writing desk. The wooden box he kept for important papers was open, and a wrinkled parchment lie on the table in front of him holding his concentration.

"There ya are, girl. Come here. I have news to tell you." He hooked a chair with his boot and dragged it to his side.

Rebekah smoothed the loose hair back from her brow, wondering at the tone of his voice. Papa was excited about something. She took a quick glance, looking for a bottle or any sign of drink. It would break her heart if he was back into his cups. The last time she'd seen him with this much vigor was the night he'd brought home that stranger.

A night best forgotten.

"What in the world could be so important?"

"Sit."

She wanted to huff, being ordered about, but his voice held a lively spark. "I don't believe I have ever seen you this keyed up."

"I have a letter here from the Lord Greystoke."

"You've already gone to town to get the mail?"

"I brung it home last night. I, uh, got something to tell ya."

Oh no. What had Papa done now?

"Ya remember that man that came home with me a few weeks back?"

Her flesh heated. She swiped a hand across her forehead.

At least her father had not brought any of his other drinking cronies home. She gave a nod. "Yes. The man who fell asleep on our couch." Then rolled to the floor, and— She dare not think about that.

"Well, now. Don't go getting on your high horse, but me and him made a bargain. An agreement. Like one of them contracts."

As soon as she heard the words *high horse*, the hair stood on the back of her neck. He had done something. Something she would not like. Then she heard the word *contract*.

"A contract? Papa, what have you done?"

"Now, like I said, don't go getting all riled up. It's a good one. One you will like."

I doubt it.

"You see. We have an understanding. I told him about you, and you not having any prospects living here with me, so we made an arrangement."

Prospects? Heaven forbid.

She curled her fingers into a fist to keep from shouting. "What sort of arrangement?"

"Wrote it up on a piece of paper, and signed it, too."

If she had not been sitting, her legs would have given out and she'd have tumbled to the floor. "Signed what?"

"The bargain, girl."

The room was beginning to spin. She desperately hoped she was not part of this bargain. Dread clawed at her stomach. "What. Have. You. Done?"

"Now, there ya go. I ain't even told ya the best part yet."

Papa could be more stubborn than an ornery donkey. His impulsive actions were always getting him into trouble. *A contract? The best part?* Good heavens, she was nearly at her wits end.

She took a deep breath and released it slowly. Counting did not help. "Papa. What is this agreement, and how does it involve me?"

"Like I said. I got a letter from the Lord Greystoke. He's coming to collect ya, girl."

"Who is Lord— He's what!"

"He's the man that's gonna be your husband. You're getting married. I found a lord for you. He's a big fish, Becky." Papa rubbed his hands together and licked his lips like he would if they were having Cod for supper.

Once Rebekah recovered from swallowing her tongue, she recounted her father's words. Either he had misspoken, or her father was hitting the bottle again. She raised her palm to his forehead searching for a fever. He swatted her hand away.

"What are ya doing? I be fine."

"Papa, I have no idea who this man is, and I have no intention of marrying anyone."

"You're already promised to him. That fella. He's Lord Greystoke. Has a great big mansion up north. He was here buying into the Anderson Shipping Line. I knew he was a rich one."

Rebekah didn't know which ludicrous statement to tackle first. "Papa, are you saying the man you brought home was a gentleman?"

Of course he was.

She'd known. His clothes were high quality, nothing one would find around here. Even partially comatose, everything about him emitted nobleman. Her mother had been a noblewoman. Since her grandfather would not accept an untitled man for his daughter's husband, she'd run away to Gretna Green. Mother often said, she was happy and never regretted her decision. But it would have been nice for Rebekah to meet her aristocratic family.

One could not miss what one did not have. Even so, Mama taught her fine English, and proper etiquette from books. She said one could never have enough learning, and should always use proper manners. Sometimes, her mother made Papa dress fancy for supper, even slicked his hair down. Just to please Mama. They didn't live in a big house or have fancy servants. Mama said they had everything they needed.

Each other.

Was the man he brought home Lord Greystoke? Why did he send a letter. What in God's name had her father said to him?

"May I see the letter?"

"It's man's business, girl."

"Papa, if you think I need a husband, then I am not a girl. I don't need a rich husband. Actually, I don't need a husband at all. When I do decide I want one, I will pick him myself."

"This is the way things are done, Becky. The father makes a match for his daughter. Don't you want better things than I can give you? Don't you want a big house, and lots of dresses?"

She prayed the letter was a ruse and the supposed contract not binding. She placed her hand over her father's. "This house is fine. I have dresses. You give me everything I need."

"I'm your father. For a husband, I picked one with lots of money? You can buy anything you wish."

Papa never spoke about such things before. Had he been ashamed? Had he worried about Mama not having nice things?

"Doesna' matter," he said with a wave of his hand. "You got a lord and he's rich."

"Papa. I don't need money and nice things. Mama had everything she wanted in you. And me. She was happy. She made us happy."

His face dropped with defeat. He looked like she'd shot him through the heart.

"Papa—"

"Now you listen here, Becky. Your mother was an angel. A God-sent angel. Why she took up with me I'll never know. But I loved her. And she loved me, thank the blessed saints. I tried to give her a good living."

"Of course, you did Papa."

"Anyway, she ain't here now, and I know she would want the best for you. I got the best."

"May I please see this contract?"

"Go on then. Have it your way." He grabbed another paper from the wooden box. "Here's his letter. That's his signature right there."

She took the parchment and read. The farther she scrolled down the page, the more horrifying the words.

This letter was confirming that Lord Greystoke had received the contract.

A marriage contract.

Dear God.

Her skin heated as she remembered that night. Fire burned her face as she recalled flashes of bare skin ... corded muscle ... and ...

"I found you a husband, Becky. A real gentlemen."

Rebekah hated the shortened version of her name. Mama called her Rebekah. The sound of each syllable rolled over her tongue. A pang pierced Rebekah's chest. How she missed her mother.

"You sent him the contract? How did you get his signature?"

"It's legal, Becky. I did right by you. Your mother's gone, God rest her soul. I've been no account since her passing, but I promised your Mama I would make it up to you." He held up the letter he'd received. "I did sweetheart. You're going to marry a lord. Lord Greystoke sent for you. He's bringing you to his grand home. He has a fine house, owns acres and acres of land. Ain't ya happy, girl?"

It was very hard not to shout when one felt like screaming. She closed her eyes and prayed she would wake up. Her father acted like her future was all planned out. Lord Greystoke had signed his name.

Why?

Had he woken the next morning feeling guilty? Was this a ploy to get out of any responsibility?

"Sweetheart. Ain't ya listening? You're gonna have a fine life. You got to get ready. Get packed. You're going to Greystoke Manor."

She had to get her father's attention. Whatever was going on, she had to stop him.

"How did you get Lord Greystoke to sign a contract?"

His eyes darted away, causing a chill to race down her spine.

"Papa?"

"Now, that ain't important. You—"

"Did he really sign it?"

"Of course he signed it."

His sheepish look told her he'd done something. What, she could not figure out.

"Don't look at me like that. It's real and it's binding. You are promised to a lord."

"I still don't understand. Are you trying to get rid of me?"

"'Course not. I'm getting old, girl."

"Papa, you're not that old. If you stay away from the bottle, you could live a long time." She'd worried about him when he drank until he passed out, but now he looked the picture of health. "Why, Papa?"

"I told ya. A man has to provide for his family. I won't be here forever, girl. And you don't want to end up being a spinster."

That last part might be too late.

"But I don't understand why he signed it. You both were well into your cups. When I came downstairs, he'd already passed out."

"But he liked ya."

"How could you possibly know that? He didn't even see me." She would pray for forgiveness tonight. Perhaps he hadn't seen her. He was inebriated.

"He was looking fer a wife."

She didn't believe a word of it. How had the two men gotten together? There had to be a reason a lord would agree to marry a pauper. The fact that he was so drunk he didn't know who she was had given her the courage to throw caution to the wind. She was glad she had. It was the most wonderful moment of her life.

She should not be admiring her recklessness, and thank goodness there had been no consequences.

"I'm telling ya—"

Rebekah held up a hand. You were drunk. He brought you home. I don't know how you got his signature, but it does not matter. That document does not mean anything." When her father interrupted again, she kept talking. "He left that next morning without saying a word. You didn't say anything either. It's been weeks."

"But I got his letter."

Rest assured I will take care of this matter with due diligence.

And it had the seal of Lord Greystoke.

"He is not agreeing to a marriage. Perhaps he never intended on honoring your contract. What is to keep him from destroying it."

"I did some checking. He's an important man. A man of his word. I have his signature."

And he has the contract.

If only she could see that paper. It amazed her that her father had gone behind her back. "You didn't even bother to ask me."

He looked bewildered. "Ask ya what?"

She shook her head. "Ask if I was willing, or even if I liked this man."

"What's not to like? He's a gentleman. A lord. He has money, a title. What more could a woman want?"

Rebekah knew her parents had loved each other. She'd seen their gentle touches, and kind gestures when her father would surprise Mama. The devastation he suffered when her mother grew ill.

"What about love?" She hadn't meant to speak aloud.

"Bah," Papa answered with a swipe of his hand, as if he were swatting a fly. "You can learn to love him."

Learn to ...

"Let me say this in a way you will understand. I love you, Papa. I am not getting married, and there is no way you can force me."

"Force you? Why, don't you want a big fancy house to live in? Don't ya want fancy dresses and servants to do your cooking and washing for you?"

She stood, placing her hands on her hips. "What I want is for you not to marry me off before I am ready.

"Becky." He placed his hands on her shoulders. "Honey. I did this for you. I've hooked you a big fish. Don't throw him back in the pond."

Frustration boiled in the pit of her belly. If it wouldn't upset Papa so much, she would cry. He thought he was doing the best thing for her.

Closing her eyes, she sighed. She wouldn't trade her one night of bliss for anything. She supposed she would marry one day. And now she knew what to expect, she would not settle for anything less than love.

"You'll be a lady, Becky. Gentry. Everything ya want at your fingertips."

How could she make her father understand? How he'd gotten the signature was anyone's guess. And now he didn't even have that paper. Lord Greystoke had no intention of marrying her then, and she suspected he cared even less now. She feared for her father's sanity. Mama's death had nearly destroyed him. But Rebekah thought he'd retained his wits.

"No. I am not."

His body froze, and his face screwed up in confusion.

"The answer is no."

"He didna' ask."

"Well, he should have. The answer is still no."

"But, he sent for you. I got his word right here. He's agreeing to the marriage. He signed a contract. We both signed it. He can't get out of it, and he's coming."

"By we, you do not mean me. It was not signed by me."

"By you? What have you got to do with a marriage contract?"

Evidently nothing. Except be the brood mare.

She took a breath and tried again. "Papa. I did not agree to this bargain that the two of you made. I am not getting married. To him, or anyone else at the moment."

"He'll give you time to get used to him. You'll be so busy in that big ole house, you won't mind him at all. Your mother would want this for you."

Please don't bring Mama into this.

She didn't know if to laugh or cry. One day, when she did marry, she would most assuredly notice her husband, and if she were lucky enough to have a marriage like her parents, her husband would love her. That is what she wanted. Not a marriage planned on a piece of paper, but one of a budding friendship, that grew into love. Maybe it was a lot to ask for, but she would not marry without love.

Nothing would come of this. Their lives would go on as usual. Hopefully her father would tire of waiting for a lord that would never come.

"Listen, girl. I'm your Papa. I must see you safely wed. I signed a contract. So did his lordship. You are betrothed. And that's that."

Not if she had anything to say about it.

Chapter 4

T hick stands of pine and oak bordered the quaint buildings
and cottages. Aaron rode through the developing town,
giving a nod to the smithy as he passed. He followed the path
he remembered to the small house just beyond the wooded hill,
gritting his teeth until his jaw ached.

Hayes was a bloody lunatic if he thought he could swindle
Aaron. Between Nathaniel and Edmund, Aaron had gotten
quite an education. In the past year, he'd tackled them both with
fierce determination and learned their secrets. Well, maybe not
all, but a great deal. Including the man who had been blackmail-
ing Edmund. The three brothers had banded together, fighting
pirates, blowing up caves of smuggled provisions, and he even
helped Nathaniel escape when he'd been shot.

An old man and a blasted girl were not about to get the best
of him.

The tiny house came into view, reminding him that the man
he'd met had little funds. Thinking back to that night, he recalled how meager the furnishings, yet the place was clean and
tidy.

A woman's touch.

He slipped from his horse and tied it to a bush. No groomsman here. A small flower bed rested below the front window.
It had been dark when he'd arrived that night, so he'd not paid

attention to the surrounding landscape. Nor had he given much notice the morning he left.

Aaron did not like this one bit. He refused to accept the matter, but he didn't see how he could ignore the situation. Especially after Nathaniel's intervention.

Bollocks.

That night was still foggy. Every time he tried to remember, he got a headache. He knew he had not over-imbibed. He had ale at the inn. After delivering the man home, they had a bit more. In too short a time, Aaron had gotten drunk in a fog, which made absolutely no sense. He liked drink, but would never get so foxed that he would lose control. Not after the way he grew up. Aaron wanted his wits about him at all times. Still, he could not explain his complete lapse in memory of that night. The next morning he had seemed back to normal.

Hayes should not be into his cups this time of day. Aaron would set the damnable man straight.

He took the two steps and knocked on the wooden door.

No one answered. He glanced to the side, and then walked around to the back.

As he strode around a corner, he saw a woman lifting a cloth from a basket, and hanging it over a line—each end was tied to a pole.

"Good afternoon," he said to the young woman. She jumped. He'd startled her. She quickly tucked a blonde curl behind her ear. He wished she would remove the cloth from her head so he could see the full mass of hair he suspected was underneath. "I beg your pardon, Miss ..." He paused. When she didn't offer her name, he went on, "My name is Aaron Greystoke. I'm looking for Mr. Hayes."

Her blue eyes filled with worry. Blue striking eyes. He suddenly had a crazy feeling of *déjà vu.*

"I know I'm a stranger, but I am quite harmless, I assure you. Do you know Mr. Hayes? I believe this is his house."

"My father is in town." Her voice came out low and uneasy.

"I don't mean to frighten you." Then Aaron realized what she'd said. He covered his surprise. "Your father? I see. Do you happen to know when he might be home?"

"I do not see." Clearly, the woman had gotten over her fright. She placed her hands on her hips, and it was clear she was angry. "Why are you here?"

Spirited chit. "I mean you no harm, Miss ..." Aaron hesitated. If Hayes was her father ...

"Rebekah Hayes," she answered forcefully. "If you plan to marry a woman, don't you think you should at least know her name?"

Good God. This was the female in question? Hayes daughter?

Was this the girl who had gotten her father to trick Aaron into a bogus marriage contract? He should have seen the ruse for what it was. The proof was standing there before him. A young woman of marriageable age. Not a little girl who'd been left at home alone, waiting on her Papa. Insolvent. Doing her own laundry.

Aaron was thunderstruck. Shell-shocked. Stuttering like a blowfish. Never, even when the bullies tried to quash him at Eaton, he had never wavered. Now, he stood here like a—

He shook the stupid off and gathered his wits.

"I presume you are the daughter Mr. Hayes mentioned in the contract? My apologies in advance, Miss Hayes, but I did not agree to marry you or any other ch—" He caught himself before he insulted her. "—female. I am here to discuss the matter with your father."

"You presume a lot, Lord Greystoke."

So. She thought he was a titled lord. No wonder Nathaniel had received the correspondence. She and her father were out to land a wealthy nobleman.

"I am not Lord Greystoke." The shock on her face was priceless. He'd assumed correctly. Aaron was a third son. If she wanted a rich, titled lord, her father would have to look elsewhere. "You and your father have targeted the wrong man."

"If you are not Lord Greystoke, then what are you doing here?"

"Your letter was sent to my brother. Since I was the one who had traveled here on business, I supposed the letter was meant for me."

She swiped at her forehead causing another curl to escape from her tied cap. "You are also a Greystoke?"

"That is my name," Aaron answered with a nod.

Rebekah was doing everything in her power not to run. Dear Lord he was tall. Her gaze drifted down over his tan britches, taut with bulging muscles, slimming down into a pair of black Hessians. He crossed his arms over his chest causing his shirt to shift over more muscles. She stuck her tongue out to lick her lips, and nearly choked on her dry throat.

Dear God, she thought she'd never see him again.

His beautiful green eyes burned. Emerald flames, scorching her on the inside. It was hot. Too hot. Then she suddenly realized—he didn't remember.

But how could he not?

She quickly thought back to that night. He was drunk, but he didn't seem drunk. His eyes were sultry and heavy lidded.

The only saving grace at the moment was that this man did not remember her.

"My mother taught me manners. May I offer you a glass of water?"

"Thank you, Miss Hayes. But this is not a social call. I'm here to find out how your father got my name on that contract and set things straight."

"What?" How her father ... He doesn't know? Dear God, what had her father done?

"Lord Greystoke, I'm afraid you've come a long way for nothing."

"I've come to set the record straight. There will be no wedding."

That was a relief. "I assure you—"

"I care not for your excuses, Miss Hayes, and even less for your assurances. Now, do you know when your father will be home?"

He was rude and arrogant. Quite different from what she would have expected.

"My father could come home any moment, or he could be all night. It varies."

"Well, he will have to find his drinking money from another poor soul. He will not get a farthing from me or the Earl of Greystoke."

Blood pumped through her veins in angry spurts. Who did this man think he was? A noble with no manners, obviously. If this was what the aristocrats were like, she was glad she wasn't near them. Papa didn't like them. He'd told her of their self-importance and high-handed ways. How the aristocrats thought they were better than common people. And now she had met one. Her father was right. No wonder her mother had run away.

Rebekah controlled her fury and tried to reason with the blunderhead.

"There is no need to speak with my father."

"Do not try your wiles on me. I will not fall for your treachery. Your father has a comeuppance coming, and I'm here to give it to him."

She could not find a trace of the gentleness he'd shown her that night. Her fear would swallow her whole if she had not seen the kinder side of this man. Even with his rough rugged, chiseled features, she had seen the smile that completely transformed his face.

That fateful night his eyes were soft, like velvet caressing her skin. Now, they were ice. She'd been wicked. Daring. Reckless. The man who held her and made her body burn, had been the most caring and desirable man. She could not have dreamed a more perfect lover.

Looking at Aaron now, seeing the harsh cynicism in his eyes, she could not believe this was the same man.

Rebekah closed her eyes in disillusion, allowing the pain to wash over her. She had made a mistake. One that might cost her soul.

"Leave my father alone," she said forcefully.

He crossed his arms over his wide chest, the movement reminding her of his corded muscles and strength. "Or what?" he goaded.

That did it.

"Listen to me, Nobleman Greystoke. I don't care if you are a highborn or the king of England. Get off of my property. And don't you ever come back." Without realizing it, she wadded up the garment she held and pointed it to a shovel leaning beside the back door.

He followed her gaze, then met it. "What do you plan to do with that?" He smirked.

If the jackass wasn't so big, she'd wallop him with the steel end. But he'd probably just take it away from her. "I was tending my garden. I won't hesitate to use it on you."

He laughed. A loud throaty laugh that tickled her all the way down to her toes. It did other things to her, too. She could not allow those memories to come forth.

"Go away, Lord Greystoke. I am not going to marry you."

He froze, as if he was stunned. "You agree?"

"Of course, I agree. There's no way on God's green earth I would ever marry a man like you."

"I am not speaking about a man like me. My brother is already married, so there is no path for you in that direction. Since I will not marry you, that contract isn't worth the ink that's on it."

"As far as I'm concerned, there is no contract. So, there is no agreement between us."

"Wait a minute. You are right. The agreement was not between us. It was between me and your father—what the hell am I saying? I will not marry you."

"How many times do you want me to repeat myself?"

"I just need to see your father."

"Answer me this, Lord Greystoke. Why did you sign a contract you had no intention of honoring?"

"What the bloody ..."

He raked a hand through his wild, long hair. It was striking in the sunlight. She recalled how it had felt within her fingers.

"I'll find your father, and I will set him straight."

She fisted her hands. "Whether you find my father or not, I wouldn't marry you if you were the only man on earth."

The vein at his temple beat a hasty rhythm, and she could hear his teeth grinding together, before he turned around and marched off.

Thank you, God.

If he'd stayed one moment longer, she feared she would have broken.

Chapter 5

"*I want you.*"

Enchanting blue eyes smoldered with dark yearning. A rush of unexpected longing hit him in his gut. She ran the tip of her finger down his chest, to his stomach, and lazily circled a ring around his navel. He sucked in a breath.

"*I don't know when I've wanted a woman more.*"

"*Pretty words.*" *The scent of blossoming roses floating in the air. His beautiful angel drifted closer, her face becoming clearer. He smiled with hope. He would see her. His hungry gaze watched her plush lips as she pressed a kiss to his upper chest, firing his hunger even more.*

"*I mean every single one.*"

Slipping his hand beneath her hair he clasped her neck and slowly drew her nearer. Her eyes invited him, her lips opened for what she wanted next.

"*Every time I see you, touch you, feel you, I want to do this.*"

He kissed her deeply as she opened her mouth to his teasing tongue. He growled and tightened his embrace. Nothing had ever felt so real.

She whimpered, and slowly faded away.

Come back. Don't go.

His body hot and hard, he reached for her.

Aaron woke with sweat running into his eyes and his heart pounding.

The woman in his dreams had disappeared. Again.

Devil take him. He'd had the same blasted dream again. It was becoming a nightly ritual. Why? He couldn't remember an incident where he might have met this woman who visited him at night. Even though she seemed so real, how could he dream of a woman he'd never met?

Why can't I see her face?

The woman in his dream felt flesh-and-bone real. But her face was always blurred. He shook his head. Maybe he hadn't met her yet. Maybe all this wedding bliss, and lost-love returning babble with his brothers, had somehow gotten into his subconscious.

Marriage was not for him. May his brothers find happiness in their euphoria. Aaron had no intention of becoming leg-shackled. Besides, he was too young. Perhaps in a few more years.

Aunt had been caught up in the wedding with Nathaniel and Serena. His oldest brother, that was a shocker. He never would have imagined Nathaniel getting married, and certainly not living at the manor they all hated.

It was the remembrances there. Their childhood left much to be desired. With an overbearing father, a man who used his oldest son for a whipping post ... Aaron shuddered and shoved those memories away.

What did any of that have to do with his dream? The same dream over and over again. Nathaniel getting married. Edmund acting like a lovesick puppy ... Christ. His brothers' affairs were drawing him in. That had to be it.

Aaron washed and dressed and strode down the corridor to begin his day. Sasha met him at the bottom of the staircase.

"Hello, girl. How are you doing this morning?" He scratched the top of the dog's head. He glanced about. "Where is that mongrel of yours? And here we thought he was the calm one of the bunch."

The dog must have heard his voice, for The Black came loping down the hall. He slid on the tiled floor before he bumped into Aaron.

"So, there you are." He gave The Black the same attention as he had the mother. "What have you been into this early in the morning? Huh?"

The dog barked. Aaron made a gesture with his hand and The Black sat. Clearly excited, his tongue was hanging out of his mouth, but the dog did obey commands.

"Good boy." Aaron strode to the front door and opened it, sending the dogs outside. After several minutes, he decided they were fine, so he came back inside and closed the door.

Nothing quite like an early morning ride.

As he entered the kitchen, Cook was firing up the stove.

"I'll have some breakfast in a jiffy."

"When I get back. For now, I'll grab one of your blueberry muffins." He snatched two out of a basket covered with cloth.

"That's still not gonna be enough for you."

"You spoil me. This will do for now."

He headed to the stables and met the stable master coming out carrying an empty bucket.

"Good morning, sire. Geldings are having their breakfast."

"Good morning, Fletcher. Glad to hear it. Is the apple barrel full? I'll need two to take with me."

"Sure is. Give me a minute to saddle up *Pride*.

"I'll do it. I've got plenty of energy to burn."

And a damsel with smoldering eyes to work out of my system.

Aaron loved riding in the mornings, when the day was starting anew. A bit of dampness in the air, after the rain last night. He breathed deep, allowing the fresh air to expand his lungs. Aunt would still be in bed. She'd had a late night at the Maverick's ball. Even so, she was usually up before noon. Aaron loved his aunt. Surprisingly, they managed living together under one roof, well. He came and went as he pleased, and the old girl never got in his away.

Life was treating him kindly, of late. Nathaniel's wedding had come off without a hitch. He and Serena had not wanted to wait, and neither of them cared for a big wedding. Of course, Aunt demanded a certain few of the ton be present. And he, nor his brothers, had heard a word about Bellingham.

Aaron knew not to believe the man was gone. He wished the bastard had gone down with his ship, but Bellingham was too damn sneaky. That thought led to Blade. Had Blade gotten off the ship?

The best way for Aaron to clear his mind was with vigorous exercise. He leaned down, patted Pride on his strong neck, and shot across the east meadow.

Chapter 6

Rebekah gazed out the window as the coach swept down the drive to a huge mansion of dark grey stones. She'd never seen anything so big in her life. The walls flowed in every direction, with towers at each corner. Lord Greystoke must be wealthy, indeed.

She had no need of money. Like she told Papa, as long as they had each other they had everything they needed. Lord Greystoke would see her as a gold digger for sure.

The arrogant poop. Was he playing with her when he denied being the earl and accusing her of setting a trap for him? He signed the blasted contract or neither of them would be in this mess. She had no intention of getting married, but she wanted to give him some of his own back. He was a nobleman. Before she was through with him, he would beg for mercy.

The tall structure intimidated. *Dear heavens.* What had his childhood been like growing up in a dreary monster like this. She should not feel sorry for Lord Greystoke. She was here to teach him a lesson. At least he had not denied her when she informed him she was coming to Greystoke Manor. But then, she'd not allowed enough time for him to receive her letter before setting out on her journey. What sort of welcome would she receive?

The coach came to a halt. She inhaled a deep breath for courage and waited for the footman. He held her hand as she alighted from the rented vehicle—charged to Lord Greystoke, of course. She looked up to see a man dressed in butler finery waiting at the open door of the three-story manor.

Meeting the lion in the lion's den.

She drew in another breath, hoping her courage would not fail her.

The steps led to a grand walkway the length of the house. Flowers in stylish pots were placed here and there, giving a cozy-bright atmosphere unlike the eerie darkness at her first glance.

"Good day, madam. My name is Josiah. I am Lord Greystoke's butler."

"Good day. Would you please tell Lord Greystoke that Rebekah Hayes is here."

"Of course. He is expecting you. Please follow me to the drawing room."

Expecting me? Rebekah glanced over her shoulder at the footman carrying her luggage.

"Don't worry, Miss Hayes. I will have your luggage sent to your room. This way, if you please."

At least he wasn't going to throw her out in the street. A large staircase swept up to the next floor. Good heavens, it was made of marble. She followed the butler to a beautifully decorated room of cream and soft blue. The large hearth had a fire burning, making the room nice and cozy after being outside in the chilly air.

The butler closed the double doors as he left to get Lord Greystoke, giving her time to look around. Her nerves were about to jump out of her skin. She took a deep breath and decided Lord Greystoke would not distress her. She was cornering him in his own home. Let's see him wiggle out of this one.

She stepped closer to the great hearth that was tall enough she could easily stand inside. A metal grate held back the logs. Flames danced tall, and vibrant colors beckoned the observer nearer. How lovely the blue and orange twisted and mingled giving beauty as well as heat.

She caught herself mutilating the handbag she carried. She'd found it in her mother's trunk, along with the dress she was wearing. As for her luggage, she didn't own much. Her clothes were not appropriate for nobility. She'd been fortunate her Papa had held on to her mother's gowns.

She took in the floral-patterned settees resting on a magnificent Persian carpet. The matching draperies in cream and blue gave the room an elegant touch, what one would expect of the nobility. This was the grand life her mother had come from. Rebekah realized now that all the times she played the game of culture graces, her mother had been teaching her about the aristocrats. She wondered if she was sophisticated enough to pull off this charade.

Footsteps echoed right before the doors opened. The time had come. She turned so she wouldn't miss the expression on his face when he saw her.

The tall, overbearing man smiled. "Miss Hayes. Welcome to my home."

Who in the world is this man? His home?

"Forgive me. Allow me to make the introductions. I am Nathaniel Greystoke, Earl of Greystoke Manor."

Dear heavens. This was Lord Greystoke? He was not ... Had Aaron given a false name?

"My wife wanted to be here when you arrived. She is with my aunt. She will be sorry she wasn't here to greet you."

Your wife? He's already married?

Rebekah felt the walls closing in. The room began to spin.

"Miss Hayes? Oh my. Here." Lord Greystoke stepped to her side and placed a hand under her elbow. "Let me help you sit down. You've had a long journey. Perhaps you would like to rest."

"May I be of service, my lord?"

"Josiah. Perfect timing. Have Anna bring tea and cake immediately." He turned back to Rebekah. Would you care to rest, and perhaps freshen up? My wife will be home directly, and you can meet her then."

"You are the earl?"

"I am Nathaniel Greystoke. Earl of Greystoke"

"Forgive me, Lord Greystoke. I'm afraid I have made a grave error. You see ... I thought ... that is ..."

"You thought you were meeting Aaron, my brother."

Rebekah stared. Her mind whirled, images of two men coming together. Yes, the resemblance was obvious, now that she had time to think. A brother.

Aaron had been telling the truth.

"Miss Hayes. I understand your dilemma. Please do not think I or my brother intended to mislead you. I believe you thought my brother, Aaron, was the Earl of Greystoke. I'm afraid that responsibility is mine. I had hoped to— Never mind. The fact is, I am the earl, and my youngest brother is Aaron. He is the one your father wrote about in his letter."

A maid entered carrying a silver tray holding tea and small cakes.

"Corinne. Would you pour Miss Hayes a cup of tea? And put some of those cakes on a plate.

The maid did as he asked, then he carried the teacup to Rebekah. "Here, Miss Hayes. Would you care for sugar in your tea? And, please have something to eat."

Rebekah's face flushed with embarrassment. Her father had assumed … Dear heavens. "I'm sorry, Lord Greystoke. What you must think? I am embarrassed."

"No need for that Miss Hayes. I'm sure after you rest from your journey, we will work everything out." He held a dainty cup on a thin saucer. "Your tea."

She accepted the China cup, admiring the delicate set with gold trim. She added sugar and used the silver spoon to stir.

"I apologize, Lord Greystoke, for showing up on your doorstep. Does…" She had to think of the name Lord Greystoke used. "Uh, Aaron, does he live here?"

"Actually no. But don't let that worry you. Serena, my wife, and I were expecting you."

Oh yes, his wife. Well, that explained that. But still.

"Please, Miss Hayes. Do not give circumstances another thought. You are welcome in our home."

She ate in silence, wondering what in the world she should do. The tea was hot, and most welcome. It gave her time to gather her wits.

The butler came back. "Excuse me, my lord. Alice has Miss Hayes's room ready."

"Miss Hayes?" Lord Greystoke addressed her. "Are you feeling well enough to climb the monstrous stairs to the next level?"

Her face flushed again. "You expect me to stay?"

"Of course, Miss Hayes. As my wife is not here at the moment, allow me to offer you our hospitality."

Who was this man? Good Heavens, he would think her a sick ninny. What had she gotten herself into? Where was the man who came to her home? She had no choice but to go along with things until she could figure out what to do.

She rose. Was she supposed to curtsy? Or was that for dukes? "Lord Greystoke. I thank you for your kindness."

"Think nothing of it. I will notify you as soon as my wife returns."

She dipped her head in polite acquiescence. It was obvious Lord Greystoke was a commanding presence. She wondered what his wife would be like.

A footman followed Serena into the house, overloaded with packages and boxes. The smile on her face smacked Nathaniel in his gut the way it did every time he saw her.

"I see you and Aunt went shopping."

"Yes, and I'll have to tell you all about it." Serena pulled off her bonnet.

"I have a surprise for you, my love."

"You know I love surprises—" Serena jerked to a stop. "Is she here?"

Nathaniel gave her a nod. "Miss Hayes is up in her chamber."

"Oh no. I wanted to be here when she arrived."

"There's no way we could have known the exact date and time. She didn't send word she was close, but she is here now."

"I hope you didn't frighten her."

"Serena, do you not think I can be cordial to a guest?"

"Cordial, yes. But your size, and if you were wearing that scowl ... At least she didn't run away."

"You need work on soothing my ego."

Serena rose on her toes to give him a kiss. On the cheek. A brief one at that.

"I did not put a guard on her door. I can only presume she is in her chambers."

"Well? What is she like?"

Nathaniel frowned. "A woman."

Serena swatted him.

"I don't know. Nor do I care." He pulled his wife to him and wrapped his arms around her. "The only woman I care about is you."

"That's lovely, Nathaniel. But—"

Before Serena could say more, he kissed her. He would never tire of kissing his wife."

She responded so nicely, he forgot for a moment they had a guest in their house.

"Nathaniel, behave." Serena gently pushed him away. When she tugged on her clothes, he realized he had completely forgotten everything.

He desired his wife. It didn't matter the time of day or night. Or even where they happened to be. Being near her, touching her, he was immediately filled with lust.

"We can go upstairs, if you like."

"I would like you to tell me about our guest."

Bollocks.

"Don't tell me you are tiring of me, Serena."

She gave him her coy—come-hither smile. "Never. However, you must remember we have a guest."

Damnation.

"Very well." He strode to the sideboard for a whisky. "Would you like a sherry, my dear?"

"Yes, thank you. Penelope helped to prepare the seamstress for Miss Hayes' arrival. Just in case, you know."

"In case what?"

"Well, the lady is not of nobility. Perhaps she will need some things. Like a wardrobe."

Nathaniel handed his wife the sherry. "Aunt is making preparations for Miss Hayes?"

"We know nothing about her. We want to make her comfortable. And it is possible she might need, oh, I don't know. Penelope is lining things up, the way she did for me."

"Lining up what things?"

"I'm not exactly sure what Penelope has in mind. But when I first came here, Penelope made me feel at home. I believe she is attempting the same for Miss Hayes."

"Does Aaron know about Aunt?"

"You know your aunt. I sincerely doubt she has confided anything to him. After all, he is against the marriage." Serena sipped her sherry, then sat on the sofa.

Nathaniel picked up his brandy and joined her.

"It seems Aunt is going along as if the two are to be married."

"I'm not sure if that is it."

Nathaniel took a hefty swallow of his brandy. "Oh?"

"Penelope doesn't want to scare the woman away, until she finds out if there is something between Aaron and this woman."

"According to Aaron, nothing."

"I don't think he would tell us if he was involved with a woman."

"You mean romantically? You're right. However, I've not seen any sign that Aaron is interested in any one woman. He likes them all."

"Your brother is not a rogue."

"Which one?"

Serena punched him.

"Ooff. All right. My brothers are not rogues."

"I remember another time when a woman came here and asked for your help."

Nathaniel raised his brow.

"Joyanna," Serena said softly.

"Yes. I had no idea Edmund was involved with a woman, let alone he was madly in love with her."

"Perhaps there is more to Miss Hayes and Aaron than we know."

"With all this business with Bellingham, I've not paid attention to ..." As soon as the words left his mouth, he wished them back. His wife's face wrinkled with concern.

"Do you have news, then?"

"I'm sorry, Serena. No. There has been nothing. We just can't be sure he is gone."

She looked down to her sherry, and said no more. Nathaniel wanted to bring the light back to her face. He finished off his brandy and then rose.

"What do you say, my love? Why don't I help you carry these boxes up to our chamber? You can get ready to meet our guest." He wiggled his brows.

Serena giggled. "I know what you have in mind. Now, be a good husband, and help me gather these packages."

Nathaniel followed his wife up the polished staircase, copiously admiring her backside.

Chapter 7

A big black ball of fur came storming at Rebekah. Before she had time to react, the big ball knocked her right on her derriere.

She tried to catch her breath, and at the same time a slobbering tongue swiped across her nose.

"What the devil!"

"Black down! Oh sir, I am so sorry. Madam, are you all right?"

"Oh dear. Nathaniel, help."

Someone was hastily apologizing, Lord Greystoke was shouting, his wife was pleading with him, and all Rebekah could do was sit and laugh. Now that she knew the big black furball was a dog, she petted the animal and tried to calm him down.

"Please forgive me, I am so sorry, my lord. Down! Black!" The servant trembled as he tried to make things right.

"Rebekah. Are you hurt?" Serena asked.

"I'm all right."

The creature was jerked from her. "Take this beast back to the kitchen! Or better yet, outside!"

"Yes, my lord. Immediately, my lord."

Two servants hurried to obey, dragging the dog away. Nathaniel held a hand out to her, while Serena fretted.

"Are you all right, Miss Hayes?"

"Yes." She used Lord Greystoke's arm to help pull herself up.

Serena looked worried. "Miss Hayes, are you sure you're all right?"

"It was just a dog," Rebekah replied. A very energetic dog.

"Nathaniel! What is going on out here?" Everyone turned at the woman's voice.

"Hello, Aunt."

So much for first impressions. Lord Greystoke had told Rebekah about his aunt living in Aaron's house. Rebekah took a quick glance of her surroundings. Aaron was nowhere in sight.

Nathaniel brushed the older woman's cheek with a kiss.

The woman's eyes passed over her to Lady Greystoke. "Serena. I'm glad you made my nephew bring you along. How are things progressing?"

Serena placed her hand over her big belly. "Wonderful. He or she is kicking up a storm."

"Where are your manners, Nathaniel?"

"Aunt, I've brought someone for you to meet."

The woman swerved her gaze from Nathaniel, straight to Rebekah.

"Aunt Penelope, this is Rebekah Hayes. Miss Hayes, this is Lady Penelope Blackburn, my aunt."

Rebekah dipped a curtsy and hoped she was doing it right. "I'm pleased to make your acquaintance. Uh, my lady."

"I must apologize, Miss Hayes, for the beast that attacked you. He should not be allowed to have run of the house. Are you all right?"

"Yes, ma'am. Uh, my lady. I will admit he caught me off guard." She gave the woman a smile.

"Please come into the drawing room. Nathaniel, help Miss Hayes into the drawing room and see there are no more incidents. I'll not have this young woman break a leg before I get to know her." The woman tucked Serena's arm in hers and led the way.

Lady Blackburn was pleasant enough. Rebekah felt sure this woman gave orders to everyone in her path. Nathaniel gave her a smile and held out his arm. She felt foolish taking it, just to walk into the next room.

"Sit over here, dear." The woman pointed to a chair next to the sofa where Serena was sitting. "Are you sure you're all right? That beast knocked you down."

Rebekah smiled. He hadn't hurt her. Not really. Not even her pride. "I'm fine."

"Berthright, have Susanna bring tea."

"Yes, my lady."

"It is a long trip from Greystoke Manor. Do you need to rest, Serena?"

"I believe I'd like tea first."

"Very well."

Nathaniel strode to the hearth and stood there. Rebekah supposed that was what lords did.

"Now, Miss Hayes. Tell me about yourself."

She shot a panicked look to Nathaniel. He simply gave her a nod of encouragement.

"Well, uh, my name is Rebekah."

"A lovely name, my dear."

"Thank you. I live with my father in Brighton." She glanced to Nathaniel again. He remained quiet. Serena patted her hand, giving her courage to continue. "Our house is much smaller than this one. My father is not an aristocrat, but my mother was."

"Oh. Has your mother passed?"

Just then a knock sounded at the door. Nathaniel walked to the set of doors and opened them, allowing the maid to bring in the refreshments.

"Thank you, Susanna."

"Cook made some lemon tarts, my lady."

"Perfect."

"Her lemon tarts are delicious." Serena snatched one from the tray.

"Rebekah, would you care for a lemon tart?"

She was too nervous to eat. She shook her head. "No, thank you."

"Well then, we'll have them after the tea has steeped. Now, we were discussing your mother."

"Yes, ma'am. Mama passed a few years ago."

"I'm sorry. It is very difficult when one loses a mother."

"Yes, ma— my lady."

"What is your mother's name?"

Lord Greystoke hadn't asked her that question. "Her surname before she married Papa was Holdsworth."

"I remember a Lord Holdsworth. I'm afraid he has passed also."

"I never knew him."

"A grandfather not knowing his granddaughter? That was his loss, not yours. Tell me, Miss Hayes, what brings you to London?"

"I suppose this is where I come in." Nathaniel stepped forward. "I have a tale to tell, Aunt. It is a long one. I hope you will hear the all of it."

"Of course, I will. Doesn't mean I won't ask questions along the way."

Rebekah chewed her lip. The woman caught her doing it.

"First off, should I be worried?

"No, Aunt. But we will seek your guidance, as we did with Serena."

The women exchanged a glance. Rebekah knew there was an underlying message between them.

"Do you remember the trip Aaron took to Brighton a few weeks ago, Aunt? While Aaron was there, he met Mr. Hayes." Lord Greystoke moved his arm toward her. "Miss Hayes' father has a contract with Aaron."

"Well, spit it out, nephew."

"A marriage contract."

The older woman's eyes grew wide. "A what?"

"Oh dear," Serena muttered.

"Yes, Aunt. I said a marriage contract."

The woman stared at Rebekah, making her desperate to find a hiding place. The lady controlled her surprise well. Rebekah wished she knew what the woman was thinking.

"Go on."

"The contract has Aaron's promise to marry Miss Hayes."

"The devil—" The older woman took a deep breath as if to compose herself.

Rebekah wished she had that kind of control over her emotions.

"Forgive me, my dear. I can be outspoken. I'm sure you can understand my surprise. However, I am wondering at your part in this Nathaniel."

"Mr. Hayes only had the name Greystoke. He sent the Earl of Greystoke a letter apprising me of the situation. I spoke to Aaron. He went to see Mr. Hayes. Aaron was under the impression the matter was settled." Lord Greystoke left out the part of Aaron not seeing her father. Maybe Aaron didn't tell him.

Lady Blackburn studied Rebekah. "How does one settle a marriage contract?"

"Aaron came to see me," Rebekah explained, "and we both agreed the contract was nothing."

"Nothing?"

"Neither of us wanted to get married. Not to each other. So, we agreed the matter over."

"Then why do I get the feeling the matter is far from over?"

She looked to Nathaniel for help.

"Aaron claims he does not remember signing the contract."

"It's not like Aaron to forget something so serious as a contract." The woman held Rebekah's gaze while she spoke.

"Agreed. But it is his signature on the contract," Nathaniel stated.

"You're sure?" The woman's gaze never left Rebekah. She now knew how a rabbit felt, just before being served up for supper.

"Aaron has identified his signature."

"Hmmm."

Rebekah had no idea how she remained seated when she wanted to run screaming from the woman's scrutiny.

"What is the conundrum?"

Nathaniel cleared his throat. "Miss Hayes has changed her mind."

A long—very long—moment passed before Lady Blackburn spoke. "Have you Miss Hayes?"

Serena reached over, placing her hand on Rebekah's "Well, that is to say ... yes."

"I see. What does Aaron have to say about this?"

Nathaniel spoke first. "He doesn't know, yet."

"That is why you're here, Miss Hayes?"

"Yes." She hated lying to this woman.

Aaron was supposed to be in the hot seat.

Not her.

Chapter 8

Aaron gave Edmund's butler his hat and marveled that the old man still had the knack to browbeat him. The solemn faced man had been his father's butler. As a child, Aaron had been afraid of him. Even now, the old coot never cracked a smile and never spoke more words than necessary.

For years, Edmund had stayed enclosed in his house, hiding his secret from everyone. Megrims behooved his brother, to the point where Aaron had thought Edmund was losing his mind. Thank God, Nathaniel returned home when he did. For he brought the truth to light about many things.

"Is my brother home?"

"Yes. He is in the library."

"Very well. Are you going to tell me to wait here?" Edmund wasn't expecting him, and usually the butler had no qualms of letting Aaron know that fact. Today he said nothing of the sort.

"No. You may go to the library, master Aaron."

Did the man think he needed his permission? Aaron strode down the corridor, his boots announcing his arrival. The door was open. Feminine laughter floated into the hall. Ah, Joyanna. Edmund's lovely wife-to-be. How he managed to snag that woman was beyond Aaron's imagining.

"May I be allowed to join the party?"

"Aaron." Joyanna rose from the settee, holding out her hands. He clasped them in his own, pressing a kiss to the back of one hand.

"You grow more lovely every day. Are you tired of this insensitive man yet?"

"It's good to see you. You're looking well. How is Aunt Penelope?" Good of her to ignore the stab at his brother.

"She is well. Visiting another matriarch, today."

"Give her my love and tell her I shall visit this week."

"I will do that." Wolf had snapped to attention when Aaron wandered in. "Come here, boy." The dog bounded over to Aaron, greedily seeking praise. "How do you like having a dog in the house, Edmund?"

"I have to admit, brother, you were right. I would be lost without him."

"I see the bounder is still growing."

"Will he get bigger?" Joyanna asked. "I thought he was fully grown."

"If that beast gets any larger, my dear, he'll have to find a new home in the stables."

"Edmund, you wouldn't dare." She knelt down to give the dog a hardy rub. Wolf immediately licked Joyanna's face, causing her to laugh again. The same sound he'd heard before he entered the library.

"I'll take him for a snack," Joyanna said as she rose.

"Good God, don't feed that beast anymore. He'll eat us out of house and home." Edmund turned to Aaron. "I have you to thank for that."

"You're welcome." Aaron grinned. "You love that dog. And it seems Joyanna is fond of Wolf."

"Come on, Wolf. Let's leave these two to their men conversations." She made a signal with her hand for the dog to follow. At the door, Joyanna turned and blew a kiss to her husband.

Aaron could not believe Edmund was the same man. Growing up, they'd gotten into their share of scrapes, but Edmund was always the level headed one. Never laughed much, and after his megrims took hold, he was an absolute bear. Amazing how the love of a good woman could change a man. The tender expression on Edmund's face made Aaron nostalgic. Secretly, he was pleased. One day, perhaps, he too would have a wife he would look at with adoration.

The expression on his brother's face quickly changed. This thundering glower was the one Aaron was used to.

"What do you want?"

Aaron's good mood altered to disappointment. Would his brother ever forgive him?

Not that long ago, Edmund had looked like walking death. Aaron was sure the bottle had a lot to do with his brother's appearance, until he found out about the megrims. Since Edmund had surgery, things seemed to be going along swimmingly. For Edmund and Joyanna. Aaron still feared Edmund resented him for sending for their eldest brother.

"Do not look as if I have an alternative motive.

"Hmmm." Edmund stepped to the sideboard where the decanter was three quarters full. He didn't bother to ask if Aaron wanted a drink. *He* never refused a good brandy.

Edmund poured two fingers of the rich amber-colored liquid, then handed a glass to Aaron.

"You have something to say?"

Aaron hated the control Edmund always seemed to have. Today was no exception. "And here I thought Joyanna had mellowed you." He took a swallow of his brandy. "I had thought to visit my brother." Aaron wanted to cringe at Edmund's raised brow.

Edmund lifted his glass and turned to stare into the fire. "The ton will be ablaze with more than one Greystoke brother off the market."

"When were you ever on the market?" Aaron asked. "Nathaniel left for years. You holed up like a bloody hermit. I was the only one who frequented the ton's events."

"Yes. The rogue brother."

Bollocks. He wasn't that bad. He took a hefty swallow.

"You seem to have the impression I dally with innocents, brother."

"No, Aaron. Just that you are the brother to keep up appearances. While Nathaniel and I ..."

Aaron looked up from the glare he had on his boot. "Yes? Go on."

"True, our father's influence on us was not completely favorable."

"Oh, I don't know. Father persecuted and terrorized Nathaniel until he fled from his loving home."

Edmund choked, causing Aaron to pause.

"What he did to our brother was insufferable, and we were not immune to his wrath. Favorable?" Aaron snorted in disgust.

"He is gone, Aaron. The man is dead and buried."

"Yet his ghosts still linger."

"No more, Aaron. Nathaniel is happily married."

"And living in the very house we all swore was haunted."

Edmund placed his glass on the oak desk. "Why are you here, Aaron?"

Yeah. Why drudge up old wounds?

"For two reasons, actually. One is to ask if you have heard news on Bellingham?"

"There's a name I wish I'd never heard."

About a year ago, a gentleman approached Edmund wanting to buy Greystoke Manor. Edmund was dealing with megrims at the time. Bellingham had taken advantage and used Edmund's condition to blackmail him. The man dealt with pirates, opium and slave traders. The color didn't matter, nor did a title; if a man was breathing, he could be waylaid and locked up in the hold of a ship.

The cur had opium hidden in the caves along the coat of Greystoke Manor. Aaron and his brothers fired the caves, and succeeded in blowing the cargo to smithereens. Bellingham had escaped, made it to his ship. Blade, and Bone, had gotten on board with a plan to blow it up, too. Aaron only wished he knew if Blade managed to get off the ship before the explosion.

"Bellingham has not been back to his country house in Kent. I doubt he will go there, but I'm leaving no stone unturned. I'm sorry, Aaron. No luck. No one has seen him."

Each of the three brothers would gladly flay the man if they could get their hands on him. First Bellingham had tried to steal Greystoke Manor. He'd blackmailed Edmund, then kidnapped Nathaniel's wife, Serena. They thought they'd gotten rid of the guttersnipe when their hired man blew up the caves on the beach. But the bastard had shown up again and threatened Edmund.

"He's popped up before. I'm not going to automatically assume he went with his ship to a watery grave."

"It's too soon for him to show himself. What about Blade?"
Blade.

"I have men searching up and down the coast in Brighton. I'm not giving up." Aaron scrubbed a hand over his worried face. "I've been asking around. No one's seen him." Aaron smacked his palm against his breeches. He felt responsible. Blade had gone on the ship at Aaron's directive.

"Maybe Blade is laying low. Don't lose hope yet, Aaron."

Don't lose hope? Don't give up? Should he wish that his brother would forgive him while he wished for the moon?

Aaron downed his drink.

"On to the lighter side of things, Aunt seems to be taken with Joyanna. You know, whenever you get tired of the old girl, I can take her off your hands for a bit."

Aaron sniggered. "She'd love hearing you put it like that. Aunt likes living in town."

"Parties, balls and all that rot?"

"That rot, as you call it, has a certain lure. She is happy. I have access to my club, and even though I am not in the chain of gossip, she keeps me informed of current happenings."

Edmund held up his empty glass, quietly asking if Aaron wanted another. As he poured brandy into both glasses, he spoke, "You said there were two reasons."

Aaron ran a hand through his hair. His brother wouldn't care, but he thought he should tell him anyway. "You're aware of Anderson Shipping?"

"Most businessmen are."

"You may as well know I am a partner."

"A partner?" Edmund handed Aaron his glass.

"Yes, Edmund. Your rogue brother has invested in the ship-ping business."

Edmund glared. "You have a chip on your shoulder? Was this something you wanted to do?"

"Yes, Edmund. This is something I wanted. As a matter of fact, I've wanted this for a long time."

"Then why didn't you invest sooner?"

Aaron saw red. The haze threatened to swallow him. Damn his brother.

Damn and blast him.

"For some insane reason, I thought you might want to know and not be caught unaware."

Edmund looked thoughtful.

What the devil was he thinking?

"Anderson Shipping is well known among the nobles. If your investment is public knowledge, someone would have mentioned it."

Well, hell. He tried.

Aaron downed the brandy, enjoying the burn. "Now you know. I'll be off." Before he could pace two steps, Edmund stopped him.

"Aaron. Is there anything else you wish to say?"

Sod off.

But he kept that to himself.

———eee———

Edmund walked to the drawing room and stood before the floor to ceiling window.

"Is anything wrong, Edmund?" As always, Joyanna's presence calmed him.

"Not at all my dear." There was a time, not so long ago, he would have answered differently. Thank Christ, he suffered no more headaches that hammered away in is skull. Megrims—the doctor had called them. "I'm simply watching Aaron leave."

"Is he well?"

Edmund turned to his wife. "All is well, my love. I just feel that something is off with him. He's holding something back."

With the cold greeting he had given Aaron the last time he came to his home, Edmund was surprised that his brother had bothered to come back. But then Edmund had been in agony, and the damned brandy did nothing to alleviate the pain.

"You know, I rebuked my little brother for tattling on me to Nathaniel."

"Your megrims?"

Edmund gave a nod. Then reached for Joyanna's hands. "'Twas bad enough, trying to hide the headaches from Aaron. I knew I wouldn't have a chance of concealing them from Nathaniel."

She leaned into his chest. "My poor darling. Surely, Aaron understands now."

"I don't know."

"Do you think he is still worried about how you feel? Him sending for Nathaniel?"

"Aaron had always been the one to intervene when Nathaniel and I would argue. Humph. We would be shouting down the house, and Aaron would step in, reminding us we were brothers. I'll always be grateful for that. He cared about Nathaniel and me."

One corner of his mouth lifted into a grin.

"Aaron was also the carefree brother. Of late, he's too solemn. He sure as hell shouldn't be worried about me. I wasn't thinking clearly then. I have no grievance with Aaron now."

"Does he know that? Have you told him—with words?

Edmund raised a brow. After a moment, he shook his head. "He can't still think—"

"What did you talk about? Can you tell me?"

"He asked if I'd heard anything about Bellingham."

"That hateful man. I hope he is dead."

"My ferocious wife." Edmund chuckled.

"Do you blame me? He threatened us, attempted blackmail. He tried to ruin things between us."

Edmund pulled Joyanna into his arms and rested his cheek on the top of her head. "I know, my love. But here we are. You and me."

She pulled away enough to see his face. "I love you."

"I know you do, darling." He kissed her lips. "I love you, too. Bellingham tried to do his worst, and failed. We're together. And we will always be together. I'll never let him or anyone else take you from me."

"I'll hold you to that." She laid her head back on his chest, close to his heart.

God, how he loved this woman.

"Aaron didn't give you any idea what he had on his mind?"

Aaron kept personal things close to his vest. He'd never been one to share. Most of their discussions were about Nathaniel. Aaron idolized him. Nothing Edmund could do about that. But Aaron seemed to be more detached since Nathaniel's return to Greystoke. Perhaps that wasn't the right word.

"It was almost as if he was worried about me?" Edmund said aloud.

"Worried about you?"

"I mean, as though he was worried about my reaction. Like I was going to berate him for something."

"What do you think he's done?"

"Nothing serious. At least I hope not. He's not himself."

"What about Aunt Penelope?"

"If there was anything in that quarter, he most assuredly would have told me. I will speak to Nathaniel. Maybe he knows something."

Chapter 9

W hen Aaron arrived home, he saw Nathaniel's carriage with the Greystoke crest. Evidently Serena had come to pay a call on Aunt.

The elderly butler opened the door before Aaron reached the top step. Aunt liked the older gentleman whose years had outgrown his duties. To please her, Aaron allowed the man to keep his post. His duties consisted of answering the door and no more. Unless it was to sit with Penelope at teatime and listen to the gossip of the ton. The man was most likely hard of hearing, so he shouldn't mind as much as Aaron or Nathaniel.

Only a slight hike of the old man's brow alerted Aaron that something was up.

"Good day, sire. His lordship is in the drawing room with Lady Blackburn."

So, his brother had accompanied his wife.

"Very well."

Aaron mentally went over his schedule. No, they did not have an appointment today. With a smile on his face, he strode to the drawing room, eager to greet his sister-in-law. It was a boon in his cap, putting a scowl on Nathaniel's face, when he sweet-talked Serena as though he were a rogue after her affection.

"Where is my favorite lady in all of London?" he called out as he stepped through the doors.

He came to a halt. Serena sat on a settee beside his aunt, with another lady in the chair at her side. The woman looked up, a glare on her beautiful face.

Good God. What was *she* doing here?

"Aaron," Aunt called smartly, bringing him to heel. "We have a guest."

His first reaction was to shout at *their guest*, then throw her out. But with the glare his aunt shot him, decorum was required at the moment. He needed to be on his best behavior. Aunt would have nothing less.

Sasha must have heard his voice and lumbered to his side. The dog gave him comfort, and the distraction he needed to calm his ire.

"I need to speak to you about your dog."

Aaron hiked a brow.

"Not Sasha. The Black."

"Am I being taken to task, Aunt Penelope?"

"That is a debate for another time. Please, come in and join us for tea."

Aaron sauntered in, holding the newcomer's gaze. "There's no need to introduce us, Aunt. The *lady* and I have already met."

Nathaniel coughed into his hand.

What the devil was going on here? And how had Nathaniel gotten involved? And Serena?

"Hello, Aaron," Serena said in a soothing voice. He supposed she was the buffer for this situation.

Bloody hell.

He gave a pat to Sasha, and then stepped to his sister-in-law.

"Forgive my bad manners, Serena. It is good to see you." He took her gloved hand and paced a kiss on the back. "Is there a party and someone forgot to invite me?"

"I will forgive your bad manners, if you collect them and greet your guest, Miss Hayes."

What else was he to do?

"Good afternoon, Miss Hayes." He gave a slight bow, holding her steely gaze.

"Good afternoon, Lord Greystoke."

"Ahh, I see no one has corrected that oversight?"

"Miss Hayes knows I'm the earl, Aaron."

"Then she also knows," he said, locking eyes with her again, "that I am a third son."

"There is no need for educating Miss Hayes on aristocracy, Aaron. Sit down, and join us for tea."

Dear Aunt.

Your wish is my command.

He strode to the hearth, signaled for Sasha to lie down, then took the seat farthest from *their guest*. She hung her head, looking at her hands carefully folded in her lap. He wondered how she managed to be so calm. He was ready to roar like an animal.

"Berthright, bring more tea," his aunt ordered.

"Yes, my lady."

"Have a lemon tart, Rebekah. Aaron has the best cook in London." His gaze jerked to Serena.

Rebekah, is it? She already has the family calling her by her given name?

"When did you arrive, Miss Hayes?"

Her eyes snapped to him.

"How did you find my home?"

Nathaniel answered for her. "I received correspondence from Miss Hayes. We were expecting her, brother."

Aaron glared at his brother. "*You* were expecting Miss Hayes?"

"Miss Hayes arrived at Greystoke Manor two days ago," Serena added. "Of course, I asked her to extend her stay. However, she was quite keen on seeing you."

"I'll bet." He didn't mean to speak out loud. A glare from his aunt made him realize she heard him. He shrugged.

He wanted to ask if it was before or after she found out Nathaniel was the heir. He didn't dare speak out of turn with Aunt sitting in the same room.

"Rebekah, you are welcome in our home."

His aunt was taking a lot for granted. Did she forget this was *his* house?

"To avoid any confusion, Miss Hayes, yes Aunt Penelope lives with me. This is her home. If she offers an invitation, you may be assured it is genuine."

When he got Miss Hayes alone, he would inform her exactly what he expected, and who was in charge.

"How kind of you for supporting your aunt. It is clear you are a close family."

Did he hear a note of sadness in her voice? What the bloody hell was she doing here?

From the corner of his eye, he saw Nathaniel's expression. His brother most likely wanted to throttle him. Why didn't Nathaniel notify him? Dammit, they had waylaid him. Thoughts ran rampant in his head as he listened to idle chit chat. He wanted answers. He wanted them now.

"Aunt, if you will forgive me," he said as he stood. "Miss Hayes and I need to have a private conversation." He turned to Rebekah. "Miss Hayes? Would you care to join me in the library?"

Her glare spoke volumes. "Of course, Honourable Greystoke."

Ah, she got it right that time.

"Miss Hayes, we will wait for you here. Then I will show you to your chamber where you can get settled before the supper hour," his aunt announced.

Assuming she was still here. He could just as well take Miss Hayes to an inn.

Nathaniel bumped his elbow. "Aaron. Mind your temper. I'll be right here."

"Miss Hayes, do not be alarmed. My family is protective of the female population. This way, if you please."

He stepped to the set of double doors, checked to see if she was following, then strode down the corridor to the library. "After you," he said, with a way of arm gesturing like any distinguished gentleman.

The click of the latch sounded like a cannon echoing in the dark room. Wooden shelves lined every wall. Good heavens, she'd never seen so many books.

Rebekah stood in awe, as the nerves shivered down her spine. She was facing the lion in the lion's den.

"Now, Miss Hayes. Would you care to tell me exactly why you are here, and how the devil you connected with my brother?"

Rebekah took a deep breath. "We left things unsettled between us."

He arched a brow over that glowering face. "Oh? You seemed to be in agreement over tearing up that contract."

Yes, well, he'd made her mad. The more she thought about his behavior, the madder she got. "I've changed my mind."

"Too late."

She'd expected him to be disagreeable. "I don't think so."

"What is it you do think, Miss Hayes?" He spoke so evenly, with no emotion.

"I've decided to make you honor that contract."

"Lord Greystoke is my brother. You've hooked the wrong Greystoke, madam. If it's a title you want, I'm not your man."

"You are nothing like your brother," she said, exasperated.

"Care to explain that?"

"*He* is kind."

A sharp snort escaped Aaron's mouth.

She gritted her teeth. "A title means nothing to me. However, your word does. You have gone back on your word. A promise you made in writing."

His eyes flashed. Still, he showed no anger. "Miss Hayes. Might I remind you that you refused me when I came to you. And now you say you have changed your mind."

The arrogant poop stood there as if he had all the time in the world. As if he had not shunned her, or the promise he'd made.

"I am going to hold you to your promise. You signed a contract. I am here to see you fulfill it." At least she sounded convincing—when underneath she was a bundle of nerves. Why had she set out on this path without thinking it through?

"You're mad."

"You think so? I have the backing of your brother, Lord Greystoke. Your aunt has also accepted me."

Take that.

"You discussed this with Aunt Penelope?"

"I had to explain my reason for showing up on your doorstep?" His brooding expression made her nervous, as if she wasn't already.

"How the bloody hell did you find me?"

She jumped at his outburst. "The Earl of Greystoke is well known. I didn't know he was your brother."

"I bet that took a feather from your bonnet."

She had not thought him so cruel. But this was the real Aaron Greystoke. "It was a shock. At first, I thought you'd given me a false name. But your brother knew. He knew about the contract."

"And he has a wife. Another stunner."

What was he hinting at?

She twisted her hands and prayed her legs would hold her up.

"Well, yes. However, they are good people. Lord Greystoke brought me to you."

Aaron shrugged. "What can I say. Brotherly love."

"You are disgraceful," she huffed.

"Why? Because I rejected you? Because my brother should have minded his own business? How do you suppose I should act? I didn't even know there was a bloody contract until your father wrote to Nathaniel."

This was not going according to plan. She should have known she was no match for the oversized, overbearing brute. "Your signature was on it."

"I believe, Miss Hayes, we've covered this ground before. We talked it out. I was under the impression we were in agreement."

She lifted her nose in the air the way she would expect a matron to do. "You owe me. You have ruined my good name."

His eyes changed from anger to predator. He slowly stepped toward her. She swallowed, forcing her feet not to run. When he was barely a breath from her, he lowered his head and stared into her eyes. "I will not marry you. Your journey here has been a waste of time."

Trying to rattle him was going to take more work. Hopefully his bark was worse than his bite. "I will simply tell your brother you took my virginity."

This time when his brow hiked, a muscle in his face twitched. Now she'd done it. He was furious. A moment later his expression calmed as if he'd gotten control of his anger.

"If you plan to use that line of blackmail, then I think I should make the threat true."

She gasped.

What?

He took a threatening step toward her. She held out a hand.

"Wait! What are you doing?"

"If I am to be labeled a scoundrel, then I want the experience. Claim my right, so to speak."

Good heavens, he was completely unpredictable. "You are ..." She backed up a step.

"Yes?" He took another step, the way a predator would stalk his prey.

"No. Wait. Stop!"

He halted, but was still too darn close. *Drat.* He'd called her bluff.

"Quite a lot of courage you have going on there, but I believe the rabbit is scared. What do you expect from me? Marriage? Money?"

She'd meant to thwart him. Shame him. Scare him, as if that were possible. Embarrass him then. Show him she was not to be trifled with. Show the mighty Aaron Greystoke how it felt to be attacked in his own home.

"I give up." She stepped away, giving her pounding heart time to slow down. "I don't want to marry you."

"You should have thought about that before you came to London, and announced to anyone who would listen, that we are betrothed." He smirked.

She crossed her arms over her chest. "Your sarcasm does not go unnoticed. Neither do you want to marry me."

He studied her for what seem like hours. "What is your real purpose for being here?" His deep voice penetrated under her skin, sending her nerves to race wildly down her back.

"Very well." She jerked her shoulders up and stiffened her spine. "You embarrassed me." There she'd said it. "You treated me as if I were dirt under your shoe."

His eyes lit with surprise. Had the fool not known how he had shamed her? He studied her for several moments more. She stared back and tried to keep her knees from shaking.

"Say what you have to say Lord Greystoke."

"How fickle you are. You don't want to marry me? Are you sure?"

"Quite sure." In for a penny ... in for a pound. "I wanted to see you squirm."

The hateful man grinned. "Miss Hayes. I do not squirm."

He was large and muscled and ... of course he didn't. Aaron looked like a man that could tackle anything and anyone, and come out the winner. She couldn't help but admire his strength, his handsomeness.

"You have won over my brother, my sister-in-law, and my aunt. That is no easy feat. If you think word has not spread of your arrival through the ton, you would be mistaken. New blood. No doubt, the hounds are already on your scent."

"What are you talking about?"

"Gossip. The ton. Rogues after the new mystery woman. And if you have declared your purpose for coming to London outside of this house ..."

"What has that to do with anything?"

The blond adonis slowly shook his head from side to side. She remembered running her hands through his long hair. Holding him close as he kissed her neck ...

She jerked the image from her mind. Her nerves were running amok as it was.

"It seems we are in a pickle, Miss Hayes. By coming here as you have, you've brought attention to our ... plight. Now our private business is public knowledge."

Which had been her intention. Good. Let him writhe under the ton's watchful eye. See how he likes being the brunt of malicious blather.

"Do you understand what you have done, Miss Hayes?" He waited only a moment before he went on. "You have made the marriage contract public."

Satisfaction made her smile. He was worried about gossip. Not her. She would return to her small home and continue on with her quiet life. He could deal with the fall out. She crossed her arms and gave a smug look of her own.

"Then I suggest you find a way to silence the gossips."

"After you have set their tongues to wagging?"

"How does it feel to have the entire upper-crust judging you? Your precious reputation in tatters."

"I don't give a farthing about *my* reputation. And my name is Aaron. Since we are betrothed, I suggest you use it."

"We are not betrothed."

That eyebrow hiked again. "As far as the ton knows, we are."

"You just said you don't care what the ton thinks."

"Personally, I don't. However, the Greystoke name is in good standing. Aunt Penelope is a matriarch of the nobility. I will not put her in a position to be ridiculed."

Aunt Penelope. That kind, dear woman.

"Perhaps you should have considered that when you ostracized me."

"Good God, you do love drama." He chuckled. "You've missed your calling on the stage."

Fury burned in her stomach. If the man wasn't so tall, she'd smack him. She stomped her foot instead.

"Miss Hayes. Did you stomp your dainty foot? How unbecoming of a lady."

"You arrogant ..."

"Ah, ah, ah," he said waving a finger. "You're a lady, remember?"

"I am not a social butterfly, nor am I a hypocrite. You have sparked my temper, lord—"

"Ah, ah, ah," That hateful finger flashed again.

Blast the man.

She counted to ten.

"I can see by your expression; you're counting in that pretty head of yours. Don't screw up your face so. You don't want to freeze that way."

Pretty?

Freeze!

She opened her mouth to shout. Scream at the injustice of it all.

Perhaps he was also trying to exasperate her. A trick.

"I will tell the truth."

"Out of the question. Your claim to be betrothed has already been heard. To tell the truth now would embroil us all in a scandal. My aunt is a matriarch of the ton. I will not allow anything to darken her reputation."

"What are you saying?"

"That your little plan has worked—or backfired. Which ever way you see it."

"It worked? You don't look rattled to me."

"On the contrary. You came here to ensnare a husband. Congratulations, Miss Hayes. You have succeeded."

Shock made her mouth drop open. She stared at him all of two seconds. "You are so devoted to the ton, you would marry a woman you don't want to avoid a scandal?"

"Devoted to my aunt. It is done among the aristocracy all the time. There are countless marriages performed quickly and quietly for that very reason."

"Well, not this one. I have no intention of marrying you."

"Yet you tracked me down in London to substantiate that very thing."

Rebekah fumed. What had she done?

"You see, Miss Hayes, we now have a very real problem." He paced to the hearth and leaned an elbow on the ledge. Silence filled the room for several minutes. Finally, he spoke. "I propose a marriage of convenience. After a reasonable amount of time, we can dissolve the vows, or if you are comfortable, we can go on. I will provide you a home, and arrange an allowance to care for your every need."

Her jaw dropped. Was he serious?

"It would also seem, Miss Hayes, I am calling your bluff. We will be married."

All she could do was stand there and shake her head. All the denial in the world would not get her out of this one. "To each other?"

He faced her. "Do you have a beau? Or a gentleman caller?"

"Of course not."

"Neither do I."

"You don't have a gentleman caller?"

"Sarcasm at this stage is wasted, Miss Hayes. And no, there is no lady I fancy. So, I think the best way to handle this situation—that you have put us in—is to move forward."

What? Had she heard him correctly?

"What if you decide later on you want to marry someone else?"

"You have no need to worry about that. As for you, we'll cross that bridge when we come to it."

Queasiness crawled into her stomach. She might be violently ill. She did not want a husband. She was used to doing as she pleased. "Can you guarantee that I will not be under your control?"

"Husbands do have control over their wives, but I would allow you to do what you wished. Within reason, of course. No lovers. Nothing to create a scandal. After all, we will be marrying to prevent one. You may be your own charge. I will not expect you to share my bed."

She gasped. She had not considered that in the least.

"We can live separate lives, if you so choose. You will have servants to cover household duties. All you will need to do is enjoy your newfound wealth."

She dropped her arms to her sides, fisting her hands. "I do not want or need your money."

"I'm not saying you do. Being my wife will open doors and provide anything you might desire."

What was she to do? Things had gotten way out of her control. "You will not force me into this?"

"I am not in the habit of forcing women to do my will. However, given the circumstances ..." he shrugged, "I believe this is the best course, Any concerns you have you may put in writing. I will agree."

"Another contract?" That's what had gotten her into this mess.

"You will end up better situated. And with funds of your own."

Good heavens. What had she done? The walls were closing in on her.

Papa pushing her, Aaron giving her a way out. Sort of. A marriage of convenience. Not a real marriage at all. Where she could live in security as a noble.

As her mother had.

As her mother chose to forego.

Was it really too late to back out?

"I will give you time to think on it, Miss Hayes. Shall we return to the drawing room, so my aunt knows I have not gobbled you up?"

Gobble. What a choice of words. At this moment, she felt like she had spent the night in a terrible storm. She was bruised and battered and needed to sleep. She supposed he meant the quip as doing his worst.

But the remark sent a tiny spark of yearning to her belly. Maybe he didn't remember, but she did. That night ... it was as if he had gobbled her up. He had devoured her.

And she desperately wanted that again.

Chapter 10

It wasn't as if Rebekah didn't know what a servant was, but she'd never had any. She'd always taken care of herself. In Aaron's house, the staff were in and out, always about. It amazed her how Penelope had them fluttering every which way, ordering them around as if she were royalty.

But then, she was. They were.

An earl. A noble.

Rebekah had never been around the aristocracy. The only noble she had known was her mother. And she'd been snubbed by her own father when she married a commoner. But it hadn't changed the way they lived. Thank goodness for that. Rebekah learned the value of love and family. Possessions were only material things. Things that were wanted, not needed.

She descended the circular stairway, admiring the beauty of the design. The woodcarver was an artist, indeed. Little carvings in each post, shining to perfection. With a house this big, no wonder Aaron had so many servants.

"Good morning, miss. Lady Blackburn is in the sitting room."

"Thank you," she told the maid. "And thank you for bringing up my breakfast. You didn't need to do that."

"Oh yes, miss, I did. The master told me to get you breakfast first thing. We suspected you might be an early riser."

"Well, it was good. Thank you. I left the tray in my room. I'll go get it."

Before she could turn, the maid stopped her. "Oh, no, miss. You mustn't. That's my job."

Rebekah supposed it was. "Thank you."

"You're welcome, miss. If you will please follow me, I'll show you where Lady Blackburn is."

She followed the maid back up the steps to the second level and down a wing with several doors.

"My lady's rooms are this entire wing. Master Aaron said this would make her feel as if she was in her own home."

"How nice." The house was rather large. Not as large as Greystoke. That place was huge.

The maid gave a soft knock, and opened the door. "Miss Hayes, my lady."

"Good, good. Come in, come in."

"Good morning, Lady Blackburn."

"Pshaw," Penelope said with a wave of her hand. "Thought we settled this yesterday. Call me Penelope. If you marry my nephew, you can call me Aunt."

Rebekah nearly choked. She was not marrying Aaron.

"Glad you're no slugabed. Neither am I. I like seeing the morning sunshine. There are times when I do sleep late. Usually after a social engagement or a ball. You'll learn all about that."

"I don't know that I will. I'm not sure how long I'll be here."

"Did my nephew ask you to leave?"

"Well, no, he didn't."

"Then you are to stay here. I told Mandy to bring you breakfast. Tomorrow morning you will join me downstairs. Be sure to give Cook your favorite dishes."

"Oh, I don't want to be any trouble."

"Dear, it's what we do. Now. Tell me about your discussion with Aaron."

Rebekah had to hide the surprise from her face. Penelope was a no-bones woman. Right to the point. No pretense of polite conversation, then sneak up on the controversial subject.

"Begin anywhere you want. Tell me what's going on."

"Lady—"

"Please don't fall back on etiquette. I told you. Please call me Penelope. I'm not an ogre, my dear." Her face screwed up. "I'll leave that impression to my nephew."

Rebekah giggled. "We spoke a little before Aaron came home." She hesitated before saying his name. It seemed so intimate. "I guess you know everything."

"I'm sorry about your mother. If you like, you can talk to me as though you would if your mother was here. I will listen."

The expression on Penelope's face made Rebekah want to cry. She wished her mother was here. She gave a slight sniff.

"Here dear. Here's a hanky."

"Thank you." Rebekah twisted the material an began her story.

"Mama was from a noble family. She fell in love with my Papa, and they were happy. She raised me with love and taught me some things that were in the aristocrat world, like dancing, and how to speak properly. I guess Papa wanted me to have what my mother gave up."

Penelope didn't say a word. She sat quietly and allowed Rebekah to speak.

"Anyway, I'm not sure how the contract came about. Papa must have slipped something into Aaron's whisky. When I came down stairs to see what was going on, Aaron was passed out on the floor. I didn't know who he was, but I recognized him as a gentleman right away."

"*Humph*. A gentleman would not have passed out on your floor."

Rebekah swallowed. I helped him up and made a bed on our sofa." She schooled her face, hoping not to give anything away. "The next morning, I woke up and he was gone.

"So, you don't know how his name or his signature came to be on the contract?"

"No." Rebekah shook her head. "Weeks later, my father told me about the ... contract. He must have written to Lord Greystoke, and his lordship replied. Papa thought Aaron was the earl. He kept saying how he done right by me. How I was going to have a fine house and fine things. I thought he was fantasizing.

"Papa took to drinking when Mama died. So, I was excited to see him come out of the despair he'd been in. He was happy. Speaking nonsense, so I thought, but more lively than he'd been in three years. Then he told me about the marriage contract."

"Must have been a shock."

"We argued. I told him I wasn't marrying anybody. And I thought that was the end of it. Papa snorted and got mad. Stomped around complaining. I ignored him."

She tried ignoring the feelings that she remembered too. But she dreamed of Aaron most nights. Everything came back as clearly as the night they were joined.

Heat flushed her face, and her breathing grew heavy. Thinking of Aaron and their night together made her want more. But it was not to be.

"Go on, child."

Rebekah blinked. "Then Aaron showed up. He was angry. Accused me of setting a trap."

"That blind fool."

"My father was wrong. And I didn't realize what he'd done until after Aaron left."

He didn't remember me.

She'd been shocked to see him. Embarrassed. Tongue tied. And he didn't even recognize her.

"He was looking for my father. When he realized I was the daughter, his whole temperament changed. He thought it was my idea. He was infuriated. There was no explaining anything to him. The more he shouted, the angrier I got, and I shouted right back."

"Good for you."

"I'm sorry, Penelope. I wasn't nice." Rebekah thought about what she was going to say and hoped the woman would let her explain. "I'm ashamed to say I plotted revenge."

"Revenge?"

"I'm getting ahead of myself. Through the shouting, we somehow managed to discover that neither one of us were going to accept the agreement."

"Did you question his signature?"

"I don't think we got that far. He refused to be trapped and I told him I wouldn't marry him if he was the only man on Earth."

"Ha. I would have liked to have seen that. Boy considers himself a ladies' man."

She could see why. Aaron was handsome, sizable, and too darn fetching not to think highly of himself. Any woman would drool over his attractive looks. Herself included.

"Then what?" Penelope asked.

"We agreed that neither one of us wanted to marry the other, and we considered the contract void."

"You both agreed?"

"Yes."

Penelope frowned like she was thinking. "Are we at the revenge part?"

Rebekah nodded. "The more I thought about his accusations, the madder I got. I thought it would serve him right if he'd gotten stuck by that contract. He needed to be taught a lesson. As far as I knew, the contract still existed."

Penelope gave a nod.

"I came up with the idea to make him pay. Make him squirm. I thought if I came to his home and demanded he honor the agreement, I would shake him."

As far as she was concerned, Aaron needed to be brought down a peg or two. He was too darn good-looking for his own good.

"That's why you came here? To rattle him? Did you change your mind about the marriage?"

"Heavens, no!" Rebekah leaped from her chair. "I'm sorry, Penelope. But your nephew is an arrogant, rude, pig-headed, condescending bully. I have no intention of marrying him. Or anyone for that matter."

"So what happened in the library yesterday?"

"He called my bluff."

"Naturally. One thing I can say about my nephews: none of them are weak. They're about as stubborn as an ox and ten time meaner when they want to be. Oh, don't get me wrong. Aaron is a good man. A respectable, upright man. He's always been the buffer between his hothead brothers. He has more patience, more tolerance when it comes to Nathaniel and Edmund, than I do. I've seen him angry. I've seen him worried. But I've never seen his temper. Usually, around ladies, he is considerate to a fault. But he is clever."

Rebekah released a long breath. What was she to do?

"He called your bluff."

"Yes," she answered with a nod. "I even told him I would tell his brother he took advantage of me." She hadn't planned to bring that up, but Aaron would most likely tell Penelope.

"As in compromise?"

Again, Rebekah nodded.

Penelope laughed. "I can only imagine what came next."

"Nothing," Rebekah hurried to explain. Anything to avoid repeating what Aaron did. "I told him I did not want to marry him and that was the end of it."

"Did Aaron accept that?"

"He will have to. He mentioned gossip. I told him that was his problem. I plan to go home and forget this whole mess."

"Hmmm. That's just it."

"What?"

"I'm afraid, my dear, you have created a bit of a muddle."

"I haven't done anything. I challenged Aaron, and he called my bluff. That's the end of it. I'm going home."

"You told him that?"

"Of course, I told hm."

"What did he say?"

"It doesn't matter. This charade is over." Rebekah rose to leave.

"Not so fast, Rebekah."

She halted in her tracks.

"Sit down, dear. Let me explain something."

What in the world was there to explain?

She turned back toward the little table and sat down.

"Let me tell you a story about three boys. Their father raised them with an iron hand. His will as strong as any devil I've ever seen. Once he set a course, there was no veering off. The oldest son was to inherit, so he started working with the boy at an early age. Then, along came a second son, and then a third where the mother died in childbirth.

"The father was not a kind man. He demanded his rules be followed and his instructions obeyed. Questions were not allowed, and no whining. "Nathaniel never whined. He was as stubborn as his father. I'm afraid that set a pattern for them. The father thought he could beat the mulish attitude out of his firstborn."

Rebekah gasped in shock. Nathaniel's father beat him? What about his brothers?

It was as if Penelope heard the unspoken question. "Mostly he ignored the second and third son. He only needed one to inherit. But still, the father was just as demanding with the younger two. It's a wonder any of them survived." Penelope looked down at her hands. Her expression one of despair. "I tried to interfere. Of course, I was sent packing." She raised her head, meeting Rebekah's eyes. "A man has control of his property. The Earl of Greystoke considered his sons his property.

"It wasn't easy for Aaron, growing up with a monster for a father. He is close to his brothers, even if it does not appear so. They are siblings. They bicker."

Rebekah shook her head to sort out everything Penelope told her. It sounded like all three boys had a horrible upbringing.

"Aaron is a good boy. A strong man. He's endured a lot for his younger years. He's as honest as men come. And he is an aristocrat. He knows what is proper, after all, he had a father who drilled it into him. He watched his brother suffer under his father's rule. I only tell you this because I want you to understand him. He is a nobleman. But he has a heart.

"I've lived in this house with him for years. He could have put me out at any time, yet he did not. I'm sure I get on his nerves, but that boy has never raised his voice to me. And I know he has a good set of lungs because I've heard him shout at his brothers."

"I believe I have seen a little of both sides of Aaron. I've seen him angry. We shouted at each other." Rebekah lowered her head timidly saying the last part. "When we spoke in private, I expected a tongue-lashing. He actually asked me what I wanted."

"What do you want, Rebekah?"

"I want to go home."

"That's not what I mean. What do you want in life?"

"What?" Her confusion, surely, must have shown on her face. "In life?"

Penelope shook her head. "What would you honestly like to have for yourself? A family perhaps? Children? Romance?"

"Doesn't every girl dream of a handsome man that will rescue her?"

"Do you need rescuing, Rebekah? Not from Aaron. Perhaps from something at home?"

Rebekah stiffened and arched her back into a straight line. "My father and I have a good life, Lady Blackburn."

"Perhaps loneliness? Perhaps you'd like a home of your own."

"Lady Blackburn, I came here to annoy Aaron Greystoke, not for any other reason. I do not want his money. I do not want a title. I make bad decisions when I'm in a temper."

"I understand," Lady Blackburn said with a nod. "However, Aaron can give you a different way of life." Rebekah opened her mouth to profess her case, but Penelope held up a hand.

"Not that you asked for it, but why turn it down? You are a lovely girl. You made a splash when you came to London. It was not your intention, but you have given food for fodder to the gossipmongers. They can be a grueling lot."

"I never meant—"

"I know dear." Penelope patted Rebekah's hand.

Her fingers ached from the strenuous punishment she was giving them.

"Aaron needs someone in his life. I think he's a likeable enough fellow. The ladies bat their eyes and pretend to swoon just to get his attention. If the two of you would spend some time together, I think you could work out a reasonable compromise. All that said, you should extend your stay here."

Was she serious? Why?

"We are not bad people, Rebekah. I think you would enjoy your stay."

Rebekah gasped. "I don't think you're bad. That is to say, I'm sure you are a kind person."

"My nephew is another matter, am I right?"

"Uh, no." Her face flushed and she knew it was turning red. "I mean, he seems a gentleman."

"Good, then you'll stay."

Rebekah closed her eyes to keep her head from spinning. She didn't think she had agreed.

"I'm asking you to think about your discussion with Aaron. Stay here with us, at least for a little while. Give us time to sort this out."

Rebekah didn't know what to do. Aunt Penelope was so nice, and her words were reasonable. No matter how much Rebekah wanted to run, she supposed she didn't need to leave right away. And what of Papa? He boasted to everyone that his daughter was marrying a nobleman. It was all too confusing.

She wished she'd never come to London.

Penelope dabbed her mouth with her napkin. "Would you like some more tea, dear?"

"No thank you."

"I'm done. Do you have plans for the day, Rebekah?"

"Um, no. I haven't thought about anything past feeling quite ridiculous."

"Nonsense. Give me a half hour to get dressed and I'll meet you downstairs. We'll talk about what to do. The first thing is to call Madame Laselle. We will order you gowns, and bonnets, and slippers, everything you will need while you are here."

"I don't need gowns and bonnets. I have clothes."

"You are betrothed to Aaron Greystoke. He can easily afford to dress you. You will have appropriate attire and I will assign you a lady's maid."

What had she gotten herself into? It seemed once Penelope got an idea in her mind, she ran with it. Rebekah still had a lot of thinking to do. For now, she would go along.

"All right." Rebekah rose to leave. Before she opened the door, Penelope called to her.

"Rebekah. Promise me you won't leave without telling me."

Chapter 11

S everal miles south, off the shore of Hampshire, a ship bobbed with the rolling waves in the water. The anchor rested on the bottom of the ocean next to a little island no one paid attention to. Rich green plants and tall willowy trees filled the wild jungle. No inhabitants, as far as anyone knew. Until *his ship* struck rock and splintered, sending them all to a watery grave—so they had thought. What a relief to find a small patch of land, overgrown with vines and sharp thistles, a jungle, so to speak.

Rainforests were often destroyed by flooding. Small islands in the ocean rarely survived the sea, and were often blasted with violent storms. The trees decayed under water. In this case, they were thriving. The men hustled to shore, dropping their exhausted bodies on the ground. Their energy came back quick enough when they realized they'd landed in a plush land of green.

Exploring, and building shelter, gave Bellingham the time he needed to disappear. No one would look for him here. He could lay low, make a plan. The men made good use of their time building another ship. The peninsula was close enough to the mainland, even a simple boat would get them across the water.

How had no one found this island before now?

He glanced about. This was not London. Nor was this Greystoke Manor. The island had a beach, but ships could not sail close, or the vessels would meet the same fate as his own. The island was perfect for a hide-away. Soon enough he would get his revenge.

His anger was a living breathing creature swelling in his chest. He fed the beast daily with memories of fiery caves and exploding ships.

Bloody hell. He could have been on that ship. So close. So close.

He could have died. His hands fisted at his sides as he realized that could have been his end. The man the crew threw over the side of the ship must have been the one to set the explosion. But then, the man had been tied up for an hour, waiting for *his* return. Seadog was with him. Thinking back, there must have been another on board.

Bellingham smacked his fist into his opposite palm.

Clearly, threatening Edmund hadn't worked. Now was a fine time for the man to develop a backbone. Another hindrance *he* didn't need. The hope of destroying the Greystokes was what kept him alive.

Bellingham no longer cared for the glowing praise from the ton. He never cared for a future of wedded bliss and children. He was a greedy bastard. No sense denying it. Money ruled the world. He'd had plenty of blunt until his cargo was destroyed. How had the brothers learned of his second supply?

Rage carved his face, twisted his mouth into a hard mask of hate. Those fools thought they were rid of him. As God was his witness, he would get even.

This time he would set a trap for the Greystoke brothers. He had time. No one would find him on this island. It wasn't even charted on the maps. No one knew it was there.

Perhaps his luck was changing. Things were looking up.

And those brothers who disrupted his plans, destroyed his shipment, would pay with their very lives.

Chapter 12

"Well, brother," Edmund said, slapping Aaron on the back. "You've cooked your goose now."

Aaron strode to the cabinet stocked with his good brandy. But then, all whisky was good. And he had plenty of it. "I suppose this occasion calls for a drink."

"Bring out the extra bottles. You're going to need them."

"Smirk all you like, Nathaniel. I remember not so long ago when your arse was in a fix."

"Brother, you don't want Aaron to get foxed, do you? His bride to be will not like a foxed groom, not to mention Aunt's reaction."

"Edmund, you know as well as I that Aaron can drink us both under the table."

"Why don't I get a bottle for each of us. Then, when Aunt sees you two, she won't look at me too closely."

Edmund chuckled. "Good try, Aaron. But you've claimed the center of attention for a while, I'm afraid."

Aaron handed each of his brothers a full glass of brandy. "To me." He held the glass up then drank a hefty gulp.

"Damn good brandy, Aaron."

"Thank you." He walked behind his desk and plopped into the hot seat. "Okay, you two. Have at me."

"I suspected you would go first, considering I'm the one who brought Miss Hayes to your door."

"Thank you for that, Nathaniel. And thank you for the warning."

"How the devil was I to give you notice with Aunt telling me what to do."

"Since when did you start following orders?"

Nathaniel studied his glass of brandy. "Since I decided you deserved to have a boot up your arse."

Aaron's hand tightened on his own glass. He set it on his desk before he crushed it with his grip.

"I say, Aaron, I agree with Nathaniel. How the hell did you get into this conundrum?"

"What else could I do? She came here bag and baggage announcing to all who would listen, we are betrothed."

"I mean how were the wheels put in motion. I gave you more credit. And you, Nathaniel, you knew about this?"

"I was a latecomer."

Aaron scrubbed a hand over his face, and tossed his hair over his shoulder. "That's the thing, Edmund. I don't know."

Edmund stared in shock. Then that cocky brow of his went up in the air. "You need to explain. From the beginning."

"You know I went to Brighton, looking for Blade, and any information on Bellingham. I also went there to speak with an agent at Anderson Shipping."

"An agent?"

"I mentioned at our last conversation, that I was interested in throwing my lot into shipping. Anderson has an excellent reputation, and I wanted to discuss a partnership. Since the American company has an office in Brighton, I went there."

I spoke with a man, and we sent correspondence to Anderson in America. He's coming to England to finalize the partnership." Aaron paused, and glanced at Nathaniel. "I thought he'd sent a formal letter to Greystoke, and Nathaniel got it by mistake."

"That is where I enter the picture," Nathaniel said. "I received a letter from Miss Hayes's father. I summoned Aaron to the manor. We had a devil of a time sorting it out because Aaron assumed the letter was from Anderson."

"You've lost me. Or you've left something out."

"Back to my trip to Brighton. I was drowning my sorrows in a tavern when I met this man."

"What sorrows? What else do I not know?"

Bollocks. Aaron hadn't meant to say that. He would need to curb his tongue.

"No, Aaron. You've already let the cat out of the clichéd bag. We brothers have not had a symposium in a while. Let's get it all out there in the open."

Damn.

"All right. I couldn't find Blade, and my guilt was weighing on me. You still haven't forgiven me for calling Nathaniel home. I was way into my cups."

"Bloody hell, Aaron. That is over and done."

"Is it," he stared at his brother. "You thought I betrayed you. You thought I was pitting Nathaniel against you."

"Now hold on." Edmund came out of his seat.

"You don't still—"

"Shut up, Nathaniel." Edmund turned back to Aaron. "I was in a bad way and not thinking straight. You probably saved me. I had no idea you still thought I blamed you for anything. Hear me, Aaron. I do not. You and Nathaniel, both, forced me out of my funk. Forced me to seek help. Thank God, you did. I've not had a bloody megrim since the surgery. I am quite happy with Joyanna. You helped me sort out that, too. I owe you, brother.

I have only good feelings for you. Now, I'm not about to hug and all that nonsense, so get over yourself."

Nathaniel laughed. "Good show, Edmund. Would you rather hug me?"

"Devil take you, Nathaniel." Edmund tossed back his drink. "Here, pour me another."

"You both have a reputation for being drunkards. Am I the only one to remain sober."

"Shut up, and match us."

Now it was Aaron's turn to laugh. But he was still trying to absorb Edmund's words. "Edmund, you truly don't hold a grudge?"

"Good God, Aaron. I meant every word. Get me a bloody brandy." He dropped back into the upholstered leather. "Let's get back to your story."

"I believe you were at the point where you were into your cups."

Aaron knew Nathaniel was making a barefaced reference to their current drinking as well.

"You need to catch up, brother." He poured more brandy, then handed the glasses over. "I was not foxed. However, I met this man, and he was singing his woes. He had a sad story to tell, and then I helped the man home. The last thing I remember, we were sitting in his house, at his table."

"You said you weren't foxed."

"That's just it, Edmund. I wasn't."

"You also said you wanted to drown your guilt."

"I did not swill myself stupid. I was in full control of my faculties."

"Until you weren't," Edmund said. "You fell asleep at the table?"

"No." Aaron shook his head, remembering back. "I woke up the next morning on the floor. In front of the sofa, with a blanket on me."

On the floor. Who covered me?

He couldn't imagine Colvin being that thoughtful. And Aaron had felt pleasantly relaxed. No headache, or cotton mouth either, which would be expected if he'd overindulged.

"I can see you're remembering something. What is it?"

"I think I was on the sofa. I must have fallen off."

"But you were not sloshed."

"No, Edmund, I was not." Damn. Why couldn't he remember? "At least I don't think I was. I don't know what was in that bottle. Rot gut whisky for sure." He scraped a hand through his hair. "Bloody hell. I don't know."

"Aaron," Nathaniel said, drawing his attention. "Did you find out what happened to Blade?"

"As far as anyone knows, he never made it off that ship."

"I'm sorry, Aaron," Edmund said. "Anything about Bellingham?"

"I've sent investigators out, searching for any news on him. There is no confirmation he was on the ship when it sank in the harbor. I've got paid men to watch in Brighton. If he surfaces, they'll send word to me."

"He's probably in some back-alley hovel, or he's left town."

"It will take time. For now," Nathaniel continued, "I'll go with the assumption Bellingham is alive. Without a body, I'm not counting him out yet."

Aaron nodded. "We'd be foolish to lower our guard."

Nathaniel growled. "The bloody cur has the luck of the devil."

"Not all of his luck is good, brother. We destroyed his shipment in the caves, sunk the one on the ship, he has to be hurting for blunt."

Aaron agreed with Edmund.

"What happened when you woke the next morning?"

"I was fine. Everything seemed normal. Mr. Hayes was jovial, I bid him goodbye and came home."

"So how did we get where we are today?"

"I've got this part," Nathaniel spoke up. "Mr. Hayes sent me a letter reminding me of a marriage contract. The contract was enclosed. Asking me when I was going to honor the contract and marry his daughter."

"You? Why you?"

Aaron answered instead. "He thought I was the Earl of Greystoke."

"The letter was addressed to the Earl of Greystoke, so naturally I got it. I was completely flummoxed. Then I saw the signature at the bottom." Nathaniel glanced to Aaron.

"My signature."

Edmund studied them both. "Obviously, he mistook one brother for the other. But how?"

"He only knew me as Greystoke. He saw my clothes, I suppose, and judged me to be a lord. I have no idea what I may have said to him, but there is no way I would have claimed the title."

"Of course not. That topic has been scoured to death."

"I confronted Aaron," Nathaniel said. "He agreed to signing the contract and asked how I got it?"

"What? You agreed—"

"Hear me out, brother. Looking back, it was rather comical. We were talking about two different things. Aaron thought I held a contract from Anderson Shipping. While in my hand, I held a marriage contract."

"I admitted to everything. I didn't like Nathaniel butting into my business, then he said I was to get married. I thought our brother had lost his mind."

"And I thought Aaron had become a rake and promised a young woman marriage."

"Clearly, you straightened the blunder out. So then what?"

Nathaniel spoke first. "That is when I found out."

"Sounds like Aaron found out at the same time."

"I had no bloody idea what Nathaniel was talking about. When I saw the contract, when I saw my signature, I think I went into shock. Of course, I denied signing the blasted thing. But there was my signature. Clear as could be." Aaron turned up his glass.

"And you have no recollection of signing that paper?"

Aaron shook his head. "None."

"That's when you went back to Brighton?"

"Yes. I found Miss Hayes, not her father. She admitted she knew about the contract, but she was not planning to get married any more than I was. As a matter of fact, when I left, she said she would not marry me if I was the only man on Earth."

"Showed her your charm, did you?" Edmund smirked.

"It's not funny, Edmund."

"Promising a young woman marriage is not funny."

Aaron glared at his brother, who glared right back.

"Down, Pup."

Aaron blanched at the nickname Nathaniel used.

"And you still don't remember anything," Nathaniel asked.

Aaron thought of the flashes in his dreams. But that couldn't have anything to do with this. "No. I thought the matter settled."

"Then Miss Hayes showed up at Greystoke Manor. Were you surprised, Nathaniel?"

"Actually, I expected someone to show up on my doorstep. After all, the letter was addressed to me. Miss Hayes landed on my doorstep clearly expecting to find Aaron, and was surprised to find me instead. She didn't mention her father. She was embarrassed by the mistake. Serena welcomed Miss Hayes as if she was family." A grin brightened Nathaniel's face as he looked at Aaron. "I brought her to the right door."

"Thank you for that, brother. I like getting waylaid in my own home."

"My pleasure, brother. I must admit, it was rejuvenating." Nathaniel chuckled.

Edmund shook his head. "Are you going to marry the girl?"

Aaron stared at his older brother. "I said I was, didn't I?"

"Thought you were blathering to pacify Aunt."

"You know how I feel about Aunt."

"How we all feel," Nathaniel added.

Aunt Penelope was important to all of them. "I will not let any hint of scandal touch her."

"You know, Aaron," Nathaniel began, "this might be a good thing."

"Good for whom? Just because you are wife pecked doesn't mean everyone has the same opinion."

"It depends on the woman, little brother."

"Don't you start, You and Joyanna have already set the date. Your wedding is to be the highlight of the season."

"I think our brother is pouting because he didn't get to choose his bride," Nathaniel said in a bored tone.

"She seems like a nice enough sort."

"Oh sure. She comes here ready to put me in my place, and suddenly you're her champion."

"I thought Nathaniel was her champion."

"I am. Who is to say she cannot have two?"

"Go ahead. Have your fun," Aaron told his brothers. "I'm the one getting leg shackled."

"I highly recommend it." Nathaniel held his glass in the air.

"Good to know, brother. Good to know."

"Of course, I didn't go through all the pomp and splendor."

"Joyanna is a viscountess. The ton is expecting posh."

"Not for my taste."

Both of his brothers were in love. The way they grew up, it was a miracle any of them even considered having a wife. Father had been a tyrant. The brothers only had each other. Thank God something good had come into their lives.

"Will you two stop? I'm about to get married. Does no one have any sympathy for me?"

Edmund and Nathaniel both burst out laughing.

At least this was better than their lives a few months ago. He hoped Bellingham was behind them.

If he was to have a wedding, by God, it would be in Surrey. The ton already knew too much of his business.

He woke in a cold sweat, his body swaying with the tide. Slowly his blurred vision began to focus. He stared at the ceiling of ... musty boards. He could smell the salt in the sea air. Was he on a ship?

He tried to move. Pain shot through his skull. He tried to slow his panicked breathing.

"Shhhh. Lie still. The fever has finally broken."

He blinked. He knew he heard an angel's voice. Had he gone to the great beyond?

A cool cloth touched his brow. He closed his eyes letting the soothing sensation wash over his face. He tried licking his lips and found them dry. What little energy he might have had drained out of him.

A metal cup touched his lips, and cool water dripped into his mouth. *Aahh, that tasted good.*

"Only a few drops. You can have more later."

Where was he?

He tried to move his tongue, but it was too heavy. His scorched throat would not work. Finally, he mumbled one word. "More."

The angel of mercy answered his need. This time, more than a few drops rolled over his tongue.

He swallowed.

Chapter 13

Whe Aaron asked her to go riding, she nearly fell to the floor. Fainting was not an option. Not if she was to get out of the muddle she'd somehow gotten herself in.

She hurried up the stairs and stood staring at the few clothes she'd brought with her, when there was a knock on the door.

"Rebekah. It's Serena. May I come in?"

Rebekah hurried over to open the chamber door. "Of course. Please, come in."

"I have something for you." She turned to a footman Rebekah didn't know was there."

"Would you bring that in, please?

The footman hefted a trunk through the open doorway.

"What is that?"

"While you are here, I thought I'd loan you a few of my things. Actually, you can keep them, but I think you have this independent streak, so I'll use the term loan." She followed the footman to the bed. "Place it over there."

He carried the trunk to the corner.

"That will be all. Thank you."

Rebekah was still staring at the trunk when the footman walked back to the hallway. Her instincts must have kicked in because she automatically closed the door.

"Come, Rebekah." Serena opened the lid, then reached in and drew out a lump of material. When she shook it free,

Rebekah swallowed the lump in her throat. It was one of the prettiest dresses she'd ever seen.

"You and Aaron had your discussion last evening, and you didn't scurry away. We are hoping you will stay. I'm sure Aaron or Aunt will plan a trip to the dressmaker for a complete trousseau. But for now, I brought a few things I thought you might need until then."

"Wait. You're going too fast."

Serena stopped, placing her hands on her hips. "Are you staying?"

Rebekah chewed on her bottom lip. "I ...I guess, for a while." She hadn't really decided yet.

"Good. As I said, you will be needing some things. I hope you don't mind they belong to me. But I haven't worn them, so they are like new. Nathaniel spoils me terribly, and Aunt insisted on me getting everything. I'm sure she will be the same with you."

"I don't need any clothes."

"I said the same thing. Did they listen? No." She pulled another item out of the chest. "With your coloring, this will look beautiful on you." She held up a blue riding habit.

Rebekah had never owned one, but she knew what it was.

"It is beautiful," she said, as she brushed the fabric. "And soft."

"Here, you must try it on. I feel we are about the same size."

"You are obviously bigger in the chest area."

Serena waved a hand. "Don't worry about that. It has buttons, see?"

Rebekah took the clothing and placed it on the bed. It was almost too nice to wear horse-back riding.

"Do you like pink? I detest bright pink. I love lavender." She held up another gown. "This is a duller shade of pink. Mauve, I believe. I think this would look nice on you."

Rebekah leaned over to look in the trunk. "How many do you have in there? Did you save some gowns for yourself?"

Serena laughed. "Rebekah, I have closets full of gowns, and dressers full of under things." She dug deeper to the bottom. "I brought some of those too. Just in case."

A lump formed in Rebekah's chest at Serena's kindness. "It would seem you've thought of everything. Thank you."

"You're welcome. All we need to do is shake them out and hang them. Do you have a personal maid yet?"

"Heavens no. I'm used to doing things for myself."

Serena laughed again. "So was I. Having servants to do things for me took some getting used to, but it's their job. You'll find that most servants like doing their job, and will be insulted if you don't let them." She leaned close. "So let them."

"I've never seen anyone with servants until I came to Greystoke Manor."

"A maid will take care of the clothes."

A timid knock vibrated on the chamber door. "Miss Hayes. Master Greystoke said to tell ya he be waiting down at the stables."

"Thank you."

"What perfect timing. You must wear the blue riding-habit. Since you don't have a maid, I will help you get ready."

In less than half an hour, Rebekah practically ran to meet Aaron at the stables. Two horses were saddled and waiting.

"Ah, Rebekah. I've chosen Gilda for you, and let me say before you ask, that was her name when I purchased her. Since she has been around for ten years, I saw no need to change her name. The mare seems tame enough. I didn't ask if you can sit a horse."

"Yes. I helped our neighbor care for his horses, and he often let me ride. I did not use a side saddle."

Aaron called the groomsman. "My lady requires a regular saddle. Take Gilda and change the saddle." He turned to Rebekah. "Do you ride well."

"I rode often. I'm not sure how well. But I never fell off."

"Good Lord, I hope not."

A few moments later, the groomsman led Gilda back outside. Aaron helped Rebekah to mount. Gilda stood steady, and the saddle felt comfortable.

"All right?" Aaron asked.

She gave him a nod and took the reins. "What is the name of your horse?"

"This one is James. I have several and ride them all. I've never cared about fancy names, so I think of them as my colleagues. Simple names are the best." He nudged his horse in a walk, so Rebekah did the same.

Gilda was easy to handle. When they came to the tree line, Aaron kept the horses at a walk.

"There's a nice glade over there," he said as he pointed. "I thought that would be a good place to rest. And we can talk in private."

She thought they had already talked. Of course, she didn't tell him she accepted his marriage proposal, if that's what one wanted to call it. Being told she had to marry to avoid scandal was as close as she would most likely get.

They rode silently until they came to a large field with tall grass. To one side, the ground sloped down to a small stream. The spot was ideal for a romantic interlude. Rebekah was sure Aaron had nothing of the sort on his mind.

Aaron reached up to help her down, and her breath caught. Just imagining his hands on her person stirred all kinds of whirling sensations. His hands burned at her waist, and then they were gone. No lingering touch. He couldn't move away fast enough.

"I've brought a blanket for the ground, so you won't get your clothes dirty. "He strode back to his horse, gathered the blanket and what looked to be a basket. "Cook wouldn't let me leave the house without food." She helped him spread the blanket and he sat the basket right in the middle. The gesture was clear, putting a halt on any fantasy one may have had for seduction.

She laughed at her thoughts, a small snicker slipping out.

Aaron arched a brow as he looked at her.

She quickly asked, "What's in the basket?"

"Bread, cheese, a bit of meat. And lemonade. Are you hungry?"

"Not at the moment, no."

"Would you care to sit?"

She thought of a smart remark, but kept it to herself. Aaron was making an attempt to be nice. She may as well, too.

He dropped down beside her, leaned back on one elbow, and crossed his boots at the ankles. The tinkling sound of the water rushing over the small rocks was surprisingly comforting. She sat with her feet to the side and reached for a wildflower at the blanket edge.

"You like flowers?"

She lifted her gaze to his. "I like nature. This is a beautiful spot." She looked at the purple wildflower in her hand and then noticed several across the grass. "This little guy has found a way to survive in the middle of a meadow. I have a flower garden at home. I like digging in the dirt with my hands. I suppose you have a gardener."

"Yes, as a matter of fact, I do. Aunt likes flowers. He cuts a fresh batch for her three mornings a week. I think the old fellow likes her."

"That's nice. Has Penelope ever married?"

"No. She says training a husband is too much work. And she doesn't like anyone telling her what to do."

Rebekah smiled. She could believe that.

"Personally, I think she was too worried about us. She didn't get to visit often, courtesy of my father. He didn't want her around making us soft."

"You seemed to have turned out well enough."

"Do I hear a compliment in there?"

She thought for a moment, then replied, "And if you do?"

He shrugged. "I didn't think there was a part of you that would see me in a favorable light."

"Even though we disagree, it does not mean you have no good qualities. Besides, if I am to consider marrying you, you would have to display something that would appeal to me."

"Do I?"

Did he want her to tell him she found him attractive? Good Lord, she found him wildly handsome. He took her breath. She knew what it was like to be held in his arms. She wanted to be there again. But how could she develop a lasting relationship with a man who didn't want her?

"I think you are fishing for flattering remarks. Let's say I am considering your words from our conversation last night."

"I think it is for the best."

"Do you?"

He sat up. "I thought all women wanted a stable home and family?"

"So, you are prepared to give me a stable home? Sacrifice your own freedom?"

"It would not be that great of a detriment. Our lives would not change that much."

She gasped. "My life would change drastically. I would be the one sacrificing my freedom while you would go on your daily routine. I would leave my home, my father, any security I have to move to a strange house, and be with people I don't know."

"Do you plan to live with your father the rest of your life?"

Well, no. But she had thought she would marry for love.

"Ah, I see that look on your face."

"What look?"

"You want what every woman wants. Romance."

Why should she feel guilty about that?

"I assure you, Aaron, I don't need poetry or sonnets or music. However, I do think it would be nice for two people to be in love when they marry."

Devil take him.

Aaron supposed every woman was a blasted romantic. "You do realize those marriages are very few. Practically all marriages are arranged. The groom or the bride gains wealth, land ... a number of things."

"I'm not used to nobility or its traditions. Mama and Papa loved each other. I was raised in a home with love. I can't imagine two people living together every day with nothing between them. I wouldn't know how to talk, or how to act."

Aaron had been quite happy as an eligible bachelor—as eligible as one could be. He had no desire to turn a woman up sweet. Even less desire to attach one to his hip, permanently. The Greystoke name had been on everyone's lips enough of late. Nathaniel and Serena were settled in at Greystoke Manor. Edmund and Joyanna were together again. Hopefully, with Bellingham in the wind, he would not bother them in the near future. Aunt needed a reprise from the brothers causing disruption.

Miss Hayes needed a man to take her in hand. Since his name was on the blasted contract, he would be the one to tackle the job. Ever since her father had sent that bloody letter to Greystoke, Aaron had been on edge.

What else could he do?

"Miss Hayes. There are couples that learn to love each other. But even if they don't, marriages succeed. Two people can co-exist amiably, I'm sure." Was he trying to convince her or himself?

What was he to do, send her back to the sorry life she'd been living? Who knew what her father might do next.

He'd been so busy going along with the idea, he hadn't stopped long enough to consider the marriage would be permanent. A wife–someone depending on him, forever. That was no hardship, he had the blunt. Servants would take care of her demands. She wouldn't have to be underfoot, unless he permitted it.

Forever? It didn't have to be.

"Rebekah, let's make an agreement."

"A pact?"

"If you so choose," he replied with a shrug. "Let's put this jumble to rest, once and for all. We will marry. After a period of time of your choosing, if you want out, all you need to do is tell me."

"You would give me my freedom?"

"If that is what you wished, of course."

Would he? He shook his head. No need to consider the chickens before the eggs hatched. He convinced himself he was doing what was necessary."

"What do you want, Rebekah?"

It drove him crazy when she chewed on her lip like that.

"I know you feel this wedding is being forced on you. I won't force you to do anything you don't want to do. But Aunt feels we should be married sooner rather than later. I feel the same way."

"How sooner?"

"Immediately. That doesn't mean we cannot have a proper wedding in a church. I just don't think there will be a large guest list. After all, we are doing this to avoid gossip."

Chapter 14

A week ago, she would have told Aaron to take the contract and eat it. A week ago, she was angry, and wanted retaliation. However, a week with his family, and watching him interact with them, made her open her eyes and consider what she really wanted.

Rebekah held her secret close to her breast. If she was being honest with herself, she wanted to experience that moment with him again. She knew he could be soft spoken. She knew he could be tender... and passionate. If she allowed it, mayhap she could have her dream.

The house was alive with activity. As soon as Aaron announced the family was moving to Surrey for the wedding, the packing began.

Another house in Surrey. How many did the Greystoke men own? Aaron may not have been the earl, but he seemed to have plenty of money. And that had nothing to do with the way she felt about him. If she was after a rich man, she wouldn't hesitate to marry Aaron. Her father would be ecstatic.

Blast. And double blast.

She wished she knew what was going through his head. He said all the right things. He offered to marry her. He promised to take care of her—which was not the same thing as caring for her, not at all. His eyes said something else, all together. He didn't really want to marry her, but he was doing everything required to prepare for a wedding.

And now they were going to Surrey. He'd said his country house was a perfect place for a wedding.

Had she agreed? She couldn't remember consenting. But then, with Aunt, Serena, and Joyanna showing their excitement, it was hard not to get caught up in the planning.

Joy filled her insides. She had to admit she loved the country. So much better than town life. Who needed parties and balls when you had fresh air and wide-open spaces? She could hardly wait.

Five carriages followed them to Surrey. The women, Serena, Aunt and herself, in the first one. Nathaniel and Aaron in the second. Personal maids in the third, and trunks in the final two. You would think they were going for the winter—and it was only spring.

They'd been on the road for two hours.

"We should be getting close," Aunt said. "Look out the window and see if you see the house."

Rebekah lifted the shade and took a look at their surroundings. Trees were blooming, the grass was a vibrant green. Up ahead, she saw stone.

Good heavens.

The house appeared to be a mansion. Or a castle. She couldn't tell from this far away.

"Penelope. Would Aaron's house in Surrey look like a castle?"

Aunt smacked her hand on her lap. "That's it. Thank the heavens. I don't want to be in this coach a moment longer than necessary."

"I agree," Serena said.

"The house is a castle?"

"It's made of stone, dear. It is quite large, built in the seventeenth century, I believe. It has all the niceties. Aaron made sure of that."

"Have you been here before, Serena?"

"No. This is my first visit."

"Oh."

"Don't be glum, Rebekah. It has running water. A water closet in the master bedchamber. Aaron hired a contractor only a few years ago to remedy this house with the same suitability of his townhouse. You'll see it has all the refinements and delicacies one could want."

"I am looking forward to it," Serena said. "Think of all the exploring we can do. Joyanna and Edmund will come tomorrow. Think of how exciting Joyanna will make our stay."

As the coach drew closer, Rebekah saw the outside looked well-tended. It wasn't the house as much as the day of her wedding drawing closer.

"Does someone live here year-round?"

"Yes. If Aaron shows up at the spur of a moment, he wants to walk in and have everything ready. Rooms ready. Food available. Fires in the hearth. Which the servants started as soon as they spotted the coaches."

"My goodness. That is a well-ordered staff."

Aunt gave a sharp nod. "Aaron demands it. Even so, the staff likes Aaron. He is good to them."

"He is good to everyone." Serena looked at Rebekah. Was she silently communicating a message?

Rebekah would agree Aaron was kind. He was many things. It was possible she was afraid of her own feelings, and that was why she was dragging her feet.

Aaron stood alone on the terrace that ran the length of the back of his country house. It was done. The argument settled; the agreement made. Tomorrow the day of his sentencing.

Rebekah managed the trip to Surrey with grace. She'd handled this whole thing with more propriety than himself. She'd been poised at supper, never once complained. He scrubbed a hand over his face. She was beautiful. Easy to talk to. She would make a good wife. Yet the woman in his dreams continued to haunt him.

"You look more like you're meeting the hangman than a groom planning for his wedding day."

Aaron tossed the cheroot over the railing and turned.

"Good evening, Serena."

"My, what a long face. I must confess, Aaron, I'm not used to seeing you so glum. You surprise me."

"I like being unpredictable. Keeps my brothers on their toes."

"Mind if I join you?"

He leaned back against the balustrade. "Shouldn't you be in bed?"

"It's a nice night. Too nice for sleeping."

"I hope my brother knows we have not planned a rendezvous. I do not think Nathaniel would give me a chance to explain if he saw the two of us, alone on the terrace."

"Since we are not going to give him a reason to be jealous, I think my husband will be fine."

Aaron shook his head. "He has a nose like a bloodhound. I thought you two were joined at the hip. He'll sniff you out soon enough."

"He is a good husband." Serena smiled as though she was remembering a moment she shared with Nathaniel. She'd done quite a lot of that since she married his brother, and so had he. One of those exceptional couples who were truly in love.

"Never thought I'd see the day. You've changed him, Serena."

Even though it was dark and shadows sprouted from the moonlight, he could tell she blushed.

"I am happy. So is he. You are still my champion." At Aaron's raised brow, she continued. "I remember a time you ran off one of my suitors."

He recalled the morning he'd arrived at Nathaniel's house and found Ackerman calling on Serena before the noon hour. Aaron had sent the rogue packing.

"Ha, Ackerman. He took advantage of the early morning, slinking in to see you before Aunt was out of bed, knowing she would not have allowed it."

Serena giggled. Then posed as if she was carefully preparing her next words. "*Lady Pettigrove has a soft tendre for fools. I do not. Now, be on your way.*"

"Hmmm. Very good impression of me."

Serena laughed. "He reminded me of a peacock. I had to bite my cheek to keep from laughing."

"Ackerman is a bore."

"I thought he was harmless."

"And I told you, no man is harmless."

"Yes, you did." She looked away into the night.

"I have the feeling you have more on your mind, Serena."

"I remember another conversation. Where you explained the ton demands decorum. There are rules to follow, but you know as well as I, many rules were broken when I came into Nathaniel's life."

"Aunt made up a tale for your background to introduce you into society."

"Yes, she did. As it turned out, I was of noble blood."

"A secret you kept well hidden from all of us."

"And now there is another." Serena faced him." Perhaps she too, is afraid to share her secret."

Serena's eyes bore into his mind. "I am not an ogre, Serena."

"Of the three of you, you are the unique bird. I love your enthusiasm for life. Your charm, your charisma. Your delight in the simple things. You have changed, Aaron."

He hiked a brow. He would expect criticism from his brothers, but not from Serena. "Are you saying I've become moody like my brothers? That I am no longer fun?"

Serena looked him straight in the eyes. "I'm saying talk to your brothers. Talk to someone. I like Rebekah. I believe she's kind. Even in arranged marriages, two people could learn to love each other."

"Speaking from experience, are you?"

Serena lowered her eyes. "I'm sorry, Aaron, for overstepping my boundaries."

He straightened, ashamed he'd offended her. "No, Serena. I am the one to apologize. I know you're trying to make me feel better. I am fine. I agreed to this ...wedding." He hoped she didn't catch his hesitation. "There is nothing for you to worry about." He shrugged, hoping to present the easy-going-air that she had reminded him of. "It is the way things are done among the aristocracy. Rebekah will be fine. Aunt will see to it."

"I'm thinking of you, too," she said softly. Then she smiled. "Do you see how happy Nathaniel is?"

His brother was happy. Something Aaron had never envisioned. He nodded. "Yes, Serena. You are an exceptional woman. Nathaniel would be crazy not to love you."

"You can be happy too, Aaron."

He wasn't all that concerned. He was a man who controlled his own destiny. To have a bride thrust upon him took some getting used to.

"Don't you worry about me. I will be fine, and so will Rebekah."

Chapter 15

T omorrow she would marry Aaron Greystoke.

Rebekah strolled in the flower garden, wondering how she'd come to this moment. A daring brainstorm flipped upside down along with her entire world. Hindsight was a grueling taskmaster. The plan had seemed logical enough at the time. And now, she saw it as insanity. Proof that one should not allow one's temper to rule.

What a catastrophe she had made for herself.

She did not know him, and he did not know her. How could either one of them profess love for the other?

A rush of warmth filled her as the memory flashed through her mind. Dare she hope for Aaron to possess her again? When she looked at him, all the sensations came rushing back. If her dream was beyond her reach, then why had she been given this chance? Aaron was the one to suggest they marry. He was agreeable.

Aaron presented strength and confidence. Not the sort of man who could be pushed into something. No, she couldn't imagine anyone forcing him to do anything.

All she had to do was reach out. Take what fate had thrown at her. It would be so easy to fall in love with Aaron. Truth be told, she feared she already had.

The heart wanted what the heart wanted. All she had to do was say yes. She wished he truly cared for her. If she married him, perhaps, one day ... was it too much to hope that one day he might love her?

She heard the ruffling of satin and turned to see Serena. "I hope I'm not intruding on your solitude."

"Of course not. I welcome the company. "We are sorry about this situation. But we welcome you to the family. We are good people, Rebekah. I hope you will give us a chance.

"I'm the interloper, and you are being beyond accepting. I wouldn't blame you if you threw me out."

"Nonsense. No matter how you came to us, you are now family."

"Of course, you are," Joyanna said, joining them.

"You two didn't wander out here by accident."

"You are correct. We thought you might have the pre-wedding jitters. We're here to help you, Rebekah. You're not alone."

Serena reached out a hand and touched Rebekah. "We want to be your friends."

Friends? She'd never had any friends.

"All the brothers are fierce looking," Joyanna said. "Don't let Aaron's brow intimidate you."

"Aaron is not one to lie, or shirk his duties," Serena told her.

"I don't want to be his duty. A marriage between us is not necessary."

"Are you going to change your mind?"

"Let's walk," Joyanna said, taking Rebekah's arm. "Think of this as an adventure. A wild one, true. But one where you will be going on a journey, and every day will get better."

"Yes," Serena joined in. "The more time you spend with Aaron, you will find he's a good man."

"You might even have fun doing it?" Joyanna giggled.

"Fun?"

"They're not a bunch of trolls. Don't get me wrong, the brothers can be fierce when protecting their family."

"Nathaniel has a brooding expression most of the time," Serena added. "He scares everyone. There are times when I need to remind him that he doesn't need to speak to people in that booming voice."

"Around you he is thoughtful and loving," Joyanna said to Serena.

"Don't let him hear you say that. Men like for everyone to believe they are strong and... manly." She giggled.

"A few months back, you would not have recognized Edmund," Joyanna told Rebekah. "He was an absolute grizzly. Hated the world."

"Edmund?"

Joyanna nodded.

"He was having megrims. Headaches that drove him mad. Well, not mad as in ..."

"Do you know what megrims are, Rebekah?" Serena interrupted.

"I've read about them."

"Then you know they can be excruciating. Edmund was hiding his headaches and dealing with his pain on his own. He'd become a recluse. His brothers forced him into the open, and he found a doctor who helped. Edmund had a bone pressing on a nerve behind his ear. The doctor performed surgery and now he is well."

Rebekah pictured Edmund's face, as he smiled at his wife when no one was looking. "I would never have known. He is so mellow. You two seem so happy."

"We are, now. That is a story for another day. But the short version is I had to win him. I loved him too much to let him push me away." Joyanna's wistful expression showed how much she loved him.

"Aaron does not have a bone pressing on a nerve. And his onery expression is from his tenacious disposition. There is no excuse for his haughty behavior."

"You have much to learn," Serena laughed. "This is a discussion we must have very soon."

"If Aaron doesn't care what the ton or anyone thinks about him, why the deception?"

The two women looked to each other, then back to her. Serena was the one who spoke. "Nathaniel, Edmund, and Aaron, all three, dearly love Penelope. But Aaron is devoted to her. They are quite close."

"Quite," Joyanna added. "For her, he would do anything."

Rebekah frowned. "Including marrying a woman he doesn't want."

Joyanna laughed. "I've seen the way he looks at you, *ma cheri*."

Rebekah blurted, "So have I. I've been the recipient of those harsh looks."

"Rebekah. When you're not looking, his eyes study you. As if he is trying to work a puzzle. He's fitting the pieces together in his mind."

"With such a small mind to work with, that must be why the strain shows on his face."

"Rebekah," Serena said softly. "If Aaron says he doesn't remember, I believe he is telling the truth. Aaron is an honest man."

"Intensely so." Joyanna added. "All three of them."

These women described a man she hadn't seen. "It would appear there is a great deal I don't know."

"Don't worry. We will tell you everything." They came to a stone bench, with delicate carvings in the design of flowers and vines. "Let us sit for a spell."

"Perhaps, if we all talk about ...," Serena began, then hesitated. "I don't want to pry, but if you could shed some light on Aaron's visit with your father, well, uh ..." She and Joyanna shared a look.

"We were hoping you could shed some light on how all this came about," Joyanna finished.

Dear heavens. The whole thing was one big muddle. How was she to explain when most of it was ambiguous?

Rebekah was embarrassed. But Serena and Joyanna were so nice. Rebekah felt like she could speak freely with them.

She quickly went over the events in her mind. Father had been to the tavern and brought home a man. Aaron passed out, but Papa hadn't been foxed. When could Aaron have put his signature to paper? Surely not the next morning. He was gone by the time she'd gotten up. Papa said Aaron must have left at dawn. Fresh from a night's sleep, he would have been aware—more so than the night before when she'd assumed he'd been drunk—and he would remember. Wouldn't he?

Did he?

No. She'd seen his eyes. He was being truthful. There were times he'd been inconsiderate, and times when he'd been understanding, even respectful. Because he was guilty?

Why would he be compassionate if Papa had tricked him?

Papa had been full of himself that morning. A skip in his step, the happiest she seen him since Mama died. Had he tricked Aaron?

"Rebekah? Are you all right?"

She shook the memories away. "Yes."

"What is it? Is something wrong?"

Everything.

"Perhaps it is just bride jitters," Joyanna said.

"I must speak with Aaron."

Rebekah jumped up and practically ran back to the house.

Papa. What have you done?

She found Aaron on the terrace.

"Rebekah? Are you all right?"

"I didn't expect to see you here."

"It is a lovely day. Thought I'd stand here and take it in for a moment. Would you care to join me?" He held out a hand.

Flustered from the thoughts rambling through her head, she took a moment to compose herself.

"Yes." She placed her hand in his, and climbed the two steps onto the terrace.

His fingers brushed her bare skin. Tingles ran from her hands, up her arms, and straight to her belly. *Dear Lord.* From an innocent touch.

He brought her even closer. "A bout of the wedding jitters?" He lifted one hand and trailed his fingers down her arm. She sucked in a breath. When he slid those fingers back up again, she thought she'd swoon.

"You have nothing to fear, Rebekah." He was trying to calm her fears. Perhaps he truly was a gentleman.

"I'm not afraid." She looked up to his face, and lost her breath again. Her eyes locked with his green, heated ones, taking her back to that night. She could almost believe time stood still, and she was in his arms again.

"If there is something bothering you, you can tell me."

She shook herself from the cloud of desire she was falling into. "Are you not bothered by this entire predicament?"

"I thought we'd ironed everything out."

She couldn't think with him this close. She stepped to the side, then put a good bit of distance between them. She gathered her composure and draped it about her like a cloak. Then she faced him. "You do not have to officially marry me."

Aaron emitted a short laugh. "Want me to unofficially marry you?"

"That's not what I mean. Is there some other way? To avoid a scandal."

"Aunt has her heart set on this wedding." He studied her. "I will not force you."

"But don't you see." The desperation showed in her voice. "I will not force you, either. I came here as a lark. To teach you a lesson." Which quickly recoiled back to her. She whirled around. "I wish I'd never come."

"But you did, sweetheart. Our engagement has been made public. Do you not like it here?"

Sweetheart?

She gave her head a little shake, then forced her feet to face him. "Aaron, your home is beautiful. I promise, I was not looking for wealth, or a title, or marriage when I came here. I just want to go home."

"Think of Blackborn Manor as your home," he said taking a step closer to her. "You will want for nothing. Your father is happy. He can come visit you anytime you want."

She bit her lip to keep from screaming.

Reach out and take what your heart wants.

"You truly do not mind?"

"I am gaining a beautiful wife."

He thought her beautiful?

He took another step and stood right in front of her. So close.

"You like Aunt Penelope. You've met my brothers' wives. I think you get along. You don't need to change anything. Don't change for me. You may continue to be yourself, carry on as you normally would. Tomorrow you will become Mrs. Aaron Greystoke."

But ... what happens after that?

"Nathaniel. Get out there and make sure Aaron doesn't scare Rebekah off. There is going to be a wedding tomorrow, or I'll give that boy my boot."

He loved Aunt, but she could try his patience. "Aaron can handle this on his own."

"Aaron is not himself," Aunt huffed.

"How do you expect him to behave? A woman shows up out of the blue, announces he is to marry her, and he should lie down and say *yes, ma'am?*"

"Shut up, Edmund. Aaron cut his own throat when he put his signature on that contract."

Nathaniel smirked, at his brother. Aunt always spoke her mind.

"He does not remember." Edmund shot back.

"He recognized his own signature."

"That's to—"

"Please," Joyanna said, placing her hand on Edmund's arm.

Leave it to Joyanna to smooth the waters. Serena shot Nathaniel a glance from her seat next to Aunt. He rather enjoyed watching Edmund squirm under Aunt's scrutiny. For his wife, he would come to Edmund's aid.

"Aunt Penelope." Nathaniel straightened from his position, leaning on the hearth. "You know Aaron would not lie."

"I did not accuse my nephew of lying. But it happened. This is what we've got. And we're going to deal with it in the right way. That boy needs Rebekah. And she needs all of us."

Well, there was a twist of view. Aunt turned her pleading gaze to him. "Go, Nathaniel. Help him."

<hr />

"Forgive me, brother, I've been sent to fetch you."

Aaron froze.

What the bloody hell was Nathaniel doing out here?

The moment was gone.

For a moment, he'd forgotten his family. It had been Rebekah and him, alone on the terrace. Alone in the quiet evening where day turned to dusk. Gazing at her beauty, he could almost forget the reason the two of them were in Surrey. Beautiful. Witty. The woman had a mind of her own. Still, she interested him. They were to be married.

Leg-shackled.

Him.

Not of his own free will. And not of hers. The ton commanded entirely too much allegiance. For decorum, for propriety, for the bloody hypocritical aristocrats, he would throw away his future and take this woman down with him.

For Aunt Penelope.

Fucking hell.

There was no escape.

"We were just on our way in." He held out his arm to Rebekah. When she placed her hand cautiously at the crook of his elbow, he realized how very much he wanted to kiss her.

Chapter 16

The rising sun told him the other occupants of the house would be stirring soon.

Judgement day.

Today was to be his wedding day. So why did it feel more like a noose was about to be put around his neck?

The entire family was there. His brothers, Aunt. Aaron had allowed no one else to get close. All his life, he'd spent wrestling with the discord of his brothers. When had he ever had time for romance? Like any healthy man, he loved women. He preferred a mistress, rather than play the rogue about the ton. It never stopped widows from approaching him, though. Nor discontented wives who were all about discretion.

Even though he'd not thought much about taking a wife, he knew someday he would. Rebekah was a beautiful woman. Any man would want her. Who said he did not?

She appealed to him. Last evening he'd been caught up in her spell. Watching his brothers, perhaps he would settle down and be faithful to one woman. He hadn't expected it to happen this soon. And he sure as hell imagined he would choose the woman. Not have her drop into his lap. Or force her way into his orderly life.

Ballocks.

He did not want anything from Rebekah. He was fulfilling an obligation. She was getting everything she wanted from this match. Money. Prestige. But one thing she would not get—was him.

He would marry her. Then he would leave her in Surrey at his country home. He rarely visited; she could have the house all to herself.

Aaron stood before his bedchamber window and stared out over the maze in the back of his house. Unbidden thoughts leaped into his head. Under other circumstances, he would have welcomed Rebekah. Perhaps in a few more years.

He was not the earl. She claimed that didn't matter. Even so, he had wealth of his own. He'd just partnered with Anderson Shipping. She didn't seem to care about that either.

She would get everything she wanted. See if that made her happy.

Perhaps this way, their marriage would have a better chance.

—ele—

Her wedding day.

Rebekah could not get over her shock. What hurt the most was everyone's sympathy. She hated being pitied. And worse, pretending that everything is fine.

It is not fine!

As for a church wedding. She wanted nothing to do with saying reluctant vows in the eyes of God. Instead, they were married at Aaron's country house in Surrey. The staff had prepared a massive amount of food. Aunt hired a wedding coordinator to arrange everything else. The ballroom was flooded with flowers of every color. All of the other decorations, ribbons and candles were accented in white. In a short time, the ballroom had been turned into a stunning wedding hall.

If Aaron regretted the marriage, why had he gone through with it? The way he had interacted with his family touched her heart. She'd seen a glimpse of the man from that night. For an illogical moment, she'd thought they could have a future together.

Men.

She would never understand them.

Even Penelope had been shocked. But she'd gone on, as if Aaron's departure had been expected. What was wrong with these people? Every minute of their lives a front. Put on a show. Don't let anyone know what was really happening. Don't let anyone see your pain.

Today, she learned from the best. She carried on, playacting as a performer on a stage. Feigning her gaiety, not daring to allow one tear to slip down her cheek. She spent the day pretending to be happy.

No one could know how miserable she was, or how crushed she'd been when Aaron walked away.

Deserted.

Her husband had discarded her.

She looked over to the beautiful wedding cake, three tiers high. More than enough for the handful of guests who'd attended. Nathaniel and Serena. Edmund and Joyanna. Aunt of course, and Papa. Aaron, and her.

Why was it necessary to marry at all? Why didn't they just pretend to get married? If Aaron had planned all along to leave her in Surrey—alone—then why marry her at all?

"That's the fanciest wedding I ever did see. You sure look beautiful, Becky. You remind me of your Ma."

Papa. The one for whom she must play her best performance. After all, it was Papa who started this entire fiasco. He wanted her to be happy. He wanted her to have the things he couldn't give his wife. Didn't he remember how happy Mama was with the simple things?

"Thank you, Papa." His arms crushed her in a bear hug. Papa had been exuberant since Aaron informed Papa of the date. Now, he was even more cheerful, as if he'd been given the world. Since his dream had been seeing his daughter married, he was on top of the world.

She'd never seen him so buoyant. For him, she would keep up the charade.

"I was invited to spend the night, but I want to get back and tell everyone about my girl's wedding."

"You're not leaving now, are you?" But then, if Papa left now, she could end her pretense sooner.

"Can't wait. Gotta tell all my friends." He took her hands and looked into her eyes. "Becky, are ya happy?"

"Happier than I can tell you, Papa."

"That's my girl." He crushed her in another hug. "I'll be going now. You write to me, ya hear? I don't expect to get a letter right away, I mean, ya just got married. But when that husband of yours give ya the time..." Papa gave her a wink. "You write and tell me all the fine things you're doing." He clogged up then.

"Papa, don't cry." If he started crying, so would she. Once she started, she might not be able to stop.

He swiped at his eye. "All right, Becky. You be happy, now. Ya hear. And don't forget your Papa."

She hugged him as tight as she possibly could. "I'll never forget you." She held on a while longer, then pushed away before a tear could escape. "Besides, I'll come visit you real soon."

"Ya promise?"

"Of course, cross my heart." She signed her fingers over her chest.

"I'm off, girly. Bye."

She waved as a feeling of relief came over her. She really was happy. Happy that Papa was far enough away he couldn't see the tears streaming down her face.

"Come with me."

Rebekah looked up through her blurred vision. Joyanna had taken her arm, and was leading her into the house.

"I'm sorry ... I can't stop."

"It's all right. Go ahead and cry. There's no one here to see you."

Rebekah had no idea where they were going. When she reached the stairs, she automatically ascended, then walked down the corridor to her chamber. Joyanna quietly closed the door.

"I'll be missed."

"Serena is having everyone fuss over her and the baby. They are occupied."

"It doesn't matter. Everyone knows. Everyone saw Aaron ..." Rebekah threw herself across the bed.

"You go right ahead and cry dear. You held this in a long time. You are overdue." Joyanna rubbed Rebekah's shoulder as she talked. "It's not the end of the world. This is but a stepping stone in your life. Deal with it today, and come out the winner tomorrow."

"I had no idea. He didn't say a word." She sniffed.

"He didn't tell anyone of his intentions, the bugger."

Rebekah sat up, wiping her face. "You didn't know he was planning to go back to London?

"No, I did not. Neither did his brothers. He was smart not to tell them, because they would have taken precautions. Edmund was just as surprised as you were."

"What about Penelope?"

"Couldn't you hear her grinding her teeth. She was completely flummoxed. We all thought Aaron had accepted you for his wife. No one had any idea he planned to hide you away in Surrey."

"Hide me?"

"I'm sorry, darling. Bad choice of words. My mouth runs away when my temper flares."

Rebekah smiled. "You're in a temper?"

"I'm controlling it. I'm in a stew, but if I allow my temper to surface, believe me, Rebekah, you would have no doubt. Perhaps it is the French in me. But I can raise the roof with the best of shouters."

"I believe you."

"That's much better. I'm glad to see you smile." Joyanna pulled a delicate kerchief from her sleeve. "Here, darling. Blow your nose. Wash your face. Then you can stay in your chamber as long as you like. Or, come downstairs where we can laugh and you can truly be yourself. No one expects you to pretend you are a blushing bride."

Chapter 17

Now that Aaron was in London, perhaps things would get back to normal.

He donned a suit of clothes and headed for his favorite haunt. He handed his hat and coat to the door's man, and went in search of his friends. Jeremy Elmsford and Noah Worthington sat at a round table, brandy glasses on the table before them.

Jeremy picked up the newspaper and stabbed his finger. "Another Greystoke has fallen. How dare you get leg-shackled without telling your friends."

His farce of a marriage was out in the open. What better way to announce his marriage than broadcast in the gossip rag.

"Who is this mysterious woman?" Noah asked. "No one seems to know anything about her."

"You've kept her well-hidden, Aaron."

"Miss Ferriweather will be in quite a stew to know you're off the market. She had her cap set for you, you know."

Regardless of his feelings, he kept the truth to himself and accepted his friends' jibes.

"Now that you have a wife—the news has jaws dropping all over Town—I suppose we will be hearing another announcement about impending children, perhaps?"

"No." When both men raised their brows in question, Aaron explained, "I mean. That is not why we married."

"Aaron," Elmsford beckoned, "You are the last man we expected to be getting leg-shackled. Why on Earth—"

"It's not a love match. And I'd prefer—" Aaron glared at each one. –"that you keep that to yourselves."

"An arranged marriage. That happens all the time. Why would you want to—"

"Lower your roar, Elmsford." *Damn*. He shouldn't have said anything.

"Well, when will we meet her?"

This part would be the most difficult. No matter how many scenarios he came up with, he still couldn't think of one believable excuse. Everyone knew about Bellingham targeting his brothers, so that would be the closest to the truth.

"We do not know if Bellingham is lurking about."

"Bellingham, you say?"

"Thought he was blown up with his ship."

"Nothing is certain," Aaron said. "Until we know for sure, I plan to keep my wife safe in the country." How bizarre the term wife came out of his mouth.

"Good idea."

"Are you not worried that he'll find her there while you're in Town?"

"No one knows where she is. I will simply say she has personal matters to attend. None will be the wiser."

"I see."

Aaron stopped by the small office of Anderson Shipping on his way home to see if there was any correspondence from Mr. Anderson. It appeared the man was excited about the merger being finalized. It was nice to have some good news, for a change.

Aaron missed lunch, and it was too soon for tea, so he headed to the kitchen to see if he could coax Cook into making him something. The dear woman had taken a liking to him and often treated him to special delicacies. It had taken some convincing to get the woman to return to London. He had not been honest about his bride returning with him. Cook didn't like it, but she still prepared him wonderful meals.

A sharp knock sounded on the front door. Aaron paused, waiting to see who might be calling.

Berthright spoke to whoever was on the other side and told them to come to the rear of the house. When the butler found Aaron lurking in the hallway, he stiffened. You could never tell by Berthright's face what was on his mind. He showed no emotion. Aunt liked him, so the man retained his position.

"It was a seagoer, my lord." Aaron's father had been the earl, and after his death the old man continued to address all the brothers as my lord. Whether he considered Aaron worthy, or he was a forgetful, arrogant old man, Aaron gave up correcting the elder man.

"What did he want?"

"To speak to you, my lord."

"Are you sure he has the correct brother?"

"He asked for you by name. By his appearance ... and smell, I suggested he come to the rear entrance, my ... sire."

Ha. He stumbled.

"Very good. I shall go see what he wants."

Aaron moved to continue on his way, but the butler cleared his throat to get Aaron's attention. He stopped.

"What is it, Berthright?"

"Forgive me for being forward, sire. Please be careful."

After everything he'd been through these past months, Berthright should certainly know Aaron could take care of himself.

By his appearance.

How many men were judged by only a glance. Murderers, thieves, or a poor sod down on his luck. Although, Berthright was a clever bastard. Perhaps he saw something that made him suspicious.

"I understand, Berthright. I will."

The butler gave a slight bow, and then turned, quietly stepping to the side.

When Aaron got to the kitchen, Cook had the man pinned at the back door.

"We don't need no beggars 'round here."

"I'll take care of this," Aaron told her. "You go back to your cooking."

Cook gave him a look between disbelief and relief. The woman had wanted to protect him. By the filthy clothes and the man's unclean smell, anyone would think that he was up to no good.

"I am Aaron Greystoke. Are you looking for me?"

"Pauly sent me."

Aaron gave a nod, recognizing the name of the man he'd met at the tavern.

"What's your name?"

The man hesitated.

"Never mind, "Aaron said quickly. He did not want to scare the man off.

"Follow me." Aaron marched down the hall to his study, and stood to the side allowing the man space to enter. "I hope you don't mind if I close the door. What you have to tell me is, most likely, for my ears alone."

He waited for the man's nod before closing the door. The man reminded him of a nervous fox hiding from the hounds on a hunt.

"Now, will you tell me your name?"

"Name don't matter. What I got to tell ya is."

"Very well," Aaron said, stepping behind the big oak desk. "Would you care to sit down?"

The fox darted his eyes to a chair and back to him. "Might get yer chair dirty."

"I think the chair can take it. Sit, if you like."

The man jerked the cap from his head, and mutilated it between his fingers. "Believe I'd rather stand."

Aaron gave a nod. "Suit yourself. What do you have to tell me?"

"Pauly said be at The Reef."

"He's here? In London?"

"Just knowd what I's supposed to tell ya. Be at the tavern when the bell strikes twelve. Bone will meet ya."

"The Reef. Done. What about Blade?"

"Don't knowd nothing else."

"That's it?"

The fox gave a nervous nod.

Aaron had to control his eagerness so not to spook the man. "Tell Pauly I'll be there."

The short man turned to go.

"Wait … uh, whatever your name is. Stop in the kitchen. Cook will give you something to eat."

"I ain't no beggar."

"Of course not. No one says you are. But you have brought me important information. I should pay you for that."

The fox seemed to think it over. Then he gave a nod.

Aaron opened his study door and heard the footsteps of the man following him. "Cook," he called, "See to it this man receives payment for his service. Since he will be waiting in the kitchen for the steward, let's not torture him with your delicious cooking. Give him a hot meal so he can see the taste is as good as the smell." He turned to the fox, who seemed to be in doubt over his good fortune.

"I'll send my steward. Please make yourself comfortable."

Aaron gave a glance to Cook. He couldn't decide who seemed more surprised. The fox, or his cook.

Why the bloody hell should a man go hungry when it was clear he needed to eat? Aaron would bet Cook made the little bugger wash his hands. He chuckled as he strode back to his study.

Closing the door, he frowned, thinking about Blade. Had Pauly received word? What about Bone? He and Pauly must have run into each other in Brighton. As far as Aaron knew, Bone had been at the docks, searching.

Aaron scrubbed a hand through his wild hair. Could Blade be alive?

He slammed a fist down on the wood desk. Devil take Bellingham. If he found that bounder, he would strike without a second thought. No warning for that blackguard. The cur had to know that the Greystoke brothers would be after him. Aaron had enough men looking for the bastard. They were bound to find something soon.

───ℓℓℓ───

Aaron kept his head down and quickened his steps. Not only was he anxious to hear what Pauly had to tell him, but he desperately wanted to know if Blade was alive. The waterfront was dangerous, but with Aaron's size, most left him alone. Reaching his destination, he slowed down to take a breath. Charging into the establishment would put all eyes on him. He'd rather keep himself on the low for tonight.

Even so, as he entered, a few men looked his way. Miscreants, every one of them. He was glad he'd put the knife in his boot. He could almost guarantee there'd be two or three waiting for him when he left. Another reason for a man to leave his purse at home when entering the bowels of hell on the London waterfront.

In the far corner, a bearded man lifted his mug of ale, and glanced at Aaron over the foam.

Pauly.

Aaron made his way to the table. "Evening. Mind if I share your table?"

"Sit down if ya like."

Aaron waved the barmaid over and ordered an ale before he sat down. "I got your message."

"Yer man has surfaced."

"Blade? He's alive?"

Pauly shook his head. "The other one. Bellingham."

Aaron knew it was only a matter of time before the hound showed up. Bellingham had more lives than a bloody cat.

Aaron nearly came out of his seat. "Where?"

"I can tell ya where he's been. He hit Brighton three days ago, with a ship. Seadog was with him. Hear tell crew came with the ship. Seadog is the new captain."

"What is the name of this ship?"

"Name won't do you no good. Bellingham is on land. Say he headed north."

"Making his way to London."

Pauly slowly nodded. "That'd be my guess."

"Anything else?"

"Yer men is looking fer 'im. He knows it."

"He'd be a fool to think we weren't."

"Someone's helping 'im. Don't know who yet, but we'll find out. What's yer plan when we do?"

"That would be better left to me," Aaron growled, recalling the churning hatred for a man who'd tried to kill Nathaniel. The bastard had tried to destroy Edmund too. Not with a pistol, but his words were just as damning. Thank Christ, Nathaniel had gotten home in time to help.

Taking the hint, Pauly held up his hands. "Not my business. Don't care, neither. But if ya need my help, send word to the barkeep. He can be trusted."

Aaron had learned the hard way not to trust any man. He chose his friends carefully. Those he called friend were bonded to his soul. Anyone else was to be watched with scrutiny.

"The minute you know where he is, I want to know. Do you understand?"

When Aaron got back to his house, he sent a message to his brothers. He couldn't imagine they had stayed in the country after his departure. Bright and early the next morning, they marched into his study.

"You two travel together?"

"I happened to be at Edmund's when your message arrived."

"Why don't you have a seat?"

Before he could make it around his desk, Nathaniel practically growled. "Spit it out, Pup."

Aaron halted. "I thought Serena had tamed you."

"Is there news on Bellingham?"

"Sit down, brother."

"Yes, do sit down Nathaniel. We will hear what Aaron has to tell us sooner."

Nathaniel dropped his large frame into a chair facing Aaron's desk.

"What news have you received?" Edmund asked.

Aaron poured two more glasses of brandy. "As you know, I've been looking for Blade since Bellingham's ship blew in the harbor." He handed the first to Edmund, then the other to Nathaniel.

"I hope that bastard is in hell." Nathaniel tossed back his drink.

Edmund rose, went to the whisky decanter, and brought it over to Nathaniel. "Looks like we're going to need it."

"I've been searching the docks from here to Brighton, visiting every rathole, every tavern, back alley I could find."

"You have no business going there alone, Aaron. You have men in your pocket for that."

"I had to do something." Blade was a good friend. Honest friend. He was on that ship because Aaron had sent him there.

"No one has found a body. He could still be alive."

"I hope so." Aaron swallowed the whisky, savoring the burn to his gut. "While I was in Brighton, at a tavern, two men approached me."

"Why are we just now hearing about this?"

"Preparing for a wedding required much of my attention." He said with as much sarcasm as he could muster. "A man showed up at my door today. He delivered a message from the man I met in Brighton. I went to meet him at The Reef."

"Tell me you did not go there alone," Nathaniel growled.

Aaron ignored his brother's outburst. "Bellingham has surfaced."

"Bloody hell," Nathaniel spat.

"I'm not surprised." Edmund turned up his glass.

"I suppose we knew the bastard didn't go down with the ship."

Aaron continued, "He has another. Apparently, got rid of the captain and confiscated the crew."

"Seadog with him?"

Aaron gave a nod. "The new captain."

"Again, I am not surprised." Edmund turned up his glass and poured more from the decanter. "The man has the luck of the devil."

Aaron took the decanter from Edmund. "He was seen on land. My guess is, he's heading for us."

"Revenge," his brother echoed.

"We've destroyed his cargo in the caves and sunk his ship. Of course, he's gunning for us."

"Let the bastard come." Nathaniel stood and started pacing.

"Come now, brother," Aaron said. "I see no reason to pace. We need a plan for when he shows up."

"You can bet your arse he will." Edmund drained his glass. Aaron offered to pour him another.

"Edmund. You know him best. What do you think he will do?"

"I know he wanted Greystoke Manor. He's a rotter. You know as much about the man as I do."

"You have no idea who might be helping him? If he's on land, and hasn't been caught, then someone must be aiding him."

"Either that, or he's found an unoccupied estate. 'Tis the season, you know. Many houses are closed for the summer."

"The only thing we can do is be on our guard," Nathaniel said. "With no idea where or when he will come at us, or which brother he will pick, each of us will need to expect the unexpected."

"Gor, brother. I would never have thought of that."

"By the by, brother. Leaving your bride without a bride month was not well done of you."

And there it was. Aaron was actually surprised Edmund hadn't demanded an explanation as soon as he came through the door.

"Are you going to tell me how to be a husband?"

Nathaniel responded. "My wife is still there. I am not happy. I would rather have my wife in Town with me."

Aaron looked up at Nathaniel, who stopped his pacing to lean an elbow on the hearth ledge.

"Yours is a love match, brother. Mine is not."

"You agreed to this marriage," Nathaniel fired back. "Hell, Aaron. You signed a bloody contract, which started this entire kettle of fish."

"I do not need reminding."

"Beg to differ, little brother," Edmund chimed in with his languid brogue. "One would think you've forgotten you have a wife."

Aaron had called his brothers here to give them news. He should have expected them to take him to task by giving their unwelcome opinions.

Good God, how much his brothers looked alike with that brooding brow. Other than that, Edmund's hair was darker, and he'd managed to keep the youthfulness to his face.

"What's that smirk?" Edmund asked.

"Looking at the two of you. You resemble each other more than I realized."

The older brothers glanced at each other, then back to him.

"You and Nathaniel are the ones who could pass for twins," Edmund muttered.

Aaron turned his lips into an arrogant smile. "But I am so much younger."

"Are you going to see her?" Nathaniel asked.

"See whom?"

"You know damn well whom."

"Clearly, you are avoiding speaking of Rebekah."

Were both of his brothers going to gang up on him.

"Imagine me having to console *your wife* on *your* wedding day."

That came as a complete surprise. For one, Nathaniel consoling anyone. The second, Rebekah needing the consoling.

"As you take great pleasure in reminding me, she is my wife. I will remind you that neither she, nor myself wanted to be leg-shackled."

Chapter 18

Dear Lord, someone should just shoot her.

Rebekah was ready to call it quits. Who knew there was so much to learn? Not only learn, but practice and watch her every move. An instructor to show her how to walk? At first, she thought Joyanna was joking. Then Serena told her that she had the same teacher.

"You had to go through this, too?"

"Like you, I thought it was unnecessary. But my mother was of noble blood. She moved with grace. I didn't recognize it when I was young, but looking back, I see her movements were like water."

"Water?"

"Well, what I mean is, fluid motions. I don't know how to explain it, but she flowed like water, or like the wind. Graceful in everything she did. Whether she walked across the room or stood cooking at the stove. Even when she brought the dishes to the table or made up the bed."

"Wow. That's some description." Rebekah turned to Joyanna. "I see it in you, Joyanna. You float across a room. You glide when you sit down."

"That's it," Serena said. "You do know what I mean."

Joyanna laughed. "I had no idea I was floating, or gliding. However, I did have an instructor. Not Mr. Bisque. I quite like Mr. Bisque. My teacher was Mr. Mason. He often told my mother I was a lost cause. He was fat and had this pointy nose he kept in the air. I never saw him point that brittle thing anywhere else."

The women laughed, and Rebekah joined them.

"I didn't mind Mr. Bisque," Serena said. "Of course, Penelope joined us for my lessons. And she was quick to take him to task if I didn't do something right."

"He taught you how to walk, right?" Rebekah asked Serena. "I've been walking all my life."

"Ah, Rebekah," Joyanna cooed, "there is walking ... and there is gliding." She giggled and Rebekah laughed too.

"I'm so glad the both of you are here. You've made this so much easier on me."

"I'm happy to help." Serena smiled. "The only person I had to lean on was Penelope. I was all alone, and I was so scared."

A shadow crossed Serena's face making Rebekah wonder if something had happened to her?

"And look at you now," Joyanna laughed. "Lady Greystoke. Not the owner of one title but two."

"Two?" It was out of her mouth before she thought better of it. "I'm sorry. I should not have asked?"

"It's no secret. My grandfather was Viscount of Rothingham Hall. Close to the shoreline, a few days from here. His son was my father. When my father ... died ..."

"Oh, Serena, I'm so sorry. If it is too painful ..."

Serena smiled. "No. Mine is a happy ending. "I'd been born a girl, so there was no one to carry on the line. Grandfather took it out on me. I escaped; Nathaniel found me. He saved me. We fell in love and here we are."

Rebekah knew there was a whole lot more to that story. Perhaps someday, after they became better friends, Serena might share it with her.

Who was she kidding? Most likely, Rebekah would not be around long enough for them to become friends. True, Aaron had married her, nut then he left. She wouldn't blame the family if they threw her out.

But Aunt Penelope was treating Rebekah as though she belonged. As though she truly was Aaron's wife—*which I guess I am*. Part of the family. Serena and Joyanna were doing the same. A tear formed in Rebekah's eye, but she quickly willed it away. They didn't know her, and still, they were being so nice.

"Want to hear *my* story?" Joyanna asked with a wink.

Rebekah blinked. "Oh yes, if you don't mind, I do." This would be interesting. Joyanna was French. This had to be exciting.

"Well, I was raised in London. My father was a very important nobleman. Mother was the *creme de la creme*," she said with a wave of her hand. "In case you don't know what that means, she was extremely fashionable and enjoyed being envied by the ton. Even so, she was well liked by the other matrons."

Joyanna's face took on a dreamy expression.

"Edmund is the love of my life. Has always been. We were together at every opportunity we could orchestrate. Everyone considered him the Earl of Greystoke. The title didn't matter to me. I loved *him*."

"Edmund the earl?"

"Oh, I left a few things out," Serena said. "Not intentionally. But Nathaniel hated Greystoke Manor. I see the questions on your face, we will answer all those questions another day. Anyway, Nathaniel left his home, and his brothers didn't know if he was ever coming back."

Rebekah gasped at that statement.

Serena nodded. "Yes, well, while he was gone, Edmund acted in his stead."

"He never pretended to be the earl. He just performed the duties as Lord Greystoke tending the Manor," Joyanna quickly explained. "He made it clear he had no claim, and he was not the heir." Joyanna looked down at her hands in her lap.

Oh dear. Rebekah feared there was a sad part to Joyanna's story.

"Edmund thought ... wait, I'm getting ahead of myself. My father invested our money with a criminal—of course he didn't know it at the time—and he lost everything. To save face, father decided we would move to France. He didn't tell a soul what happened. He wouldn't have been able to stand the embarrassment." Joyanna looked directly at Rebekah.

"So, you see, the ton is a dangerous weapon. They can make you or break you. Aristocrats believe they are privileged. Due to their titles, they consider themselves most qualified to rule. They hold the power."

"This is why Penelope arranged a cover for you and Aaron. She did the same thing for Nathaniel and me."

"What do you mean?"

"I was a young woman living with a popular bachelor. Aunt had to chaperone. She made up a story about her relative being my mother and I was Nathaniel's ward. Then we fell madly in love—that part is true—and we married."

"Oh, I have got to hear the rest of that story."

"If your dance instructor wasn't due this afternoon, we would have time," Joyanna said. "I'll be quick."

"I don't want you to leave anything out," Rebekah blurted.

Joyanna smiled.

"As I said, another day. For now, the basics. Let me see, where was I? Oh, yes. Father lost all our money and was taking us to France. I couldn't tell Edmund the truth, so I allowed him to believe I wouldn't have him because he was not the earl."

"You mean, he offered for you, and you refused him?"

Joyanna nodded. "I thought I was doing the right thing, even though I broke both our hearts." She removed a handkerchief from her reticule and dabbed at her eyes. "Goodness, I can still see the pain on his face. The anger."

Serena patted Joyanna's hand for comfort. "Get to the good part."

"Oh yes, well," Joyanna waved her hand. "I went to France, married an old man who was a Viscount—father arranged the marriage. I didn't care who I married. I didn't care about anything."

"Joyanna," Serena drew her attention. "The good part."

The corners of her mouth lifted into a bright smile. Rebekah released the breath she'd been holding.

"My husband was old. He died, poor man. But I was free. I came back to London, and went after the man I loved. It wasn't easy."

Serena giggled.

"But we're together, and we are very happy."

"I can see that," Rebekah told her. "I also see another long story. One day the three of us need to get together and plan a day of stories."

"That sounds like a fine idea. Doesn't it, Joyanna?"

Joyanna clapped her hands. "I can hardly wait."

"Did Penelope have to make up a story for you, too?" Rebekah asked.

"No. It wasn't necessary. The ton was presented with the new Viscountess from France. A high-born lady with a title."

"There was a grand introduction into society. Everyone knew the famous lady from France before even we knew of her connection to Edmund."

"Before? I know, another long story. I think we will need more than one day." Rebekah laughed, feeling liberated, and pleased that she had these ladies for friends.

Aaron left the small office of Anderson Shipping feeling better than he had in quite a long while. The merger was complete. He owned fifty percent of the company, an equal partner. He decided to stop by Whites to celebrate, and ran into his rollicking friends.

"I say, Aaron. The betting book has your name in it."

"I'm used to the ton gossiping about me and my brothers."

Jeremy chuckled. "This is ripe."

"If it has your interest," Aaron said to Noah, "then pray tell me what the gossipmongers are whispering."

"You are married, are you not?"

Aaron, tensed. Then he tilted his head. "I am."

"Where is your bride?"

"I thought I'd settled that weeks ago."

"And still you have not presented said bride."

"We only have your word to go on, Aaron."

Anger flared in his chest. He knew the ton would be curious about his unexpected wedding nuptials, but he had not suspected the ton would question its authenticity. "Are you questioning my word, Elmsford?"

"God no," he sputtered. "There's no need for pistols at dawn."

Worthington chimed in, "Good God, no!"

"Not a 'tall."

Aaron waited for Jeremy to stop sputtering. "Then explain yourself."

"Well, you've been in this..." Jeremy looked to Noah and back. "...mood." The men shifted in their seats, clearly uncomfortable. They had witnessed Aaron's wrath, but none of the three had been on the receiving end of it.

"Mood?"

"You've turned into a downright sullen man," Worthington admitted. "Not your usual rascally self."

"Where is the charming man who brought laughter into a room with him," Jeremy asked. "I say, you are not my friend Aaron. What have you done with him?"

"Go to the devil, Jeremy."

"The season is half over, and your bride still has not made an appearance. One cannot help but wonder why?"

Before Aaron could answer, his friend spit out, "Our friends think you have a case of the blue devils."

His indignation simmered. He had a lot on his mind, but he didn't think he'd been that bad. They were mad. "You are aware I have a mistress." He glared at them. He'd given her up, but they didn't need to know that.

"And quite a fine one she is. Why her reputation—"

"Hold, Jeremy. Are you eager to face Aaron on the dueling field? That's twice you've managed to tread on his toes."

"What?" His gaze jerked between them. "Now see here. I'm only repeating—"

"Don't worry. Aaron is not as sensitive as all that. Why don't you get to the point?"

"Well." Jeremy cleared his throat. "When you did not bring your wife to London, after a time, the wager was placed if you were leg-shackled at all. You must admit, it's hard to believe of you, old chap."

"And now?" Aaron growled.

"Oh, no, you settled that one," Noah was quick to amend. "Now lords are wondering why, or if your lady wife will ever come to Town."

The fools. They had nothing better to do than waste their money on speculation. Aaron did not like being the brunt of supposition. "What is your wager, Noah?"

"The betting goes from she is too beautiful that you want to keep her to yourself ..." He hesitated.

"And?"

"Well, uh ..."

"Spit it out," Aaron growled

"Or if she is pock-marked and too ugly," Jeremy finished.

"I didn't say that?" Noah huffed.

Aaron thought his friends were imbeciles. "Perhaps I should take a look for myself." He stood, and Noah fluttered about like a hen protecting her chicks. He followed Aaron over to the betting book, where a large group was already gathered.

"Chapman. The man in question is right here. Let's see what he had to say."

Aaron's glower had several men quickly stepping aside. He read the last few entries until he found the one he was looking for. Not only his friends, but half the ton had made wagers. There was nothing for him to do.

He slammed the book closed, turned on his heel, and left.

Rebekah embarked on her task with all the determination of one of Sasha's puppies finding mischief. Her curiosity burned as deep as the critters' inquisitiveness. She poured over volumes of conduct, convention, and protocol. What she did not learn in books, Serena and Joyanna happily filled in for her.

Serena and Joyanna were nothing like what she had expected. They were nice, and fun, and not snooty at all. Not like one would expect aristocrats to be. True, Rebekah had not been around nobles, but from what she gathered from her Mama and Papa, lords and ladies were a bunch of fakes. Pretending to be better than anyone else, yet sneaking about, with less morals than a commoner.

She and Papa were ordinary people. Her mother had turned her back on the upper-class. Or rather, the bluebloods had turned their noses up to her, after she married Papa. Mama never regretted her choice, and she made the three of them a happy family.

Rebekah had been happy.

So why was she trying so hard to prove she could fit in?

Aaron had gone through with the wedding—grudgingly, of course. The frown on his face never changed the entire time during the ceremony, and after. Especially when several men offered congratulations. His grim expression was one of attending a funeral instead of a joyous occasion. As soon as the vows were spoken, the groom made a hasty retreat, and she hadn't seen him since. She'd been lost and alone until Aunt showed up. Penelope was not happy with Aaron's desertion.

Then Serena and Joyanna showed up, cooing and clucking over Rebekah like a couple of hens. They were happy to spend an afternoon practicing the social graces and rehearsing polite conversation.

In four months, Rebekah had gained the stamped approval of Aunt Penelope.

"Aaron is a fool. I have half a mind to tan that boy's hide."

Rebekah grinned. She would dearly love to see that, but she knew Aunt cared a great deal about Aaron. "Whatever for? He's done nothing."

Aunt huffed—very unlady-like. "That's just it. He has ignored his wife for far too long."

Rebekah couldn't argue with that. What surprised her was how much she missed him. Even after that night, when she'd been alone with her father, she'd thought of Aaron constantly and remembered their passionate night with fondness.

At the moment, the last thing she felt for Aaron was affection. Angry. Distaste. Antipathy. Those were the words she used lately.

"Perhaps the answer is to take her to London." All eyes turned to Joyanna. Her gaze was locked with Penelope.

"Why not show Aaron exactly what he's been missing?"

Aunt looked thoughtful. "You may be right. If Muhammed won't come to the mountain, the mountain must come to Muhammed"

"What does that mean?" Rebekah asked.

Serena explained. "It is a proverbial saying. According to the story, when Muhammad was asked to provide proofs of his teachings, he ordered Mount Safa to come to him. It didn't. So, he went to the mountain. My grandfather had an extensive library."

"You my dear," Aunt said, "are about to be Muhammed."

Rebekah stared.

"Oh, that's what I think too," Joyanna said. "Rebekah, if something cannot or will not happen the easy way, then sometimes it must be done the hard way. We adjust our approach, take a different path to achieve our goals."

"Aaron will be angry," Serena muttered.

Joyanna waved a hand. "He deserves it."

"My head is spinning. What are you talking about?"

"Rebekah," Aunt said, drawing her attention. "It is time for you to make your debut."

Joyanna clapped her hands. "We are going to London."

Chapter 19

T he large ballroom glimmered with candlelight, brandishing the grandeur of the mansion, exhibiting every aspect, displaying every item to perfection. An air of magic and mystery drifted aimlessly, captivating the guests and luring them into enchantment. In the center of the room, a group of reflective stars hung above a crystal waterfall. Clouds of white lined with beads were draped between columns surrounding the dance floor of sparkling glass. Rebekah stared in awe.

"Lady Mayweather has outdone every matriarch in London. Her ball shall be on the tongues of every member of the ton," Penelope said.

At the moment, all Rebekah could do was stare. She could hardly contain her excitement—and her dread. The room was filled to overflowing. How would she spot Aaron in this crush of nobles.

Her heart did a little flutter. How could she not? Aaron was taller than most, a broad chest with muscle, and his hair held the brilliance of the sun. Most likely he would have it tied back this evening.

Even though Rebekah tried to prepare herself and develop an attitude of languid nonchalance, on the inside she was a bundle of nerves. She was a participant in a well manufactured sham. Aunt had helped her choose the perfect gown, and of course Madame Lasselle had assured her it was the latest fashion.

Joyanna's personal maid did Rebekah's hair. When she'd seen herself in the mirror, she could barely believe the woman staring back at her. She'd felt like a princess attending her first ball.

Sorrow loomed with her role of achievement, hiding her broken heart. Playing the lovely, cheerful woman who cared not a whit about her husband's indiscretions. She tried not to judge him too harshly. He had given her a house to live in—without him. He'd saved her reputation—which she didn't give a hoot about. He promised to take care of her father—Papa was happy. And he'd given her a ready-made family—that treated her better than he did.

She held her head high, pasted a smile on her face, and damned her husband to hell.

And then she saw him.

Of course he was breathtaking.

Aaron cut a fine figure in his tailor-made clothes. Taller than she remembered, and his coat stretched tight over his broad shoulders. Aaron was no dandy with lace at his cuffs. But the diamond pin in his neckcloth drew her gaze to his throat. Men were handsome, but Aaron was so much more. Dashing, with an air of danger. His waistcoat with silver embroidery stretched over his sizeable muscles. He held the strong presence of a confident stallion. His trousers clung to his well-defined thighs. He was most handsome and sharp with nary a piece out of place. His long hair had been tied back showing his prominent jaw.

She lifted her gaze to his eyes. His stark gaze frightened her, and at the same time sent a zinging heat to her core. His eyes roamed over the entire length of her, then ever so slowly returned to her face. A knot formed in her chest. Tingles of apprehension shot through her limbs, and she silently prayed her knees would hold her steady. While their eyes were locked on each other, one corner of his mouth lifted in a forced grin.

Good. Let him be angry. He'd ignored her long enough. She'd been left to survive on her own, she was not about to fall at his feet. The arrogant poop was too sure of himself. Their sham of a marriage was about to be put to the test.

Aunt watched her. Waiting to see if Rebekah was made of the starch that Aunt had assured *her* she was. She postured as she'd been taught, remembering the last few months, and why she was here.

There was no going back.

Aaron strode toward her. The entire room had gone quiet. The world was watching, waiting, to see the lovebirds unite. She would not give them the satisfaction—give *him* the satisfaction—of seeing her falter. If the ton wanted a polished lady, then they would get one.

"Hello, wife." Aaron's words pierced her, quiet enough only she heard. The evil grin on his face looked like a wolf ready to devour everything in his path. He took her gloved hand and bent low, kissing the back. Even through her glove, she felt his heat.

She shook off the moment of weakness, and mentally kicked herself for being drawn in. Placing her fan in front of her face, she whispered in the same tone he had used. "So, you do remember."

His gaze shot to hers, letting her know the mark had hit its target.

She lowered the fan, and said loudly for the onlookers, "How perceptive you are, dear husband. Thank you for allowing me my ... private time. I have missed you." Let the ton think of that what they will.

Whispers murmured at once, the buzz growing louder around the room. Someone signaled the orchestra, and a melody filled the hall.

Never releasing her hand, Aaron placed her fingers on the sleeve of his coat. Instinct made her jerk away, but he caught her hand with his own, forcing her to leave it in the crook of his elbow.

"Don't worry, husband," she snapped, keeping a smile on her face. "I won't embarrass you."

His brow furrowed, and the vein at his temple jerked.

Not so sure of yourself now are you?

Let him see she was no meek mouse.

"May I have this dance, darling?"

Darling. She wanted to snarl in his face.

"Of course, my love." She beamed at him. Flashing her eyelashes was too much, so she decided not to do it. She was no simpering miss, no debutante with stars in her eyes. She knew the real Aaron Greystoke. No one should envy his wife.

He led her to the dance floor, with the courtliness of an aristocrat. At that moment, she was thankful she had paid attention to Serena and Joyanna.

Aaron's face softened as he placed his hand at her waist. Rebekah accepted his gallantry, knowing it was for the benefit of the observers. For the evening, she would keep up the pretense of doting wife.

As Aaron whirled her on the highly polished dance floor, she refused to be intimidated by his perfect steps. It was no great surprise that he was a superb dancer. She was a fast learner. The instructor Aunt hired to tutor Rebekah had even given her a compliment, saying she had a natural talent.

Aaron gripped her hand tighter. He bent close, his voice low enough so others would not hear.

"Have you grown bored in Surrey, wife?"

It was now out in the open. The ton now saw with their own eyes that Aaron Greystoke had a wife.

"Did you think your wife so ugly you had to hide me away?"

His brows rose with his surprise.

Yes, Aaron, I am no meek mouse.

"Or perhaps you thought I would embarrass you?"

He gritted his teeth, his jaw so tight she thought it might crack. "It appears, dear wife, we need to have a serious discussion."

"Certainly," she said with a nod. "Would you prefer to check your calendar to see when you might be available to fit me in?"

"Do not test me, Rebekah. There are limits—even for a wife."

"Oh, then, you do remember you have one."

"Bloody hell."

"Be cautious, husband. You do want to keep up appearances, do you not?"

"I would rather not have scandal reach Aunt Penelope."

"Hiding your bride in Surrey and attending parties and balls as a bachelor is not scandalous? But then, there is a separate set of rules for gentlemen. And I use that term loosely."

Good God, she was lovely. More lovely than he remembered. If he was not so shocked, so stunned, he could truly enjoy Rebekah's beauty. If he was not angry, he could allow his lust free rein. Rebekah was a beautiful, desirable woman. Her hair had grown into glossy waves that tumbled over her shoulders. Sooty lashes enhanced the bright blue in her eyes. Her curves had filled out rather nicely drawing any man's gaze.

She looked delectable enough to shake any man's control. Her low-cut bodice had half the bucks in this room already with their tongues hanging out, and most likely planning a rendezvous with *his* wife.

Aaron took a peek at her bosom. Her lush, creamy bosom. He could almost feel his hands grasping her flesh.

Bloody hell. Snap out of it.

Just what was she and Aunt up to? He knew Rebekah showing up in London, coming to Haverson's ball, had been his aunt's idea. She was forcing him to acknowledge his wife. He thought about the betting book at White's. Let the ton go hang.

"What are you doing here?"

"Are you not happy to see me?" Sweet and docile would not describe Rebekah, yet here she was, acting like a cheerful debutante.

"You should have told me you wanted to come to Town."

"And how, pray tell, was I to communicate with my absent husband? By carrier pigeon? Or perhaps the widows of the ton. After all, those ladies know more regarding your whereabouts than I do."

And there was the woman he knew.

Aaron forced the smile to stay on his lips while the muscle in his jaw clenched. "Since you are here with Aunt Penelope, I will assume she had a hand in this."

"You may assume whatever you like, dear husband."

"Smile, darling. Your facade is slipping."

Her eyes flashed with fire. "I should think, Husband, if you are going to bring up duplicity, perhaps you should look to yourself. Were the ladies of the ton aware of your matrimonial state?"

Anger impaled him. No one dared to call him a liar. "You go too far, dear *Wife*," he growled. "You know very well the news of our nuptials spread before the wedding ceremony took place."

"And what a lovely ceremony it was." Her smile flashed and she moved with the music expertly. Her eyes glared daggers and promises that he would pay later.

Just what did she think she could do?

"Whatever will you do now that the cat is out of the bag? Or should I say the jailed wife has broken free from her prison."

"Prison?" If they were not in front of a million curious eyes, he would throttle her.

"Yes, Aaron. The only thing worse than being married to you is being pitied." She tried darting off, but he would not let her go.

"Oh, no, my butterfly. You will not stalk off in the middle of our dance."

She surprised him by continuing with their steps.

"Would that be humiliating?"

"Not only to me," he ground out. She would suffer more than anyone else. "Now, shut up and pretend you want to dance with me."

She seemed to consider her options. Then she placed an alarming smile on her face and gave the appearance she was enjoying herself.

Talk about two very different sides to one's personality.

"I had no idea what parties awaited me in London."

The cheeky chit was toying with him. "You like parties, do you?"

"Since you never took me to any, I have nothing to compare. However, if they are like this one, I think I shall have a grand time during the season."

Over my dead body.

"Aaron. You look distressed? Is anything amiss?"

"I believe it is time for us to leave."

She looked surprised. Then the blasted luring smile was back on her face. He would get her out of here before another randy buck took notice and was tempted by her appeal. Good God, he would not fight admirers for his wife's attention.

He took her arm, and escorted her from the throng of dancers.

"Where are we going, darling?"

"We are leaving."

She dug in her heels. "You may do as you wish. I am going to stay."

Aaron was so stunned he could only stare. His wife was defying him? In a room full of onlookers?

Devil take her.

His grip on her arm tightened. "You are coming with me, *Wife.*"

"Are you going somewhere, Rebekah?"

He recognized that voice immediately. Edmund. Damn him for his interference.

"Step aside, brother. My wife is leaving with me."

"Joyanna," Edmund spoke to his wife keeping his gaze on Aaron. Why don't you and Rebekah go to Aunt Penelope, while I discuss manners with my brother."

Joyanna looped her arm through Rebekah's and waved her fan. "I agree, Rebekah. Shall we join Penelope?"

Aaron glared at Edmund as the women walked away. "Enjoy your sneering grin while you can, brother. If you try to stop me, you may lose a few of those shining teeth."

Edmund threw his head back and laughed. "Damned good one, Aaron. Damned good one. Now, shall we discuss this in private?"

"Glad to see you making jokes. Because a moment ago, it looked as though you were about to cause a scene, Aaron."

Aaron cringed. *Another brother.* "Good of you to join us, Nathaniel. I have a bone to pick with you."

"Pick away, brother. Just remember Aunt, and as well as the rest of the ton, is watching."

Damn the bloody ton.

"Very well. We'll discuss the matter later. As for now, we are leaving."

"We?" Nathaniel raised a brow.

"Don't goad me, brother." Aaron moved to step around Nathaniel, Edmund blocked him.

"Stop right there, brother. Wife or no, you will not manhandle Rebekah. Did you not even notice you were bruising her arm?"

What? Bollocks. No, he hadn't.

"She came with me," Nathaniel pointed out. "When she is ready, I will take her home?"

Aaron snapped his head to Nathaniel. There were so many things wrong with that statement. One—who did his damn brother think he was? Two—why was Nathaniel sticking his nose in Aaron's business. Three—when she was ready?

"Where is Serena?"

"How kind of you to ask. As you know she is heavy with child, and her time nears. She is indisposed."

"So, you decided to bring *my wife* to a ball?"

"Down, Pup." Nathaniel growled in a whisper.

"Aaron, watch your words," Edmund intervened. "You've had a shock. You need time to process."

Being the unreasonable one was new to him. He took a breath and faced Nathaniel. "I don't know how *my wife* came to be in your company, but I suggest you go home and take care of your own."

Nathaniel gritted his teeth, showing his temper was close to the surface.

"Might I remind both of you we are at a bloody ball," Edmund said, then turned to Aaron. "You surprise me. Usually, it is you who shows a cool head and reasons with us."

"Stay out of this, Edmund."

"Sorry, brother. Not happening. Not while there's a lovely young woman caught between the two of you."

"Bollocks." Aaron glared at Nathaniel. "Rebekah is mine."

"Need I remind you she came to me?"

"She came to Greystoke Manor only because she thought I was the Earl of Greystoke."

"And what did you do? You deposited your wife at Surrey, then came to London for the season, living as a bachelor."

Aaron took stock of their situation. He and his brothers were the center of attention. He placed a huge grin on his face and spoke to Nathaniel in a voice low enough the damn gossip hungry matrons wouldn't hear. "Don't tell me how to live my life, Nathaniel. Rebekah didn't want this marriage any more than I did. You know nothing of how I've been spending my time in London."

"There is no excuse to desert Rebekah and act like she doesn't exist!" Then Nathaniel gave him the look he'd given when they were youths, and Aaron knew his brother would not back down.

Aaron had always looked up to his eldest brother. Wanted to be just like him. But Nathaniel sticking his nose in Aaron's so-called marriage—no matter the ludicrous state—was crossing a line he had no business crossing.

"You may be the oldest, Nathaniel, but I remember how you flouted father's teachings. You not only disobeyed, but you challenged him. I am a grown man. You are not my father. As a matter of fact, you disappeared—"

"Shut up, Aaron," Edmund said. "Our father was a tyrant, but the one thing he instilled in each of us was decorum, and how to behave while in public." He grinned, and continued, "You wouldn't want to upset Aunt this evening, would you?"

Aaron steamed. He glanced over to where Aunt and Rebekah sat with the other matriarchs. "Some bloody brother you are. I see you stand with Nathaniel."

"I'm not taking sides. But I'll not have you embarrass Aunt by creating a scene. Aunt is the one who brought Rebekah here. She had Nathaniel escort them. If you don't like the situation, then do something about it."

Aaron thought about his decision for two seconds, then spoke, "I shall do exactly that." He spun on his heel and made a bee line for Rebekah, leaving his brothers to follow or stand there as they liked.

"Good evening, Aunt."

"You rascal. What are you and your brothers arguing about?" Aunt might sound in a temper, but she masked her true feelings by her guarded expression

"How observant, Aunt. Actually, we were discussing the ball."

"Of course, you were."

He may have been her favorite, but Penelope would take him to task if need be. "Aunt, I hope you will forgive me, but I have not seen my wife in quite a while."

"Whose fault is that?" she mumbled.

Crafty old woman.

"There are things we need to discuss." He kept his gaze on Rebekah as he talked to his aunt. She flinched at the mention of her name.

Again, he was taken with her beauty. She was more lovely than he could have imagined. The gown of lilac complimented her creamy skin and her light hair. Her eyes met his and quickly darted away. Not as confident as the woman spouting bangers at him on the dance floor. He squinted his eyes, studying her. She was nervous. Or frightened.

Of him?

Bloody hell.

"Rebekah, I apologize. I did not mean for my grip to be so strong." He managed a grin. "I'm not as bad as all that, am I?"

When her eyes met his, they were filled with confusion. At least it wasn't fear. He never wanted her—or any woman—to fear him.

"If I promise to be on my best behavior, would you leave with me?"

"We only just arrived, Aaron," Aunt scolded. "You will allow her a chance to experience her first ball."

"You lay me low pointing out my thoughtlessness, Aunt. I digress. Rebekah, I shall do whatever is in my power to see you take pleasure in this evening's festivities."

Aunt gave a nod of agreement. Rebekah looked as if she'd been poleaxed. And his damned brothers stood there, ready to pounce if he stepped out of line.

Chapter 20

Rebekah felt every muscle in her tense body. If she changed the expression on her smiling face, it would most likely crack. The cushion on her chair could have been filled with needles and her skin would not be pricklier than the apprehension of Aaron standing by her side. He'd not moved since joining her after their dance.

Aunt was in her element, introducing nobles to her nephew's wife. The question never arose why Aaron's wife had been absent while her husband had been relishing the season. Aunt said no one would dare. Still, Rebekah felt like prey while hungry vultures circled around her.

Why did she let Penelope talk her into this?

For that matter, why had she agreed to marry Aaron?

She sat staring into space when she realized a gentleman was staring back at her. *Oh no.* Lost in thought, she'd unthinkingly caught the attention of this man. He loomed in her sight, then moved toward her. The breath caught in her throat. Was he going to ask her to dance? What should she do?

As it turned out, she didn't have to do anything. The man glanced up to Aaron, then halted. He dropped his head and turned about, going back in the other direction. Suspicion tackled the back of her neck. She glanced up to see a harsh glare on Aaron's face.

So that's what he'd been doing. Scaring potential dance partners away.

"Aaron," Aunt said sharply, "Surely you won't object to your brother dancing with Rebekah?"

The statement caught him off guard, and he gave Penelope a look of confusion. Or guilt. "Of course not, Aunt."

"Forgive me for being remise," Nathaniel spoke up. "Rebekah, would you care to dance?"

"Yes," Rebekah answered quickly, before Aaron could object. She did not want to sit under his watchful eye all evening. She didn't even look at him as she took Nathaniel's arm.

Once they reached the dance floor, Nathaniel spoke, "You can relax now. "

Rebekah released her breath, not realizing she'd been holding it. "Thank you."

Nathaniel expertly led her as he spoke, not missing a step. He made her feel comfortable, and she had no trouble keeping up.

"My brother is being ridiculous."

"He is being suddenly possessive."

"You have made him the center of attention. He must play the role of dutiful husband."

"As far as I'm concerned, no, he does not. He's been an absent husband for weeks. I have found, quite pleasingly, that I do not need him at my side every minute."

Nathaniel chuckled. "Now that you have been introduced to society, he's not about to let you go out alone."

"Whyever not?"

"My dear, Rebekah. You do not realize how lovely you are." His kind eyes showed her he meant what he said.

She had no idea what to say. She looked down, feeling slightly embarrassed.

"I didn't mean to make you uncomfortable. You are a beautiful woman, and you've captured the eye of every man here. I dare say Aaron is jealous."

She jerked her gaze to his. Then she laughed, she couldn't help herself. "I'm sorry," she said with a shake of her head. "You're mistaken. Aaron cares nothing for me, so that idea is absurd."

"I think you're wrong." He waited for her to meet his gaze, then said, "He married you."

"Which means absolutely nothing." She lowered her voice so not to be overheard. "Ours was a marriage to avoid a scandal."

"You could have had a long engagement. Broken it off, and no worse for wear."

"I wasn't exactly given that option."

"Aunt, of course, thinks her ideas are best. She has her own reasons."

"Oh? What reasons?"

"What most matrons want. We are her nephews, but she clucks around us like a mother hen. She could see this as an opportunity to see the last of us married."

His words shocked her. "You think—"

He interrupted. "I think, Rebekah, that my brother can make up his own mind. He married you."

"I believe the term used was *leg-shackled*, and that he was too young. I suppose Penelope is the one who changed his mind."

"I know my brother. No one can force him to do anything."

"Yet, we are wed."

"Exactly." Nathaniel held her gaze, giving her time to think.

Rebekah rolled the possibility around in her mind. Could Aaron have wanted to marry her? For what reason? So, he could be a rogue and discourage the idea of another young woman trapping him?

The dance ended. Before Nathaniel could lead her back to her seat, a sharp dressed gentleman stepped in front of them.

"Greystoke." The man gave a nod. "Might I be introduced to your lovely companion?"

"May I present Rebekah Greystoke, Aaron's wife. Rebekah, this is Christian Henebry, Earl of Dankworth."

The earl lifted her hand and kissed the back. A thrill of delight rushed through her at the contact. "My pleasure, Mrs. Greystoke. Would you do me the honor of being my partner in the next dance?"

"I think that is a fine idea, Dankworth." Nathaniel slapped him on the back and gave her a wink.

A wink.

What did that mean?

Dankworth took her gloved hand. "Your husband and I met at Eton. We've been friends ever since. I would welcome it, if you would call me Chris. All my friends do."

"We've only just met, Lord Dankworth."

Dankworth placed his hand at her side. "I will keep an appropriate amount of distance between us, Mrs. Greystoke. I would not want to provoke Aaron's temper."

"Since you are his friend, you may call me Rebekah."

He grinned, the most handsome grin she'd ever seen. Lord Dankworth put her right at ease. "I shall, and you must call me Chris."

"What the hell?" Aaron set off to intercept Rebekah and her new partner. Nathaniel grabbed his arm.

"Woah, brother."

"Why the blessed hell did you do that?"

"Do what? Oh, you mean formally introduce Christian and Rebekah?"

"Why did you let him dance with her?"

"You were making a spectacle of yourself. Glaring at every man like you were going to take a piece of his hide."

"Dankworth will be the first."

Nathaniel grinned. "I thought he was your friend."

"That was before he decided to dance with my wife." Aaron watched Rebekah smile and dance as if she belonged among the circle of admirers. She was exceedingly lovely. Her eyes met his with an amused stare of ridicule, taunting him, daring him to take notice.

"Aaron, don't you think you should examine that statement?"

Aaron glared at his brother. He had to concentrate to remember what he'd said.

"Had you bothered to visit your wife in Surrey, perhaps there would have been no need for her to seek you out. Maybe you need to ask yourself why you're getting so upset."

"Because ..." *Wait.* Was he upset? Surely not. "I'm not upset."

"Smile, brother, while I tell you, you're acting like an arse."

Bollocks. He was behaving like a bear with a sore paw. He glanced to Aunt. She had a smirk on her face, too. He was playing right into her hands.

"I see." Aunt set up this little demonstration to garner his reaction. Damned if he hadn't fallen for the bait.

"Do you see yourself, Aaron? That you're acting like an idiot? Like a possessive husband?"

"You're one to talk," he grumbled. "I'm surprised you left your wife at home. You normally won't let her out of your sight."

"Ah, but then I am in love with my wife."

Good God. Nathaniel could not possibly think ... "I will not rise to the bait, brother. As for my actions, I am merely being cautious. Protecting Rebekah from rakes."

"Rakes?" Nathaniel chuckled, damn his hide. "If you care not for her, then why do you care who she dances with?"

"Rebekah is not a piece of fruit ripe for picking. I will not allow young bucks to treat her thus."

"What about old lechers?"

"Make fun, as you will, Nathaniel. I think I will take my bride home."

"Where she belongs?" Aaron looked at his brother. Being of equal height, he could glare at him, eye to eye. Don't make the mistake of thinking you can rule her. Showing up this evening as she did, clearly, the woman has a mind of her own."

"Sod off, Nathaniel."

Aaron made sure he was the first to reach Rebekah when the music stopped.

"I believe I shall escort my wife now."

"Felicitations, Aaron. Please allow me to compliment you on the choice you've made for a wife. Rebekah is a remarkable dancer."

Rebekah?

Chris was enjoying his annoying mockery. As he kissed the back of Rebekah's gloved hand, Aaron gritted his teeth.

"Thank you for your delightful company. Your servant," Chris said to Rebekah.

Aaron wanted to wipe the grin off the arrogant devil's face.

"You are too kind, Chris."

Chris?

As his former friend walked off, Aaron's jaw was ready to crack. "You two seemed rather chummy."

"He is your friend, is he not?"

Aaron leaned close to her ear. "We are leaving. Do not fight me on this, Rebekah. Tell Aunt it is your decision to leave."

She gave a soft laugh. "You think she will believe that?"

"We have much to discuss."

"Why Aaron, it is almost as if you *want* to speak with me. Here I thought you had nothing to say to me. I mean, me in Surrey, you in London ... You couldn't get away fast enough on our wedding day."

The jibe hit its mark. He'd been a jackass, but he could not allow his wife the upper hand.

Penelope studied Rebekah's face, looking to see if she was consenting to leave with Aaron, or if he was forcing her against her will. She gave a slight shrug, letting Penelope know it didn't matter. Rebekah had agreed to ambush Aaron. She'd known he would not be happy, but at least he was willing to voice his opinion in private.

Aaron presented his arm and helped her into his carriage. Whether he liked it or not, she was the woman by his side. When he climbed in, she expected him to take the opposite seat. Instead, he sat next to her. Heat emanated from his body as his muscled thigh burned into her. She scooted further away.

"I'm not going to bite, Rebekah."

She glared at him, then smoothed her skirts. She refused to allow him to intimidate her. Taking a deep breath to calm her awareness, she breathed in his alluring scent. Dear heavens, how could she remain strong when everything about him drew her. It didn't help that she clearly remembered his soft lips against her skin, or how his sensuous touch flamed a fire that had raged out of control. After yearning for her lover night after night, it was difficult to believe this was the same man.

"I can hear you breathing, Rebekah."

She bit her lip, drawing on her anger as a shield. "Just because I agreed to leave with you, doesn't mean I am surrendering to your authority. I've been getting along quite well on my own, without a husband. I will not be a biddable, compliant wife."

"I see no need to discuss this in a carriage."

"You swept me out of there so fast, why delay the inevitable?" She wasn't ready for this conversation, didn't know if she would ever be ready, but it had to happen.

Aaron scrubbed a hand over his face as he released a sigh. "Why are you here, Rebekah?"

"I missed my long-lost husband," she couldn't help throwing at him.

"You did not come to my townhouse. Yet you show up at Haverson's ball."

"'Twould seem the only way to find you. You have quite the active schedule."

Aaron sighed as he shook his head. "This is why I think we should wait until we get home. Your sarcasm is wasted. Did you know your eyes give away what you're thinking? I want to see your eyes when we have our ... reunification."

Chills raced along her spine. Her emotions ran close to the surface, and she'd always been loud and expressive when she tried making her point. But she knew in a moment, Aaron could shatter her resolve if she listened to her heart instead of her head.

Every girl imagined a knight in shining armor saving her, or hoping some day she might marry a handsome prince. As Rebekah grew older, she realized those were fairy tales, but she still held hope that she would one day marry for love. That didn't happen.

Maybe she should have been satisfied with staying at Surrey. At least she had her dream of one perfect night. Coming to London only crushed her dreams and made her see her husband for what he was. An arrogant poop who never wanted her. Perhaps the memories of that night were all in her imagination. Clearly, it was hopeless to think this man would sweep her up and promise her everything would be all right. No matter how much she wished it, no matter how much she'd hoped, no matter how much she fought to hold on, Aaron would not meet her halfway.

What a fool she was. Penelope had been wrong. Rebekah might be Aaron's wife, but obviously that didn't mean a thing. Fate had tossed her into a new world, ripping away her aspirations of home and family.

"We do not need to battle, Rebekah. Neither am I of a mind to coddle you like a child."

"Then allow me to live my life, as you have these past months. You go your way, and I am perfectly happy to go mine."

"I can't let you do that."

"Oh? Pray tell, why not? It's been working so far"

The carriage stopped. "We are here."

When Rebekah alighted, she glanced up at the grandeur of Aaron's home. Before she had a chance to truly relish its beauty, he grasped her elbow and escorted her up the few steps to the main door.

The house was nowhere near as large as the earl's, but the grandeur was impressionable. This is where her husband had been living without her. All at once, everything from the past few months began to crowd her. Her mind swirled so fast, she froze from the onslaught. Aaron accusing her of trickery. Aaron refusing to honor the agreement. Aaron demanding they marry. Aaron deserting her.

She was his wife. This was supposed to be her home. She glanced up at him. Did he have to be so tall and intense?

Her stomach rolled, making her want to throw up. She closed her eyes. The room swayed, and she quickly knew that wasn't going to work. Her hand shot out to latch on to anything solid that would hold her.

"Are you all right?"

Dear Heavens, please don't let me faint.

She took a deep breath and suddenly her feet left the floor. Strong arms carried her. Her head rested on Aaron's shoulder, soaking up his assurance. For a moment—just for a moment-she allowed herself to savor his warmth, his strength, his ...

Aaron placed her on a soft cushion. "Rebekah. Look at me."

She slowly opened her eyes. Worry? Caring? Was this the same man who had glared so harshly at her only moments ago?

"What the bloody devil is wrong with you?"

Well, that moment was over.

Rebekah pushed him away as she sat up, mindful of the chiseled muscle under her hand. Clear thought was impossible when Aaron was such an attractive man. Everything about him screamed enticement. Although, she'd never seen a man glower as much as him.

"Give me a moment, Aaron. All of this is coming at me too fast."

"Are you going to faint?"

It was her turn to glare. "And if I do?" She'd shocked him. "What do you expect? You show up in my life, turn it upside down, then abandon me, and now you are dragging me about like you have every right. Let a girl catch her breath, for heaven's sake."

"You were the one who came to me."

"What makes you think I came to London to find you? Perhaps, I wanted to see what I was missing. Parties and balls sound like a lot of fun. And I had not been asked to one. Unless you clearly accepted invitations for both of us and forgot to tell me."

"I did no such thing."

"Did I spoil your plans for the evening? Perhaps you can still save them. With your wife safely at home out of the way, you can keep your assignation."

"What the devil are you going on about?"

"The way you dragged me out of that ballroom, I thought you were in a hurry to get rid of me. Don't worry, husband. I've been without you for weeks. I can take care of myself for one night—while you go see your ladybird."

"My what?"

"Have I shocked you? Being your wife, I suppose I am not supposed to know about such things as your mistress."

"What makes you think I have a mistress?"

"Don't lie to me, Aaron. Every man in London has a mistress. I'm not that naive."

"I have not been with another woman since our marriage."

"Should I thank you for that? I don't believe you. You did tell me—very clearly, I might add—that I was not to share your bed." She put a finger to her chin. "The thing I cannot fathom is why you want to remain married to a woman you don't even want."

She jumped, when a burst of laughter came from him.

He studied her, delving into her eyes as if he was reaching into her soul.

"You're a very desirable woman, Rebekah. Any man would want you. When I look at you, I feel something achingly familiar, and I want to reach out and pull you close. But I made you a promise, so I put temptation out of my reach. Yet, here you are. How can I keep my word, if we are in the same room and my desire to kiss you overwhelms me?"

"Now you're making fun of me."

"You think I don't desire you?"

"No more than you would feel for any beautiful woman."

Silence stretched for several moments.

How she wished Aaron desired her for herself. She wished he loved her and would look at her with longing. Like he had that night. She was only kidding herself.

Aaron hated her. His abandonment was proof of that. And if more was needed, her encroaching into his world, forcing him to accept her in public, would most likely be the end of them. The two of them were at the mercy of a plan put into motion not of their choosing. How could she make the best of a situation when her husband despised her?

Pretend?

There wasn't enough acting in the world she could pull off. Sometimes, one had to let a dead horse lie.

There was no future for them. She would never be happy; she saw that now. For he would never allow her to love him. Never again would she see his tender expression for her, or feel his wonderful lips against hers. She would forever be yearning ... wishing ...

"What do you want from me?"

Startled, she blinked. Her heart was so heavy, she could barely get the words out. "I want to be free of you."

He took a step toward her. She immediately held up a hand to stop him. "Your desire for me will pass the moment I am out of sight. Save yourself for the next woman in line.

Aaron shook his head. "Being obtuse doesn't become you."

"How could you possibly know anything about me from the two minutes you spent as my husband?"

A sob caught in her throat.

She dropped her gaze to the floor and concentrated on putting one foot in front of the other, until she reached the foyer.

If Aaron said anything else, she didn't hear it. Tears filled her eyes, making the steps wavy. She placed her hand on the polished rail, and ascended the staircase.

One step at a time.

The same way her heart was breaking.

One crack at a time.

Chapter 21

R ebekah rose to the morning sun shining through the
curtains. She was not one to sleep late even though she'd
gone to bed in the wee hours of the morning. She made her
bed—yes, servants were supposed to make the bed, but she'd
done it every day for the last twenty years.

Her mind drifted to last evening. The ball was divine. Everything about the ball was divine. The decorations, the lights, the
orchestra... Thank goodness Penelope had made her take dance
lessons. She never knew people danced all night. Her feet were
complaining this morning. She stepped to the dresser to get a jar
of salve. Not only was it good for her skin, but it would sooth
away the ache.

After Aaron's shock, he played the gentleman doting on his
wife. All it took was a tilt of Penelope's head, and Aaron jumped
to do her bidding. He'd introduced Rebekah as his wife.

His wife.

Without a grimace, too. It seemed strange and took some
getting used to. As long as she smiled and nodded her head, she
realized she gave the impression she fit right in. And she had
fun doing it. After she got over her nervousness of catching her
husband off guard.

Aaron had been angry, no doubt about that. She had noticed
the signs when they argued about the contract. He had tried to
leave the ball straightaway, but Penelope put a stop to that right

quick. Then she bragged about her nephew being married to such a lovely woman. Rebekah could almost believe the charade.

But it was a sham. A faux marriage. She had tried pushing that depressing tidbit out of her mind. Eventually, she relaxed and enjoyed herself.

Since she missed her own mother so very much, it was nice having Penelope hover over her.

Rebekah went through her morning routine, fiddled about the room a bit, and decided she'd wasted enough time. Surely someone would be up. Someone other than Aaron. She wasn't quite ready to meet him.

Looking in the mirror, she supposed she was presentable. She left her bedchamber, closing the door softly behind her, then headed for the stairs. At the landing, she met Penelope coming from the opposite stairway.

"Good morning, Rebekah."

"Is it still morning?" she asked.

"Yes. The clock struck eleven a few moments ago. Shall we go down to breakfast?"

Would Cook still be serving breakfast? Rebekah reminded herself they were in Town. The ton kept different hours than in the country. Penelope had told Rebekah how Cook spoiled Aaron. Most likely, she would prepare anything they wanted any time of the day.

"Will Aaron be joining us?" Rebekah asked as they descended the stairway.

"I'm sure he left the house hours ago."

Rebekah released a sigh of relief.

"Normally he is up and tending to business, or he might be with the horses at this hour."

When they entered the breakfast room, two place settings were on the long table. A maid greeted them.

"Is that beast tied up?"

"The Black is outside with Sasha, my lady."

"Good. We can eat in peace."

Rebekah wanted to believe Penelope spoke of Aaron, but Rebekah was beginning to believe she was the only one who thought of Aaron in that light.

"Penelope, may I ask what beast you are referring to?"

"Do you not know of Aaron's breed? Dogs, he calls them. Sasha is the female mother. She's had two litters, and recently a third. Aaron has found homes for the puppies, but kept The Black. That rascal started out as the most subdued of the litter. He's growing, and is becoming the size of a horse. Aaron loves the animals. I cannot believe he hasn't told you about the Malamutes."

"The night Nathaniel brought me to Aaron's house, I remember a large dog. He nearly knocked me over. He was black. Quite large, and frisky."

"That's the one. Aaron calls the dog The Black. He is still a puppy."

"A puppy? The dog that came at me was fully grown."

"*Pshaw*. That was The Black. He is barely half the size he will be. Have you seen Sasha? The Black will grow bigger than his mother."

"I cannot imagine." She followed Penelope to the sideboard.

"The servants serve our supper, but I know how independent you are. So, if you want, we can serve ourselves. Let's see what we have." Penelope lifted the first silver dome. "Ahh, ham. You do like ham, Rebekah, or would you prefer bacon?" She lifted the lid from another dish. "Yes, as I thought. Bacon."

The large cupboard held several silver domes in a long line. There must be fifteen food choices. By the time she sat down beside Penelope, Rebekah had a dab of almost everything on her China plate. She stared at the monstrosity of food. Good Lord. She would never be able to eat all of this. Ham, bacon, and sausage, eggs scrambled with cheese—yum. Sunny side up were in one of the platters, but she got the scrambled because of the cheese. There were potatoes, tomatoes, various fruit. She had picked up a branch of grapes for later. And melon. She loved honey dew melon. Since she wanted the fruit, she passed on the pancakes and syrup. There were even waffles. Who in the world was going to eat all this food?

"Eat, child. Or are you going to sit there and stare at your plate?"

"Oh." She lifted a fork. "This is a lot of food."

Penelope giggled. "It sure is. You must be hungry."

"Cook should not offer so many choices."

"Had trouble choosing? Perhaps your tastebuds wanted to try everything."

Rebekah shook her head. "I will pop out of my clothes in no time if I eat like this."

"Aaron will buy you more."

"Good heavens. I do not need more clothes."

"He can afford it, dear."

As though that explained why she needed more.

"Mama taught me not to waste." She glanced at the sideboard loaded with food.

Penelope noticed. "It won't go to waste dear. There are a lot of mouths to feed."

That's good.

"After breakfast, I will send a note to Madame Laselle. She is very discreet. She will be delighted to work on a new wardrobe for you."

"A new wardrobe. I haven't worn some of the gowns I have."

Penelope chewed her food, then replied, "You need party clothes for London. You cannot wear the same ball gown to another ball. It simply is not done. You are in Town now, dear. There will be events and parties every evening."

"Every evening?"

"Yes. Outdoor soirees. Balls. You will need your rest in the mornings."

Rebekah laid down her fork and wiped her lips with the napkin. "I'm not sure Aaron wants me here."

"It doesn't matter. You are here now, and here you will stay."

His angry image came to life in her mind. "He has no right to order me about."

Penelope placed her fork beside her plate, then spoke in a firm, clear voice. "He has every right, my dear girl. A husband has the right to treat his wife any way he wishes."

"I am not an object."

"But you are his property."

Rebekah's mouth flew open in shock.

"I'm sorry, dear. Among the aristocrats, the wife has very little say in anything."

"I shall get a divorce."

"Do not spout nonsense," Aunt said as she picked up her fork. "That's your pride talking. Aaron has pride too. Men and their damnable pride."

With Penelope's confidence and forte, there was no doubt in Rebekah's mind who was in charge. "What if he decides to send me back to the country house."

"You were presented to the ton last night. Aaron would not dare. If you were to disappear, he would have to face questions he cannot answer. I'm sure he has already had difficulty explaining his estranged wife."

Her chest tingled with excitement. She would be staying. She scooped a bite of pudding. Who had pudding for breakfast?

"Berthright told me invitations have been pouring in all morning. You are the toast of the ton."

Rebekah paused with her spoon halfway to her mouth. "Me?"

"As soon as we finish, we'll go to the parlor and take a look at them."

"What sort of invitations?"

"Inviting you to soirees. Everyone who is anyone wants to be the first to show you off at their social event. It's a competition between the noble matrons. See who can out-do the other. One-up, so to speak."

Every night? Wow. She scooped another dollop of pudding, thinking she was bound to need the extra sugar for energy.

⁓ℰℓℓ⁓

Aaron closed his book full of figures and sums. Adding should not be done when a man's mind was occupied elsewhere.

His wife.

Aunt was behind Rebekah's sudden appearance; he was sure of it.

Good God, when he'd seen her, his heart nearly stopped. Her beauty had stunned him, enveloped him. A dozen emotions swamped him all at once. Shock overpowered them all.

Rebekah was in Town, and the entire ton knew it.

There would be no question now whether he was married or not. Every noble at Haverson's ball had seen for themselves. The rumormongers would spread the word to anyone who'd been absent.

He had yet to have a *tête-à-tête* with his wife. Surely, she would be up by now.

Aaron rose and went in search of his bride. He found her with Aunt in the parlor.

"Good afternoon, ladies."

"Oh Aaron, good. We are going through these invitations. Apparently, they've been coming in non-stop all morning."

"Aunt, do you mind if I steal Rebekah away? My wife and I must have a long-awaited conversation."

"And whose fault is that?" Penelope snipped.

"Forgive me, Aunt, for being outspoken, but I should have been informed of my wife's surprising arrival."

"Since your leaving came as quite a surprise, I would think you would not complain."

"Are you saying this was recompence?"

"Not at all, Aaron. Rebekah was following your lead. After all, what does she know about this family—or our habits. She is learning by example."

"I stand duly noted, Aunt." Aaron turned to Rebekah and held out a hand. "Would you join me ... Rebekah?" He almost said *wife* in a derogatory manner, but Aunt would have chastised him for that.

Rebekah stood, and he noticed her hands slightly shook. She did not take the hand he offered.

"Where are we going?"

"To the library, if you will."

"You will need to show me where it is."

Of course. He'd forgotten she would not know the way. He'd thought he found a means of escape from their dilemma without brewing scandlebroth. Her appearance at the ball last night had merely fueled the gossip.

He led her to the library and closed the set of doors behind them.

"Would you care for a sherry?"

She dipped her head. "Thank you."

He poured a small amount in a tiny wine glass, wondering how the devil women held the fragile things without snapping the stems. Then he poured a brandy for himself. He carried them over to the sofa and placed the glasses on the center table. Most likely, she wouldn't want him to see her hand shake as she accepted her glass.

"Well. I see you have gammoned me," he began. "By showing up in London, you've brought attention to us once again. I was completely gob-smacked. I suppose that was your intention. To catch me off guard?"

"I am not going back to Surrey."

"I see." He steepled his fingers as he thought about that. Then, he reached for his glass, needing the sustenance.

"You left me," she blurted. "What was I to do? Did you think I would not like to go to parties with my husband? Or are you ashamed of me?"

He'd been about to swallow a pull of brandy, and nearly coughed up a lung. Finally, he got his voice back. "That is utter balderdash. I have no reason to be ashamed, and neither do you."

"Then why did you leave me? At the altar, I might add."

Good God, he didn't know. He'd not thought things through completely. Other than he supposed she would be happier without him, since she didn't want a husband—and he sure as hell had not wanted a wife.

An image of sultry eyes in a fuzzy cloud looked back at him. It was useless to indulge in fantasies. He shook the image away.

Had he really told his wife he did not expect her to share his bed? He must be ready for bedlam.

"I beg your pardon, Rebekah. At the time it seemed the reasonable thing to do. Apparently, I am losing my mind along with my dignity."

Her shock turned to confusion. "Why would you say that?"

"Because I have bungled things badly." He would never know the woman in his dreams. He should be content with his wife.

"You are here now; you will stay here."

"I hadn't planned on going anywhere." Her pointed nose turned up in the air.

Did she not understand?

"In my *home*," he pointed out.

"I am staying with Serena in their townhouse."

"Not anymore. You will stay here under my roof where you belong. And that is final."

Her brow arched. "Giving orders, Aaron? You gave up the right to take charge of my life when you left me in Surrey. I will not allow you to rule my every move."

The guilt he'd felt left in an instant, squashed by her ire.

"I am your husband," he said with force.

"I am not the one who forgot!"

Blasted female. He tossed back his drink and stood.

"That song is getting old, my dear. Since you are in London, you will behave according to the rules of etiquette. We will be in the same house, we must tolerate each other. Aunt will be here, so you will have a champion in your pocket. All I ask is that you consult me before you leave the house."

GREYSTOKE'S CONFLICTION 211

"You mean, ask permission?"

Good God, the woman was fierce with her accusations. If she was his wife in truth, he would fix all this poppycock by taking her to his bed.

Imagine waking with his tempting wife every morning. Then retiring each night with her long hair spread out like a halo over her pillow. Her lips swollen from their passionate kisses. Her eyes all stary and glorious from their lovemaking.

Good God. He shook himself. He was giving himself a growing erection.

Did he not just convince himself he would no longer indulge in fantasies?

He took a steadying breath and tried being reasonable.

"You are new to London. There are many dangers for a woman, that come in all forms."

She gave a faux laugh. "Be careful, Aaron. You sound very much like a protective husband. You wouldn't want to give the wrong impression."

She glared at him as if he had sprouted another head.

"You are my wife, and that is not going to change. We can stand here and shout at each other all night, or we can accept our circumstances."

He raked a hand through his hair. Damn and blast. She was beautiful in all her brusque fury. A strong woman. He liked strong women.

He walked to the hearth, setting his glass on the ledge. "I'm sorry your feelings were hurt."

"Climb down off that pedestal of self-importance, Aaron. You give yourself way too much credit. Your brothers' wives took it upon themselves to befriend me.

The sharp pain of rejection was lessened a little by the promise Rebekah had made to herself. She would learn everything there was to learn. And she would not give Aaron any reason to be ashamed. She'd been determined to show him. Show the ton. She made a vow to stand up for herself. Face the ton. And be more compelling with Aaron.

She had promised to be a good wife. Aaron did not love her, nor she him. But the hope had been there—maybe someday.

Hindsight was such a bothersome fiend. She'd brought this on herself. She should have stayed in Brighton, but her foolish pride demanded she seek retribution. She had set out to humiliate him, serve the arrogant man the same cold dish of rejection, only to be caught in her own snare. He'd married her. Turned her whole world upside down. Then he'd left. Couldn't get away from his bride fast enough. They didn't even have a wedding night. What did that say about her?

Humiliation.

She shot Aaron a killing, pain-filled glance. The hurt became her *métier.*

Would they forever be crossing swords?

He took a step forward. Her instant response was to draw back. He stopped.

He raked a hand through his long hair and mumbled something like, *"Devil take it."*

Her chest pounded. Not from fear, but from exasperating anger.

"Rebekah, I humbly apologize. It's true I did not take your feelings into consideration when I left Surrey. I had assumed that you preferred to be left alone. I thought the best way to do that was to give you time and space; therefore, I left."

She glanced about the library. "And came back to your normal way of life."

"I did give you a home. Servants. Aunt saw that you had a complete wardrobe."

"That excuses you?" She tilted her head to the side. "Did you think of me even once, Aaron?"

The arrow found its mark. His expression was sad with guilt.

"Did you think of your wife when you went to your fancy balls?" She stood, anger radiating in every bone of her body. "I mean, the whole point of our marriage was to avoid a scandal. Did the ton even know you had a wife?"

"Of course they knew," he shouted.

She narrowed her eyes as her anger rose. "Did anyone ask about your absent wife, or ask why she wasn't with you? I'm sure the widows didn't care—"

"Enough, Rebekah," he said on a harsh breath, looking defeated. "I am not a rake."

Enough?

Damn him for his condescension. "Is this the way it is to be then? War between us?"

"I hope not." He lifted a hand to touch her, then paused.

"I am willing to give this a chance if we can come to an understanding. Besides..." He gave her an emphatic grin. "You may find I am not the ogre you think me to be."

"Don't count on it."

"You don't really know me. I don't know you. How do you suggest we remedy that?"

"Huh." She crossed her arms over her chest. "A husband must spend time with his wife if he wants to know her."

"In other words, you living in Surrey and me in London is not working out."

She glared at him.

"No. I suppose distance is not the answer. There is only one way for us to spend time together. We must occupy the same house. That is why you will stay here, with me."

"I might fight you every step of the way." Her voice lacked the fervor of her words.

"Be my guest, wife." He gave her a lazy grin. "Mayhap you will win a battle, here and there. But you will never win the war."

Chapter 22

A aron skipped down the staircase, with his mind on Rebekah, where it stayed most of the time. As of late, he'd been unable to think of anything else. His aunt was in her corner. His staff had taken an instant liking to her. His house was not his own.

Bollocks.

This is what having a wife in the house was like?

He reached the bottom of the stairs and turned toward his study, passing the drawing room. He caught his breath, smelling an achingly familiar soft fragrance. Rebekah's fresh scent was everywhere in his home.

He'd been able to avoid her as long as she'd been at his country house in Surrey. Now that his wife was under his nose, not only did he have to accept her presence, he had to interact with her. See her. Talk to her. Admit he had a wife.

His wife.

Damn and blast.

Speaking to her was no hard task. Being in the same room while his mind ran rambunctious with unsavory thoughts was another matter entirely. Her creamy breasts were exposed to his gaze which only made him want to release them from their confinement. He couldn't control the thrill of anticipation every time he thought about caressing her sweet mounds.

Her eyes captivated him. It made him angry when she quickly turned her gaze away. He loved the color of her eyes. He just didn't get to look into them long enough.

He'd spent the morning convincing himself—not successfully—that the marriage was not a complete mistake. Rebekah was intelligent, and clearly had a backbone, showing up in London without any warning.

Good God, she'd taken the ton by storm.

And him.

A wolfish grin sneaked up on him as he recalled his first glimpse of her. His body had tightened at her beauty, and dammit, several times since then. It would appear he was becoming infatuated with his wife.

When had Rebekah crept under his very thick skin? No woman had such an effect on him. Not even his mistress. Which he had not visited since *his wife* had become his wife.

Devil take him. He shouldn't be thinking of cuckolding his wife.

The best course of action would be to carry on as though his schedule—his life—had not completely changed. Yet, of late, when he left the town house, he'd been unable to purge Rebekah from his mind. She'd taken residence in his brain and now he rarely thought of anything else.

Supper was at eight, sharp. Usually, he had a light repast. Or ate at the gentleman's club. With Aunt back in town, his schedule swiftly changed. She required sticking to the particulars regarding tradition.

Yet, tonight, she would be eating in her chamber.

There was little to gain making Rebekah think he did not want her here.

He opened his pocket watch and saw the supper hour only a few minutes away. He and Rebekah would be dining alone. As he replaced his watch in its pocket, he glanced up—and his heart lurched. His breath caught in his throat. If the moon suddenly fell out of the sky, he couldn't be more surprised by his reaction.

He shifted uneasily.

For days, Aunt had been Rebekah's shadow. Her protector, more like. So having Rebekah to himself was a mixture of excitement and dread.

He drew a breath. Every time he saw *his wife*, she was more beautiful. More real. Something akin to pride filled his chest, even though he knew he did not deserve her, let alone merit the satisfaction. She was no lightskirt for him to lay claim to a lustful evening. But he couldn't help thinking of the idea of a night with her in his bed.

She was his wife, for God's sake.

He may have the right as her wedded husband, but the cad who left her in the country should be horse-whipped.

Good God, he was a mixture of emotions. He needed to get his head out of his arse and play his part.

"Good evening, Rebekah." He held out his hand as she reached the last step. The blue of her gown enhanced the color of her bright eyes. A man could drown in such striking eyes. "Aunt is having dinner sent to her chamber."

She regarded him for a few seconds. He had a feeling if Rebekah had known in advance, she would have stayed in her room, as well. Making her decision, she placed her hand in his. He escorted her to the dining room, and then held her chair as she sat down.

Aunt would be proud.

"You look very nice this evening," Aaron said as he pulled out his chair at the head of the table. He'd purposely placed her to his right. He didn't like the idea of her at the other end, so far

away. He sat down, and when he looked up, her eyes were wide
with surprise.

"Thank you."

For what? Then he quickly remembered his compliment. He
turned to the maid. "We are ready for the first course."

"I hope Penelope is all right."

"If I know my aunt, this was her way of giving us time alone."

"We were alone this afternoon," Rebekah said.

"Yes, we were. Discussing our arrangement. Perhaps at supper, we will speak of mundane things."

"I would not want to bore you."

Aaron snorted. "I don't think you could ever bore me, my
dear." Yes, this was better than dreading their circumstance.

He watched her as she lifted her spoon.

"Ah, turtle soup. One of my favorites. Do you like turtle
soup, Rebekah?"

She was staring down at her bowl in horror. "I've not had it
before."

He wanted to chuckle. "You should taste it. If you don't like
it, I'll order for something else. But I think you should try it."

"Do you? Will you be telling me what to eat during my stay
here?"

Bloody hell. If he wanted peace with his wife, he would need
to try harder.

He laid his own spoon down. "This is your home, Rebekah.
As much as it is mine. As for how long you stay here, that is
entirely up to you."

"You will not send me back to Surrey?"

"If you want to go, then yes. Until you do, we will both
remain here."

She took a few bites and so did he. He supposed she liked the
soup. Somehow, it seemed ridiculous to ask.

"Will you escort me to the next ball?"

Her choice of topic surprised him. "Of course."

She scrunched up her pretty nose. "What do you mean, of course? You don't have to, you know."

He grinned. "I wouldn't think of letting my wife go without me. Besides, don't you want me to escort you?"

She hesitated. What did his lovely wife have on her mind now?

"I thought you would prefer to go elsewhere."

"Elsewhere?"

"Anywhere that I am not."

Good God. Had he hurt her that badly?

He laid his spoon down again. "Rebekah, I was unkind. I didn't mean to be, but that is neither here, nor there. A husband should escort his wife wherever she wants to go. Unless, of course, you go shopping with Aunt. I would much rather see the things you buy, instead of helping you choose. It seems more the sort of thing a woman does."

"Afraid I'll embarrass you while picking out unmentionables?"

Ahh. Finally, a smile.

He took a swallow of his soup. "Actually, I think you would be the one embarrassed."

He enjoyed watching her eyes go round. This is something he should get used to, he supposed. After all, they were husband and wife. Even if in name only.

"Come back here!"

A big black dog came hurdling around the corner with a slippery footman right behind. He slid to a halt. "Oh, sire. I'm sorry."

The Black loped to Aaron's side.

"Sit, Black." The dog obeyed immediately. "It appears he's looking for me."

"Yes, sire. I believe he heard your voice."

"Hello, Black." Aaron fondly rubbed the dog's head and ears. "Rebekah, this is The Black. Odd name, I know, but that's what it is."

"Penelope mentioned he is still a puppy."

"That he is. Another six months should see him fully grown."

"Six months? He's so large."

"He's an Alaskan Malamute. One of the oldest and most impressive dog breeds in the world. They are powerful, intelligent, and devoted to their owners."

"I can see that."

Black turned to Rebekah.

"He is curious about you. Have you been properly introduced?"

"The night I arrived; he came at me."

Aaron's brows shot to his hairline, then lowered into a deep frown. "What do you mean came at you?"

"He knocked me down. I'm sure he didn't mean to. I was caught off guard. Surprised is all."

Why am I just now hearing about this?

"Were you all right?"

"Yes. Nathaniel helped me up. I was fine."

The night his brother brought Rebekah to his home.

"I apologize for him. Black is not usually so rough with the ladies. My brother is a different story."

"Really? Which one?"

"Nathaniel is the one who charges into a room like thunder. Actually, I gave Black's sibling to Edmund. He didn't want a dog, but they became fast friends."

The dog's excitement grew. "He won't stop until he sniffs you. Do you mind?"

"He won't knock me out of my chair, will he?"

"Absolutely not," Aaron nearly roared.

"Very well." Rebekah smiled, and suddenly Aaron wanted to be the one at her feet, begging for her to like him.

"Hello, Black."

The dog hurried to her side and sniffed her hands. She rubbed his head, then he placed it on her thigh. Dear God, Aaron had to stop this line of thinking immediately.

The Black was quite taken with her—the cur. Soaking up all of her praise and attention.

The kitchen maid stepped into the dining room. "Oh dear."

"Bring some bowls for washing, Corinne." The maid hurried to do his bidding. "Enough, Black. Go have your own supper." Aaron twisted his finger in a twirl, and the dog loped back to the kitchen.

"He seems well behaved."

"The Black is trained. But he forgets how to behave when a pretty woman comes to the house."

Rebekah blushed and Aaron couldn't believe his eyes. Did his casual comment please her?

There were so many layers to this woman. He would enjoy peeling back each one.

Aaron was about to close the study door, when his butler hurried down the hall. As much as the older man could hurry. If Berthright was anxious, something must be afoot.

"A runner is here with a message."

"Is it the same man?"

"No, sire. He gave me this."

Aaron tore open the missive.

The Reef
Come now.

"Berthright. I'm going out."

Feeling the need to hurry, Aaron grabbed his coat and stormed off. Every step he took, he prayed Pauly had news of Blade.

When he got to The Reef, he found Pauly at the same table. Aaron slowed his movements, not wanting to draw attention. He slid into the chair opposite Pauly.

Aaron signaled the barkeep for an ale, then turned back to Pauly. "Well?"

"Bone told me to set this up."

"Where is he?"

"Don't get yer breeches in a bind."

Aaron glared as his temper surfaced. "I have little patience. My brother has none. Be glad I am not my brother."

Pauly's eyes narrowed, and his expression darkened. Aaron knew he should be more careful around cutthroats, but he didn't care. He had to know. Where the hell was Bone?

Pauly leaned back in his chair like he hadn't a worry in the world. "You ain't makin' no threat now, are ye?"

A man grabbed a chair and spun it around. Then sat.

Basil.

Basil jerked his attention to Pauly, then back to Aaron—and never said a word.

"If you have any information concerning Blade, I want to hear it. And nothing else."

"I guess I can understand yer worry over a friend. Blade is a good 'un. He's alive."

Aaron stared in shock.

Thank Christ.

"How do you know? Where is he?"

"What we know, and what we think, can't say right now. Bone went to find him. That's all I know."

Joyanna had stopped by on the pretense she'd just purchased a new gown and was, frankly, parched. Serena was already there. Penelope was taking a rest in preparation for the ball this evening. So, the three of them had tea, while Serena and Joyanna regaled stories. Rebekah hung onto their every word.

"Of the three brothers, Aaron is the more relaxed. He loves living in Town and is known for having his fun." Joyanna took a sip of her tea.

Fun and Aaron did not belong in the same sentence.

"I'm sure he's having loads of fun, without me."

Joyanna replaced her cup in its saucer. "It's his natural way. A smile is always on his face."

Rebekah gaped. "Who are we discussing? It certainly cannot be Aaron. He has a grin now and then, when he wants something, or tries to get one to see things his way. But a real smile, I cannot believe it."

Joyanna laughed. "Edmund is truly the brooding one. He's serious minded, analytical. Accountable for everything, whether it belongs to him, or his opinion of another, He has an explanation for everything."

"Now I know you jest. Your husband worships you. He acts like a man hopelessly in love. He appears to be the more relaxed one."

Joyanna waved a hand. "He is that way now. I mean, he's still methodical and reasons everything, he just takes more time to play now."

"Play?"

"She's right, Rebekah," Serena replied. "You should have seen him before Joyanna came back to London. He was brooding, moody, always angry. Of course that could have had something to do with the headaches."

"Of course, it did," Joyanna agreed. "But you are also right about the former. He is happier now."

"Clearly, you make him happy," Rebekah said. "I cannot believe he was as moody as you make him sound."

"Nathaniel is moody." Serena rolled her eyes. "He has to have everything his way. He has the aura of commanding attention when he enters a room."

"Aren't most lords like that?"

Serena and Joyanna both laughed.

"Oh heavens, if you knew how much he hated the title … Nathaniel never wanted to be an earl. As a matter of fact, he left Greystoke Manor for years. It was going to ruin. Thank goodness he came back and had the place restored. But he's always been moody, so I'm told."

"Yes, Serena, but nowhere near as bad as his brother."

"You can say that again," Rebekah piped up.

"Not Aaron," Joyanna said to Rebekah. "I'm talking about Edmund. I told you, Aaron is the fun brother."

"I still don't believe it."

"It's true. Edmund was a bear. Even to me, until we cleared the air. He was furious with me when I went to France and married someone else."

"That would make any man grumpy, I'm sure."

"I've always loved Edmund, and now we are together. So yes, I suppose he does seem happier."

"He's in love with you," Serena said quietly.

Joyanna beamed.

"He is wonderful with me. Since he had performed the duties of the earl for a while, I'd wondered how the ton would treat him after Nathaniel's return. Not that Edmund cares, none of them do, but I am happy he is still respected by all."

"I assumed all three brothers were well respected."

"For different reasons. But what I'm trying to say is Aaron is normally a ... rascal." Joyanna grinned. "He's intelligent, strong, and very likeable. Seeing him so serene is a side I've not seen." She caught Rebekah's gaze. "Until you."

Until I came into his life.

She would love to see this side of Aaron. Was she the cause of his temperamental state?

"Oh lovely. I'm making Aaron miserable."

"No!" Serena cried. "That's not true at all."

Joyanna laughed. "Not the way you think."

Rebekah gaped. If she didn't stop dropping her mouth open, she would get lockjaw. "See." She glanced to Serena. "Even Joyanna thinks so."

Joyanna held up a finger, slightly waving it a bit. "Perhaps he is *moody* because he is unsure of you."

Of me? Huh. Aaron is filled with confidence. He simply tolerated her. "What do you mean?"

"He does not know how to behave around you. You've only just met. The arrangement is uncanny. Perhaps he is as confused as you."

"Ha. That man knows exactly what he is doing. You'll not convince me otherwise. He seems very capable of saying and doing exactly as he pleases."

"Give it time, Rebekah. I think you will find he likes you more than even he realizes."

"Ha. Now I know you're joking. He can't stand me.

Joyanna gasped. "Where on Earth did you get that idea?"

"For one thing he hid me away at his country estate. Since I've been here, he's gone most of the time. If I enter a room, he leaves. I go to soirées alone. With Penelope, of course."

"You are wrong." Serena said. "I don't think that's the reason. He watches you."

"I know."

"Do you pay attention to the way he looks at you? It's a possessive look. Men don't look at their wives like that, unless there is a personal interest."

"Serena is right. Most men have mistresses. Lords and Ladies live separate lives."

"Like me and Aaron."

"No. You began a bit uniquely, but that's changed since you came to London."

Tears threatened to break free. She had foolishly hoped and prayed Aaron would come to love her. But she had to face reality. If he liked her, it would be a bonus.

"Oh, Rebekah. I didn't mean to upset you."

"It's nothing. Sometimes I feel sorry for myself, but I truly have a grand life. And you two are my best friends."

Aaron filled his brothers in on what he'd just learned. Good news in small doses.

"That's all he said?"

"Didn't know much more. Someone Bone knows must have spotted Blade or knew he was on a ship."

"What happened to him? Where's he been all this time?"

"He's not even sure it is Blade. This bloke was tossed into the sea. Had a stab wound, and was delirious. A crewman spotted him floating on a piece of wood. Dropped him off at the next port, and when the man healed, he signed on another ship. But Bone thinks it's Blade."

"I suppose we'll find out soon enough." Nathaniel tossed back the last dollop of brandy. "My wife tells me Rebekah is not a happy woman."

Aaron stood at the hearth, staring down into an empty glass. "She has fooled me. She goes to parties every day and balls every night. It would appear she is having a splendid time."

"With you glaring right over her shoulder."

He shrugged. "What would you have me do, brother? Act like a devoting husband and kiss her toes?"

"Don't be impudent."

Good God, he was tired of all of this. "Why not? There are those who already considered me the neglecting husband who abandoned his wife."

Edmund had to add his own assessment. "The gossipmongers were calling her the estranged wife. Now, they are trying to figure out why? She is likeable. The ton adores her. Therefore, the fault lies with you."

Aaron stretched to his full height. "You may be older, Edmund, but I am taller."

Edmund stood and faced him. "Give it your best shot, brother."

"You two stop." Nathaniel growled.

"Isn't this ironic," Edmund said. "You being the intermediary rather than the adversary."

"Now you know how I felt all those years of playing facilitator to the both of you." Aaron shoved his hair out of his face, as he stomped across the carpet.

"Aaron, you're being ridiculous."

"Am I? She has every randy cock aimed in her direction. I'm her bloody sentry. No one cares that she is married."

Edmund laughed. "You remind them indubiously."

"If rakes think she is estranged, Aaron, you have only yourself to blame. What excuse did you give the ton?"

"I didn't realize you were a sponge for the gossip mill, Nathaniel. Am I to believe you have taken your title seriously?"

"You had to tell them something," Edmund added.

"My wife—God, I'll never get used to saying that."

"You'd better!"

Aaron glared at Nathaniel. "Lucky for you, fratricide is considered quite beyond the pale."

"I will remind you that you are the one who got into this mess."

He did at that. A mess of his own making. And the entire family was paying for his blunder. "The rumor mill believes my wife needed time due to personal family needs, requiring time adjusting to the idea of marriage."

"Good God, what a bunch of balderdash."

"Now see here, Edmund. When did you go over to Nathaniel's court?"

"I am your brother, not your bloody kowtower."

Aaron went to the sidebar and refilled his glass.

God give me strength with officious brothers.

"Why not accept her, Aaron?"

He whirled about. "I already have, you clod."

"No," Edmund stood and brought his own glass with him. "I believe our brother means accept her as a true wife. You do like her, don't you?"

Bloody hell. How was he to answer that. He more than liked Rebekah. The drawback was he did want her for his wife. He wanted the rights of her husband every time he saw her in a bloody gown. He wanted to kill every man who looked at her.

"You know, Aaron, I believe she would accept you. I think she already has a fondness for you."

"Hard to believe with the way you've been acting," Nathaniel added.

Aaron lifted his brandy glass. "A ruse. Nothing more."

"You think she's pretending when hurt fills her eyes?"

Hurt? He whirled to his brother. "What do you see that I have not?"

"Apparently, quite a lot," Edmund said.

Bloody hell.

Would this farce never end? He was in no mood to deal with his brothers tonight. He was trying to woo his wife. Clearly, she was not making it easy.

"She got what she wanted," he said aloud, mainly to convince himself.

"I'm not so sure." Edmund shook his head. "A marriage, yes. In all seriousness, Aaron, the way she looks at you ... I believe Rebekah has feelings for you."

Chapter 23

The day of Lady Cobblestone's ball, Rebekah was feeling herself again. The powder took care of any tear stains on her face. Joyanna informed her that a touch of coal at the corner of each eye made her more mysterious. Rebekah would settle for average, but being among the ton, she feared they would only see her as puzzling. Not as in bamboozling or perplexing. No, with her, it would be more along the lines of awkward, or inconvenient, intolerable.

She shook herself. Tonight, she would be a new woman.

At the time of her decision to marry Aaron, she'd been under pressure. There were a hundred reasons where she'd convinced herself to go through with the wedding. Foolishly, she'd imagined that she and Aaron would have a life together. He'd shot that down with one arrow clean to the heart on the very day of their wedding. She hadn't had one inkling that he had any intention of leaving Surrey. As for the last few days, Aaron had been as polite and distant as ever.

Aunt Penelope and Rebekah took the carriage, and Aaron rode by himself. The evening was off to a grand start. She was never so glad to see another human being in her life as she was when Joyanna and Edmund came into view.

"Good evening, Rebekah. My, you look stunning." Joyanna gave her an air kiss on her cheek.

"Thank you."

"Aunt," Joyanna gave Penelope a kiss as well.

Rebekah glanced at Aaron, tuning everyone else out. He was such a handsome man. Quite tall, he commanded attention just by standing there. He'd worn his hair down, and she wanted to run her hands through the strands. Pull his head to her for a kiss. Tell him, she truly wanted to be his wife and to please, please be her husband.

"Don't you?"

Oh dear. She hadn't been paying attention. Thank goodness, Aaron answered.

"Of course, I do. I told her this evening before we left."

"When?" Penelope asked him. "You were outside by the time we came downstairs."

Aaron stared at his aunt like he'd been caught dipping his finger into a cherry pie.

"Come ladies, let us escort you to the seating." Clearly Edmund stepped in to cut the tension. He offered his arm to Joyanna and Penelope.

Aaron was left to escort Rebekah.

She would need to be more careful and stop dreaming of something that would never happen.

She and Aaron followed Edmund as he guided them to the right of the room where a row of matriarchs were already sitting. Rebekah sighed as she struggled over the nobles' names. There were too many to keep up with.

After several *good evenings* were tossed about, Rebekah sat beside Penelope and listened as the dear woman filled her in on the ton's gossip.

"That is Lord Feriweather, there." Penelope pointed with a tilt of her head. Heaven forbid she use her finger. "His daughter set her cap for my nephew. If you had not showed up, I suppose she would still be chasing him."

Rebekah knew Penelope was talking about Aaron. That was the first anyone had mentioned he might have had a sweetheart. Was he in love with another woman? He had denied any special feelings for anyone, or a relationship.

"Over there is Lord Wiltshire. If he asks you to dance, you should refuse."

"How would I do that?"

Penelope looked at her as if she'd grown two heads. "Say no."

I would never have thought of that.

She wanted to laugh, then the sudden thought struck her. "Why?"

Uh oh. She said that out loud.

"He's a rake. For one thing, it would ruin your reputation."

What reputation? She was married to a man who didn't want her. That reputation?

"Who knows what might happen if he pilfered you away from us."

"I don't see how that will happen, with Aaron glaring at every man that comes near me. I wouldn't be given the chance to accept or decline."

Joyanna reached over and patted Rebekah's hand. "He cares for you."

Rebekah swung her head so fast, the room blurred. "That's a good one. I didn't know you had such wild ideas, Joyanna."

"Hmmm. You like him too."

Like. Huh? *Love?* She wished she didn't. This ache in her chest convinced her otherwise.

"You're in love with him."

Rebekah's mouth dropped open. "Certainly not." If only denial made it so.

Joyanna smiled. "You can deny it all you want. It is clearly written on your face every time he enters a room."

Rebekah released a burdensome sigh at the same time she gave a reluctant nod.

"I knew it," Joyanna crowed.

"Shhh. Don't let anyone else hear you." Rebekah glanced to Penelope. She was engrossed in conversation with a duchess. "I will admit when I see him, I get a fluttery feeling in my stomach. It's the querist sort of feeling."

"I'm happy for you."

Rebekah smiled even though she felt a little sad.

Too bad her feelings were clearly one-sided.

───ele───

From the time Edmund had said them, Aaron had not been able to get the words out of his head.

Feelings for you.

Could Rebekah have feelings for him?

Ballocks.

It didn't help that the woman in his dreams had taken on the face of his wife. The woman in his dreams stirred his desire. Just when he was about to claim her, she floated out of reach. He wondered if he would ever know her true identity.

That thought made his heart hurt. He'd dreamed of the woman for too long to let her go so easily. His wife was already slipping under his skin. She was beautiful, but something else about her attracted him. Drew him like an acquainted magnet.

He gazed over the throng of aristocrats, and zeroed in on Rebekah. An air of mystery surrounded her. Yet something almost recognizable. He supposed he should give the marriage a chance.

Good God. He was infatuated with his own wife.

He shook his head and tried concentrating on the evening.

This was not going to work. Not as long as Rebekah stood there in her alluring gown, showing off her tempting charms. Her provocative breasts would draw any man's attention, let alone have the blood pounding in his ears.

His wife.

His anger faded to frustration.

"Forgive me, old man, you seem to be otherwise occupied."

Hell. He'd not been paying attention to the bloody bore. "Suppose we talk in the morning, Sherwood."

"Given the lateness of the hour, I suppose business can wait." The man gave a nod and turned to the throng of dancers.

Good God, how was he to carry on a normal conversation when his wife was quite possibly the most enchanting woman he'd ever met?

And the most infuriating.

"Brother, you look unusually somber for a husband who has just been reunited with his bride."

"Two weeks."

"What's that?"

"She's been here two weeks. How could you bring her here without telling me?"

"It was not I who abandoned his wife."

"Still, to waylay me at a bloody ball. That's low, Nathaniel." Aaron had been shocked to say the least, but he thought he'd covered it well.

"Aunt Penelope is in charge of this parade."

"Aunt needs to tend to her own business."

"I suggest you not tell her. Besides, she likes Rebekah. She thinks you should present your wife to society."

Aaron glowered at his brother. "It is obvious she doesn't care what I think."

Nathaniel shrugged and sipped a glass of brandy.

"That's not punch."

"Your powers of deduction are equal to none, Aaron."

"Bloody blowhard. Where'd you get it?"

"Cobblestone's study."

"You just helped yourself?"

"I'm the earl."

Aaron glared at his brother.

"Cobblestone wanted a word, and we had brandy. He freshened it up before we came out here."

"Any chance I can get the same treatment?"

"Go ask."

Aaron looked around the room, then decided he didn't want to be absent from his wife. He'd damned near lost his tongue when he'd helped her remove her pelisse. As stunning a creature as he'd ever seen. Quite desirable in her Emerald green gown with the low decolletage showing entirely too much bosom. Just as he liked.

On another woman. Not his bloody wife!

"You know Aaron, you could be happy," Nathaniel said, drawing his attention. "Why not make the marriage a real one?"

Aaron had no comeback for that. His damn brother was serious. True, Rebekah was *his* wife. They were still playing the part of a loving couple.

"You know, brother, I didn't know if I ever wanted to marry," Aaron told him. "With the upbringing we had, I certainly never expected *you* to wed. Let alone, living in the very house you hated as a child. Yet here you are."

Nathaniel met his gaze, eye to eye. "Life has a way of changing our minds."

"Life, huh? I suspect Serena had a lot to do with it."

Nathaniel grinned. "You'd be right, little brother."

"I guess anything is possible." He glanced back to the droning crowd.

"Would it be so bad to give the girl a chance?"

Aaron lifted a flute of champagne from a silver tray. "I wonder what you would do, brother, if you were suddenly saddled with a wife not of your choosing." He downed the entire glass. Scowling, he turned to glare at Nathaniel. "Stay out of it." He turned to make his exit, but Nathaniel stepped directly in front of him.

"What are you planning to do?"

"Are you her protector, now, Nathaniel?" Since they were of an even height—almost—Aaron could meet him eye to eye.

"What I do with *my wife* is my concern."

—ell—

Rebekah could feel the hair standing on the back of her neck. Great. Now she could feel him staring from across the room.

"Rebekah, I think you are wrong. Aaron does have feelings for you."

Serena drew her from her doldrums. What would Rebekah do without Serena and Joyanna? They had befriended her, carrying her through the ordeal of being Aaron's wife in public.

"I can't imagine what feelings he has, other than considering me a burden." Her eyes got all misty. She could not cry now.

"You are in love with him," Serena said softly.

Rebekah took her hanky and held it to her nose, afraid she would break down and sob. Joyanna quickly tried to comfort her.

"Oh, Rebekah. Don't be sad. I do believe Aaron cares for you, and I know just how to prove it."

"Joyanna," Serena cautioned. "What are you thinking?"

"I have an idea." She glanced about the ballroom. "Look. There's Lord Belgrave. Come along, Rebekah. I will introduce you."

"Joyanna, you can't. He's a well-known rake."

"Exactly," Joyanna replied with a smile. She guided Rebekah in his direction, and then made it seem as if the women were suddenly in Lord Belgrave's path. Joyanna pretended not to see him.

"Lady Mirabeau," he called in a loud voice. Lord Belgrave was very handsome, and all smiles. Although, his clothes seemed a bit elaborate for a man.

Joyanna fluttered her fan. "Why, Lord Belgrave. Fancy meeting you here."

"Always a pleasure. May I say, Lady Mirabeau, how utterly ravishing you look this evening?"

"Of course, you may say it, as long as my betrothed is not within hearing. He does tend to be jealous."

"I can understand. And where is my nemesis?"

Joyanna giggled. "You *are* a rogue, aren't you, Lord Belgrave?"

His grin was devastating. Then he looked to Rebekah. "And who is your charming companion, Lady Mirabeau?"

"Allow me to introduce you to Rebekah Greystoke." She paused for effect. "Mrs. Aaron Greystoke."

He bent slightly at the waist, but his head suddenly jerked up when Joyanna mentioned *Aaron.* "The devil you say. This lovely creature cannot be married."

"Rebekah," Joyanna pronounced enticingly. "This is Lord Belgrave. A known flirt. Do not believe anything he tells you."

"Now, Lady Mirabeau. Do not scare the poor dear. Mrs. Greystoke, I am charmed to make your acquaintance." He gave a bow worthy of any gentleman at court.

"Your gallantry is endearing, Lord Belgrave."

His eyes snapped with interest. "Forgive me for speaking out of turn, but your husband is the last person I would have expected to take a wife." His smile reminded her of a fat cat that had just swallowed a canary. He took her gloved hand. "Now that I have met you, I certainly understand how he became so besotted."

His thumb stroked the back of her fingers, making her a bit uncomfortable.

"May I say you are the most beautiful woman here this evening." His eyes drifted to her decolletage.

Rebekah had already been self-conscious of her low neckline showing so much bosom. Seeing this man staring at her chest so blatantly had her discomfort quickly changing to anger.

"My eyes are up here, Lord Belgrave." She tapped a finger to her cheek, just below her eye.

His shocked expression was comical. Joyanna laughed, holding her fan to cover most of her face.

"I must beg your forgiveness, again. My only excuse is that your beauty makes a man forget—only for a moment—to behave like a gentleman."

He couldn't mistake her glare for anything other than anger. She allowed him to stew, then another voice came over her shoulder.

"Belgrave." Aaron glared at the man. "Don't you have somewhere else you need to be?"

Lord Belgrave smirked. Then he centered his gaze back on her.

"A pleasure to make your acquaintance Mrs. Greystoke. Good evening, Lady Mirabeau." He took another quick glance at Aaron, then turned on his heels and sauntered off.

"You are to stay away from that man."

"More orders, Aaron?"

He lifted her hand, bringing it to his lips, playing the part of devoted husband. She gritted her teeth to keep her mouth from hanging open. He placed her hand upon his sleeve. Then, Aaron lowered his head, speaking directly into her ear.

"We are leaving. Now. You may come quietly, or I will carry you kicking and screaming. The choice is yours."

Her eyes flew wide with surprise. She heard his anger in every word.

Some choice.

She glared, but his expression dared her to defy him.

"Joyanna, would you please tell Aunt Penelope, that Rebekah and I are going home?"

Joyanna grinned as if Aaron was joking. "How do you know she is ready to leave? It looked to me like she was enjoying herself."

"Too much for my liking."

Joyanna smiled at Rebekah with a coy expression. Had the woman lost her mind?

Rebekah nearly stumbled as Aaron took her arm and steered her outside. He helped her into their carriage without saying a word. He remained silent—brooding, his temple pulsing—on the ride back to the house. She thought over her actions, and came up with no reason he should be annoyed.

Chapter 24

When they arrived at Aaron's house, he advised his butler," We are not to be disturbed!" Gripping Rebekah's arm, he directed her straight to the drawing room, her steps echoing quickly to keep up with him. He closed the double doors, then spun around to face her. His temper had cooled somewhat, but his bloody irritation hit a new level when she took off her pelisse.

His eyes narrowed and lust filled his veins.

He railed at his jealousy. A completely new emotion he'd never felt before.

"What is the matter with you?" He'd been too angry to notice at the ball. His cronies were salivating at the mouth. No doubt, the bastards had been planning on how to get a moment alone with her.

"What have I done that has offended you?"

He smacked a fist into the palm of his other hand. Bloody hell. She was ravishing. He would have to lock her up. Throw away the key.

"Just what did you think you were doing? Were you trying to get the attention of every man there?" He paced to the hearth and back again. Damn if he would allow the dandies and rogues to lust after her with their tongues hanging out. She belonged to him. And he would not be cuckolded. He would be the only one who would see her beauty. To see her eyes glaze over in the throes of her passion.

"Belgrave. Is that what you want? A bloody popinjay? He's a rake. I will not have my wife flirting behind my back."

"Behind ... We were at a ball in plain sight."

"Then you admit it. In sight of everyone. The entire ton saw my wife being—" He caught himself before he insulted her.

"Being what, exactly?"

"He would ravish you in the garden in an instant. Were you planning on taking him as your lover?"

Hell will freeze over before I allow another man near my wife.

"Aaron!"

He whirled around. "What?"

"I have no idea why you are shouting at me. Will you please stop?"

The more he thought about her, the angrier he got. The fools at the ball looked at her. Saw his wife. In that damned dress that covered nothing. Her breasts were ready to pop out.

"Why are you wearing that gown?"

Her eyes widened with confusion. "It is a ball gown. Madame Laselle—"

"It looks striking on you. Christ, Rebekah." He took the maddening steps that brought him directly in front of her. "You look like a harlot. Must you act like one too?"

Crack!

Aaron froze. And stared in awe. Had his wife truly just slapped him?

Good God, he deserved it.

He stepped back and dropped his gaze to the carpet. Holy mother of Christ, he'd gone barmy.

"Your aunt approved this gown. I don't think she would want me to look like a harlot."

Aaron drew himself up, deserving the tongue-lashing he expected.

Rebekah released a sigh. "Perhaps it is time we talk of dissolving this marriage."

That was the last thing he expected her to say. "Is that what you want?"

"Since I've been in London, my wants have not mattered."

He wanted to tell her she was wrong.

"I've tried to fit in. I would not wear a gown that would shame you. I have tried my best. I've learned how to be a proper lady. Serena and Joyanna—" Her voice caught, making him feel even more like a cad.

What the devil had gotten into him? The green-eyed monster had Aaron entirely in its thrall. True, he'd never experienced the emotion, so he hardly recognized it for what it was. He should not be taking his temper out on Rebekah.

"Do you have any idea how lonely, how scary it is to be in a strange place, knowing no one, and depending on them for your very existence?"

His head jerked to her.

"Of course not." She dropped her gaze to the floor. "You never thought about how I might have felt. You only thought about you. What was happening to you." When her eyes lifted back to his, what he saw in them brought him low.

Aaron stared at the woman who was his wife.

Devil take it.

Rebekah spoke the truth. He had not once considered her feelings toward his actions. He'd convinced himself that he had done the proper thing. Done what they both wanted.

Who was he kidding? Neither one of them wanted the marriage, but they both had to deal with the fall out.

Only he had handled things as he saw fit. What an arse. He'd set out to fix a conundrum, and once done, he presumed that was the end of it. He'd given her everything she wanted. So he thought.

He hadn't considered that a woman alone might be scared. He had not taken into account that every person in the house with her was a stranger. He'd left Rebekah with no way to leave if she wished.

What a bastard.

Damn étiquette.

Damn the ton.

It wasn't supposed to be like this. Marriage should have made her happy. So what, if it had been a marriage of convenience. She had said yes.

Damn his soul to hell.

"You are wrong, Rebekah. Your wants do matter. I owe you an apology."

"An apology?"

"Well, yes, and a lot more."

Her wide eyes told him of her surprise. He did not normally apologize to women. To anyone, for that matter. But he'd never behaved in such an ungentlemanly fashion.

"I beg your forgiveness; at the same time, I ask you to hear me out."

"I've heard enough already. Unless you change your attitude toward me, I don't want to hear any more from you."

"I am trying to explain. And I did offer an apology."

She stared at him as if she was searching his soul. "Why the sudden about-face?"

"I see your side of it. I came to my townhouse, familiar surroundings. I carried on almost as normal. You were in a strange house with strangers. I know my family. However, you did not.

I knew they were safe. You did not know you were safe." He
yanked a hand through his hair. "I did not realize it was fright-
ening, nay terrifying for you. I'm not normally a thoughtless or
uncharitable man."

She had the softest looking lips. A million thoughts drifted
through his mind, yet all he could think of was kissing his wife.
He took a step toward her. She didn't run or draw back. He held
her gaze as he took another.

"I ask for your forgiveness. And I promise to be more considerate."

"You asked me once before to allow you time. You said I
would find you not the ogre I thought you to be."

"Then I went right ahead and proved myself a liar. I'm not a
liar, Rebekah."

Did he dare confess his jealousy? He could not give her that
much power. He took another step, hoping to close the gap
between them as he closed the distance.

"I do not at all like the way you behaved this evening."

"Again, I apologize. I have no excuse. You are a beautiful
woman, Rebekah. I resented other men looking at you."

She gasped, her hand slapping to her chest, drawing his attention to her full breasts. Good God, she was luscious. He took
another step, close enough to reach out and touch her.

He had no right.

He had every right.

She screwed up her face as if she didn't believe what he'd
just revealed. What man in his right mind would want to admit
jealousy over his wife?

Damn, she was desirable when she was mad. He raked his eyes
over her exquisite form. Her breasts rose with every deep breath.
He wondered if she was a passionate creature. Since she was his
wife, he was bound to find out. One day.

Why not today?

He took the final step that brought him so close, without actually touching.

The steam seemed to float out of her. Her shoulders drooped a bit, she looked tired. In one swoop, he could snatch her off her feet and carry her to a bed chamber. But if he did that, he knew he would not want to leave.

She stood close enough for him to feel her breath on his face. He inhaled her sweet fragrance. Not sickly sweet, like a room full of flowers. No, it was more like sunshine, and ... something familiar crossed his mind, and then it was gone. Had he recognized the scent? Knew it from someplace before?

As he stared into her eyes, he saw the darker crown around the iris. Magnificent and vibrant. Her hair, such a lovely shade of blonde, lighter than his own, he wondered how he hadn't noticed it before. Rebekah was quite lovely. Remarkable, really.

He tilted his head slightly to the side. "I also asked you, once before, what you wanted. Your answer was to be free. If I ask you again—now—will your answer be different?"

"Let me ask *you* that question. And be truthful."

"I am always truthful." His voice had lowered almost to a growl.

"Hmmm. What do *you* want?"

"I do not want to end our marriage."

"Why, for heaven's sake?/ You don't want me."

"Wrong." He slid closer. "I want you with every fiber of my being."

Her breathing kicked up, which meant her pulse was beating faster. She might deny her attraction, but he sensed it. He saw it in the way she held her body. In the way she tried not to move her eyes.

Rebekah was his wife.

His!

He should be allowed to touch her.

Yes, he was her husband. He had the right. Judging from her heavy breathing, she would welcome it. After all, she'd come to London looking for him.

Her mouth opened and his groin tightened.

"I won't let you go. I've gotten used to having a wife. Having you for my wife."

Perhaps ... perhaps what?

He leaned to her. Just a bit.

Her eyes flashed fire. The color on her cheeks brightened, and her breath grew harsh. He lifted a loose curl and smoothed it behind her ear. She leaned into his hand, a sigh escaping from her mouth.

Hell's Teeth, she was stunning. His gut tightened.

"I want you to stay. We can have a real marriage?"

She closed her eyes as she shook her head. "Why are you saying these things?"

He lifted his arms and gently placed his hands on her shoulders. "Seeing you laugh, seeing you with Belgrave drove me mad with longing. I want you to look at me that way. I want to see happiness on your face when you look at me." His voice lowered. "I want to see desire in your eyes."

Her face was tilted up to his, exposing her throat. The desire to run his tongue over her creamy flesh, dip down to the swells of her breasts, was too tempting. All he had to do was lean down. Instead, he lifted a finger and gently traced the outline of her bodice. She shivered.

A thrill shot through him that she was not unaffected. An even bigger thrill hit him when he realized she allowed his finger to remain where it was.

He whispered, "I want ... you to want me."

She closed her eyes, her head tilting to the side. Her moan triggered a reaction in his groin. He savored the moment. He slid his hands around her waist.

"I have neglected my wife." He pressed a kiss below her ear. She sucked in a breath. "Would you allow me ..." he placed another kiss to the side of her mouth. Her eyes opened. "To remedy my negligence?"

Her mouth opened, but no words came out. He could feel her heart racing. His hands added pressure, bringing her flush against his chest—and against his arousal.

Her hands grasped his shoulders, then his nape. When her tongue slipped out to wet her lips, he was lost.

He seized her mouth in a deep kiss. Desire exploded the moment his lips touched hers. So soft. So sweet. And to his absolute amazement, Rebekah was kissing him back.

Thank God.

Rebekah's hands were in his hair, tugging, pulling him to her. He locked his arms around her and let her steal his breath. She tasted magnificent. She tasted divine. He kissed her with all the longing he'd denied himself since their wedding. She met him lick for lick, allowing her passion free rein, pouring everything of herself into the kiss. As if she had been starving for him.

Good God, it was glorious.

He couldn't get enough. Their tongues danced around each other, their mouths merged together, and still he tried to get closer. The need to devour her surged within him.

Something teased at the edge of the realm of possibilities.

Something familiar.

More.

More. He wanted everything she had to give. And she gave so sweetly. So passionately. He was swimming in deep, and he kept going. Somehow knowing she would not turn him away.

He kissed her as though he would never get enough of her, as though he would never let her go.

He was drowning ... his passion so great he shuddered with the power of it. A familiar heavenly gale rushed over him, as though he'd done this before. A welcoming sensation, as though he knew her scent, her taste. He'd craved it. With her. With Rebekah.

A pair of stunning eyes, flashing with desire, blinked into his mind. At the same time, his hand was moving up to fondle her breast, as though he knew the way.

Rebekah moaned, and it was music to his ears. He loved the breathtaking sound of her desire. Together, they were spiraling to a magical moment. He wanted to give her that magic. Give her what she longed for and what he desperately desired. Visions of another kiss pierced his brain. Moans of ecstasy ...

This time, he could not ignore the familiarity.

Aaron tore his lips from hers and shoved her away. His fingers were like steel bands clamped on her upper arms. He stared. Then blinked, shaking another image from his mind. But as he stood, staring into her eyes, he saw the same ones looking back at him with passion. The same ones as in his dreams.

Rebekah?

Her eyes filled with horror, but they were the same eyes. His gaze dropped to her swollen lips. He remembered them on his body. How ...

"Aaron ..."

That voice. Her voice. How had he not recognized it before?

He raked his eyes over her features again, and again. He closed his eyes as the truth struck him like a blow. Pain, raw and fierce, gouged his chest.

"It's you," he whispered.

Rebekah melted under Aaron's insistence, opening her mouth, opening her heart to him. Her mind floating back to that perfect night, where she could no longer think. Only feel as she fell deeper and deeper into Aaron's kiss. She forgot where she was. Who she was. Her dream of Aaron holding her in his arms, kissing the living daylights out of her, was real. And it was as wonderful—no, even more magnificent than she remembered.

Until her worst nightmare flashed its killing blow.

Aaron remembered.

Shock kept her frozen in place. She stared, unbelieving, not knowing what to say. What to do.

When his eyes snapped open, she gasped, then realized she'd been holding her breath.

His hands were like iron grips, forcing her to look at him. Dear God, what could she do? Her body began to shake. She bit her lip, to keep from screaming, and waited for Aaron's wrath.

"Do you have nothing to say for yourself?" he shouted.

She opened her mouth, but could not get any words out. What was she supposed to say? *I'm sorry?* She was not sorry. She would never be sorry for the night he made love to her. A night full of loving and passion. The most wonderful feeling in the world. Aaron had given that to her.

"Speak, Rebekah. Tell me it was real. Tell me it wasn't a dream. It was you!" He shoved her as he released her arms. She stumbled back.

"I ... I don't—"

"Do not lie. I know it was you." His voice dropped to almost pleading. "It had to be you."

"I don't know what you want me to say." She hung her head.

He spun to face her. "The truth!"

"I have not lied to you."

He froze. His entire body language changed. "You can't be serious. My God, I can't think. My brain is scrambling in every direction." He started pacing the carpet. "You did not tell me the truth. Omission is a lie. You know what happened. I thought you were a dream. Yet, it seemed so real."

He talked as he paced. She wasn't sure if he was talking to her or himself.

"You were there. It was real." He stopped and whirled to her. "*You* are real."

The only thing she could think to do was stand there until he finished. Afraid to move, afraid to speak, she stared at the floor.

"Damn you!" He paced. "Damn you!" When he came stomping toward her, she gathered her skirts and fled.

She had no idea where she was going, she just ran. But she'd made a wrong turn and now she appeared to be going deeper into the house. She saw the stairway at the same time she heard his boots pounding on the floor behind her. She felt like a fox being chased in a hunt. Her heart pounded so hard, she prayed it would not jump out of her chest.

"Rebekah! Don't you dare run from me."

She made a bee line for the stairs. Her slippered feet climbed as fast as she could go.

"Rebekah!"

Dear Lord, he was much too close. She turned at the landing and raced up the next set of stairs. Turning down the corridor, she panicked. *Which door?*

She heard his boots on the stairway. She ran by several doors before she quickly darted into one. Having no idea where she was, she looked down and saw a key in the lock. She flipped it. The lock slid into place with a *click*.

She turned her back to the door and prayed he would not find her. That was silly, he knew she was in the house.

"Rebekah! Damn you. Do not hide from me. You owe me answers." A door banged against a wall causing her to shriek. She slapped a hand over her mouth.

"Aha. I know where you are."

The vein at her temple throbbed with her heartbeat. She feared it would burst. When the door handle rattled, she nearly screamed.

"Open this door."

She ran to the bed and grabbed a post, holding on for dear life. "No. Go away."

"This is my house, Rebekah. There will be no locked doors between us."

"I'm sorry, Aaron." Tears slipped down her face as she cried in earnest. "I'm so sorry."

"Open this bloody door!"

"I will not!" Dear Lord, would he hurt her? She'd never seen a man in such a rage. "Aaron, please. I did not lie to you."

Silence. Maybe he was listening.

"Aaron. If you will allow me to explain. The day you showed up at our house, I was shocked. I was afraid." Her hair had come loose from its pins. She shoved the wild mess out of the way. "Aaron. Please listen. When I realized you didn't remember me—"

"Stand back!" he shouted. "This is your last chance to unlock that door."

What?

"Aaron, please."

"So be it."

Crash!

Rebekah smacked her hands over her ears and stared at the splintered wood flying through the air as a chair came hurdling through the chamber door.

Chapter 25

"Aaron!"

Aaron shoved the hair out of his eyes. The ringing in his ears came from every direction. His chest heaved from hurling a chair through the heavy wood door. Rage filled his vision. He was going in that damned room after her.

His arm was yanked, and he swung about. His reflexes had him drawing back his fist.

"Have you lost your bloody mind?"

Aaron blinked. His damn brother. "Stay out of my way."

"What the bloody hell is going on here?"

He glared through the busted hole in the door. "She has locked the goddamned door."

"Aaron! What is the meaning of this?"

His attention snapped past Nathaniel. *God's teeth.*

"This does not concern you, Aunt."

"What are you doing? Where is Rebekah?"

Aaron took the time to gather his composure—what was left of it. "Rebekah is in there. She is perfectly fine." Then he said to Nathaniel. "Go away. And take Aunt with you."

"Like hell I will. Explain yourself."

Aaron raised a brow, letting his brother know of his irritation. "I have no intention of laying my soul bare to you this evening, Nathaniel." He turned his gaze back to the hole and caught Rebekah's gaze. "However, my wife and I have quite a bit of talking to do."

Nathaniel swung his arm toward the scattered wood. "Is this what you call talk?"

"Get out of my way, brother."

Nathaniel ignored him and shouted to Rebekah. "Are you all right?"

"Mind your own business, brother," Aaron warned.

"Aaron. For God's sake, snap out of this."

Aaron stood there allowing his fury to engulf him. Too many questions. He would not rest until he had the answers to them all.

Devil take her. She lied. So many emotions attacked him he didn't know how to deal with any of them, or which one first.

Hurt. Shock. Anger. Fury. Betrayal. Hurt. Nausea. Broken.

"Aaron. Can we talk about this? You and me?"

His fury was barely in check. "You overstep, brother. This is between me and *my wife.*"

"You'll not get the answers you seek while in a fit of rage? Good God, what happened? You seemed calm enough when you left the ball."

He glared at Rebekah. "That was before I found out—" Damn if he would say any more. He didn't know what he was so mad about. He wouldn't know if he should be angry until Rebekah told him all.

"I need answers, Nathaniel. I need my wife to give them to me. No bloody locked door will keep me from finding out what she should have told me a long time ago."

"I cannot allow—"

"Nathaniel," Rebekah said quietly. "Aaron is right. We need to have a long conversation."

"It doesn't have to be tonight."

"Yes, it does." Aaron couldn't keep the growl from his voice. "Right now."

"I don't think—"

"I don't care what you think. I will have my answers."

"Aaron—"

"Brother, give me my due." Aaron ran his hands through his tousled hair, ready to tear it from his skull. He inhaled. Then exhaled. "I will not harm Rebekah. She locked the door. It is open now." With his fists clenched at his sides, Aaron locked his eyes with Nathaniel's gaze, hoping his brother would see his earnestness. "I am not mad. However, I am in complete control of my faculties. Get out of my house. Take Aunt with you."

Nathaniel looked to Rebekah. She gave a nod.

"I don't like ... Are you sure?"

"Do you not accept my word, brother?" His word was his bond. If Nathaniel could not believe him, then fuck him. He should know Aaron would never hurt a woman. Even one who'd lied to him. Betrayed him. *Hurt* him.

And there lay the rub. He didn't want to admit that Rebekah had hurt him. Nathaniel's decision could hurt him, too.

"Nathaniel," Aunt called. "Please take me home with you. Aaron has given his word. I am ready to leave."

Until then, Nathaniel's gaze, nor Aaron's, did not waver. His brother continued to study him. Did his brother trust him? Or not?

After too many achingly long seconds, Nathaniel gave a sharp nod. "Coming, Aunt."

Aaron stood there waiting for his breathing to return to normal.

Would he ever feel normal again? His entire world had been turned upside down. He no longer knew what normal was. As the minutes passed, his temple stopped its throbbing. The feeling was beginning to return to his fingers that had been clenched into tight fists. He lifted his gaze to what was left of the bedchamber door. The woman inside looked more worried than frightened.

His emotions were running rampant, like lightning in a raging storm. He swallowed his fury, and hoped he could control the volcano erupting inside. He was vehement when he found the locked door. How could he expect Rebekah to know he would not hurt her. He just wanted answers.

"Rebekah," he finally got out. "Breaking down the door was not well done of me. I will not hurt you. I will give you time to collect yourself. Meet me downstairs in the library in a quarter of an hour. I will not break anything else. At the very least I will try to keep my temper in check. Please believe I would never hurt a woman, but our conversation is far from finished."

At that, he turned on his heel and left.

He marched down two flights of stairs, and found Berthright standing as stiff as a statue at the bottom.

"Might I be of assistance, master Aaron?"

"I hope my brother didn't give you too much grief."

"No, he did not. Lady Blackburn left with Lord Greystoke."

"Good. My wife and I will be having a discussion in the library. Would you have some food prepared and sent straight away."

"Yes, master Aaron." Berthright gave a gentlemanly bow, and said nothing else, letting Aaron know the man was there if he needed him. But Berthright was smart enough to stay out of the way.

—eℓℓ—

Rebekah collapsed on the big bed as soon as she was alone. She had to get away from Aaron.

How had she gotten herself into such a spin? Nothing was turning out like she'd planned. It was time to take off the blinders and remove the stars from her eyes. She'd pictured a blue sky, brilliant sun, and the two of them sharing a dream. She had given her heart to the man she'd married, and then fate plunged her world into despair.

No matter how much she wanted Aaron to sweep her up and promise everything would be all right, she saw things clearly now. Aaron would never be a true husband to her.

A tear trickled down her cheek. If she allowed one, there would be no stopping the others. She furiously brushed her cheek and hated herself for her weakness.

Damn and blast the man.

Aaron's temper was as contradictory as day and night. His actions from one extreme to the other. He'd completely shocked her. The man who'd splintered the chamber door had been a mad man. And yet, he had spoken to his brother as though he was in control of his emotions.

What had she done?

It didn't matter now. She'd set the wheels in motion. Now she would have to see it played out. Her husband was a stranger.

Her silly heart was breaking.

—elle—

Good God. What a bloody night.

Aaron marched right to the sideboard and poured a glass full of brandy. He tossed half of it back and nearly growled at the burn blazing down to his gut.

He wished this was a nightmare he would wake up from.

Rebekah.

He saw the eyes of the woman in his dreams. He heard her sigh as he kissed her from her breasts to her knees. Her moans of ecstasy driving him crazy. Was it Rebekah?

Hell and blast.

He wanted to rip the woman from his dreams. He had fantasized about her every bloody night.

The grandfather clock in the hallway struck the hour. He counted along as it chimed twice. Many couples were finishing up the midnight supper and had gone back to dancing. He was sitting in the library waiting for his *wife*.

Perhaps he should wait until later today to confront his wife. She wouldn't be too keen to see him after he smashed a bloody chair through the chamber door. But he'd be damned if he would wait another bloody minute to find out what the hell all this nonsense was about. It had happened to him. Why couldn't he remember?

Just when he thought his wife would not be joining him, her silhouette filled the doorway.

Aaron saw no need to rise from the chair he'd flopped in. He didn't want to see the fear leap back into her eyes.

"Come in, Rebekah."

She timidly took a few steps forward. "I prefer to stand."

"There is no need. I will not jump at you."

Just then, Berthright rolled in a table laden with several silver dishes.

"Ah, Berthright. Fabulous timing, as always," he said rising to meet the butler. "Surely you did not do all this yourself?"

"Cook was already up. She insisted on preparing a meal for you and the misses."

"Please thank her for me." Aaron waited for his butler to leave, then closed the library door. "I thought you might like something to chew on besides me."

As soon as the words were out of his mouth, he fathomed the double entendre. He'd meant it as a lark. When he looked up, all he saw on Rebekah's face was confusion. At least she wasn't frightened.

"Thank you for joining me. Please. You must be hungry." Aaron filled a plate and decided to give her space. He walked to the hearth and sat down in one of the two leather chairs. Before long, she sat in the opposite one.

"I suppose I should apologize for scaring you. It is my house. I will have no locked doors between you and me."

She didn't look at him, but she didn't comment either.

"I see there is tea. I have sherry, if you would prefer one."

He waited in silence to see if she would answer.

"Perhaps after I eat. Tea is fine for now. I'll pour. Would you care for tea?"

Good God, she was actually going to serve him?

He stood, holding out his glass. "It's brandy for me."

She stayed silent as he poured another glass of brandy. He marveled at the meal cook had prepared in the middle of the night. There was bacon, kippers, onions, and cheese. Even the bread was warm. They ate in silence, and he allowed her time to relax. As much as she could. He had no doubt she expected him to pounce at any moment.

"Rebekah, I don't want you to be afraid of me. Surely, you can understand my anger."

She finally met his gaze. Her turquoise eyes shining like the morning glen. "You did not remember. You didn't mention it, so ..."

"Ignorance is bliss? Were you surprised that I did not remember? Or did you think I was pretending?"

"The thought crossed my mind. A nobleman wanting to forget his folly."

"Christ." Aaron scrubbed a hand over his face. He gritted his teeth, shook his head, completely at a loss of what to say. "You thought I would bed you, and then act like it didn't happen?"

She flinched. "I ... I didn't know what to believe. At first. When I realized you truly did not remember, I didn't know what to do."

"So, you stayed silent."

She gave a slight nod.

"What happened? What about your father? I can't put my finger on it. Things are very blurred. I don't get foxed. I drink, but not excessively. Yet I must have passed out."

"Will you allow me to tell the all of it? Before you get angry again?"

He placed his plate on the table, then rested his elbows on his knees. "Is what you're hiding bad enough to fire my anger again?"

She chewed on her bottom lip, and a flash of arousal hit his groin. Damn. From what he could remember, he wanted her. He had wanted her then, and he wanted her now.

"All right. I will keep my distance, but I have to know. Please, tell me the truth. All of it."

"I'm sorry. It is rather humiliating."

"Please." He leaned back into the soft leather of his chair.

"I don't know where he got it, but ... I believe my father drugged you."

Aaron had considered the possibility. His mind was too foggy for him to have swilled so much whisky.

"It took me a while to figure it out. With the way you treated me, it makes sense. I'm shamed by it. My father is a good man. His heart is in the right place, it's just his mind. He doesn't think ... Anyway. He wanted me to marry a gentleman. To have a fine home and money. He didn't ask me what I wanted."

Aaron remained quiet, giving her time to tell him everything.

Rebekah stared into the fire as she spoke. "My mother was a wonderful woman. She was everything to my father. Her father cut her off when she wanted to marry a commoner. But she loved my father, and they were happy. She told me about the aristocracy. How nobles behaved differently, but she taught me that material things were not important. The three of us were a family, and nothing was more important. Our love for each other was more valuable than money."

She looked at him.

"You may not believe me. I mean, after all, my father did trick you into signing a contract."

"I honestly don't remember that, but I did recognize my signature. I had a devil of a time trying to explain that one."

"I'm sorry. When I found out, I was livid. I thought you ..." Rebekah clutched her hands together. "I didn't know what to think. I couldn't imagine why a lord would want to marry me. And then leave. It made no sense. I gave Papa what for, you can believe that. I was furious with him. I told him I was not going to marry anyone. We argued, but I stood my ground. I thought that was the end of it ... then you showed up."

Then I showed up.

He wanted to know about their lovemaking, for that is what it had been. God, he wished he could remember more. His frustration was eating at him, but he had to allow her time to come to grips with her story. If he rushed her, she might clam up. Then where would he be?

Rebekah hated what happened. With her father, that is. Not what happened with Aaron. She hated talking about this. Bringing into the open the intimacy she had kept hidden for so long. It was personal.

Blast her father.

"Aaron, I'm sorry—"

"Please stop apologizing. Will you just tell me what happened?"

She could understand his impatience. It wasn't easy for her to bare her soul, and that is what he was asking her to do.

She took a deep breath. "When you showed up at the house, I was shocked. I remembered you right away. My heart started pounding. I couldn't believe you were standing right in front of me. I thought I'd never see you again."

She stared into the fire, watching the flames, letting them carry her back to that day.

"You didn't know me. You didn't recognize me."

"I'm sorry."

"At first, I thought you were trying to hide what happened. You were an aristocrat. The nobles did not air their dirty laundry. Yes, I believed you were pretending that you did not remember. You accused me of tricking you. I didn't know then what my father had done to you. Only that you signed that paper. I'm afraid I also have a temper. Our conversation grew heated, and we said some terrible things." She sat the empty cup on the oval table between them.

"You said you had no intention of marrying me."

She turned to look at him. "That was true."

"Then you showed up at Greystoke Manor."

"After you left..." She turned back to the fire. "I replayed our argument over and over in my mind. The more I thought about it, the madder I got. Papa was mad at me, and I thought 'why don't I teach him,' meaning you, 'a lesson.' You were arrogant, officious, and nothing at all like ... I ..."

Like that night.

She stiffened her backbone and continued. "I packed with the intention of staying long enough to make you squirm. I didn't want to marry you, and I hadn't truly planned to force you into a wedding. I was foolish. Everything got turned around."

"When you met my brother, when you knew I wasn't the earl, then what?"

"I assumed you lied about that too."

"I do not lie." Aaron said forcefully.

"I—"

"Do not apologize."

Good heavens. How was she to keep her wits about her when he was calm and gentle one minute, and ferocious the next. She twisted her hands in her lap.

"I didn't know you or your brother. However, Lord Greystoke was nice to me. I never expected that."

"Even though I have not shown you the courtesy due to you, I can understand your suspicions. I haven't behaved like a gentleman. I am the one who should apologize. For scaring you. For goading you. For being an unworthy husband."

"That came as a shock. I had no intention of getting married."

"At least we were calm enough to discuss our situation and come up with a reasonable solution."

"A solution that neither of us wanted. I still don't know how I ended up agreeing."

"Some part of you must have wanted to marry me," he said softly.

Her face grew hot, and she knew the red flush was enveloping her entire body. She stood, and hurriedly walked to the window, gathering her thoughts.

"However it happened, it did. We are here now. Have you had any more thoughts on dissolving our marriage?"

"After tonight's fiasco, the ton will be watching our every move with a magnifying glass."

She spun to him. "Is it so important to please the ton?"

"I've never cared much for pleasing the ton," he said. "It's my life. Right this minute, I don't give a tinker's damn about them or any bloody aristocrat." He stood and took a step toward her. "All I care about is you and me."

His voice rumbled over her shoulders and down her spine. She heard the words and caressed them. Was he being sincere? Did he care about her? Or just their situation. She could not let her heart interfere.

"Rebekah."

Oh, how she loved her name on his lips.

"Something drew us together. I've felt it. And now I know there was more. I dreamed of you. I woke up willing you to life. I couldn't let you go. I felt it. I knew you were real. Will you tell me about that night? About the two of us?"

Her hand flew to her mouth at the same time she spun to the window. She bit her knuckles to keep from falling apart. "How can you ask? You cannot expect me to talk about it."

"You have your memories. Mine are slowly creeping in. Even so, they do not tell me how we came together."

Dear God, how can I ...

"Please."

She nearly jumped out of her skin. He was standing directly behind her. She felt his breath on her neck. She shivered from the thrilling sensations overwhelming her body. Remembering, recognizing, wanting ...

"Rebekah," he whispered. Then his hands were on her shoulders, the heat burning through her clothes to her skin.

Her body betrayed her. She leaned back into his embrace. His arms slid around her.

"You feel wonderful. I've got you. You can tell me anything."

Flashes of memories scorched her mind.

The same need, the same emotions, swamping her once again.

Chapter 26

H is arm scorched her, making her relive that night in her mind. Aaron was here. He was holding her now. She wallowed in comfort for as long as she dared. Guilt ate at her. She wanted to erase everything that had happened since that night. Take back the awful words between them.

But she could not. There was no going back in time. She could not undo the hurt and blame, nor her rash actions. Maybe she wasn't to blame for her father's part, but she had agreed to the marriage to prevent scandal.

One could lose oneself on *what ifs?*

She'd been a fool. Determined to prick his pride, taunt him, and then came the powerful urge to kiss him. A romantic notion that had caused dire consequences. Yet here she was with him now. His soothing arms about her, reassuring her.

"I judged you one of father's cronies, but I knew you were a lord by the way you were dressed. I put blankets on the sofa, and tried to help you there. You were limber, and heavy. You fell to the floor and pulled me with you."

His arms never moved. He said not a word. She opened her soul.

"You kissed me. Held me like you are now, and I liked it. I'd never felt such closeness to anyone. You made me feel things. My body heated and responded to your touch. I thought ... I thought *this is heaven*. And I was too weak to push you away. Weak with longing. I wanted your touch."

His lips brushed her neck.

"Yes, just like that. I loved what you did, and ... I wanted more. I wanted to see what was next. I didn't have the power to let you go." She let her head fall back, into his shoulder. Even now, she could not stop herself from enjoying his touch. Even now, she wanted more.

She froze. She had to stop. Stop him.

"Is that enough? Please don't make me say more. I have the memory of our night together. It means nothing to you ... and everything to me." She tried to pry his fingers loose from her waist.

"Wait, Rebekah. Please." He refused to let her go. "I want to know more. If you don't want to talk, will you let me hold you."

Did she dare? How had they gone from crashing a door to a heartfelt embrace?

"Let me absorb everything I've learned tonight. Let me tell you how it's been for me these past months."

Good or bad, she wanted to know. She needed to know.

"I dreamed of a woman." His voice rumbled at her jaw. "A woman with golden hair, it felt like silk against my fingers." He lifted a curl of her hair as he spoke.

He pressed his cheek to the back of her head, the way a lover would.

"Unforgettable turquoise eyes, flashing in the dark of night, yet as blue as a warm summer sky. Those eyes haunted me every night. They belonged to a woman I couldn't find. A woman I desperately wanted to touch and feel. Yet when I woke, she was gone."

His lips were back at her ear.

"I remember her hands on my body."

Rebekah trembled at his words. His hand opened and flattened against her belly. She bit her lip to keep from moaning.

"Ah, I see you remember, too. But I only have my dreams. Can you understand, Rebekah? I had to know her. I had to know if she was real. And now that I've finally found her, I don't want to lose her again."

A lone tear slipped from her eye and ran down over her cheek.

"Look at me, Rebekah. Tell me it is you. Tell me my dreams were real."

Dear God. What should she do? What could she do but follow her heart. She slowly turned. His hands loosened a bit, but never left her.

When she faced him fully, she drew a sharp breath. His emerald eyes burned like fire, scorching her own. She felt the heat sizzling in her bones. Desire. And more.

"You are very beautiful," he said, smoothing a whisp of hair from her brow. "You *are* the woman in my dreams."

"Yes. I hope so."

"You are," he breathed as his lips met hers.

Aaron tried not to think of how magnificent it felt to hold Rebekah in his arms. He tried not to think of her lips, or how alluring her sweet scent. And her eyes, the trust in them sent something alien burrowing into his chest.

He gave into his impulse, inching closer, giving her time to get used to the idea that he was about to kiss her.

When his lips met hers, he was lost once again. So soft, so delicious. Her fingers threaded through his hair, and tickled the back of his neck. He pulled her closer and molded his lips over hers, claiming them completely. Passion flared between them instantly, and he reveled in every blissful second. He slid his tongue over her lips, inviting her to open them, then he delved into her mouth, claiming every space, claiming her for his own.

Emotions and sensations racked his body. Having the woman of his dreams kiss him the way he wanted nearly brought him to his knees. Desire fired in every cell, demanding he make her his own. Her heart beat to the rhythm of his, pounding mercilessly, urging him forward. God help him, he must surrender to the raging desire inside.

He couldn't stop himself. His hands roamed, caressing every delectable inch. Rebekah gave him her all, merging her mouth with his.

Good God, he was on fire.

He tugged at the ties of her bodice, freeing her breasts. Blood surged to his temple as his eyes devoured her full flesh.

"Rebekah," he breathed. She was the most beautiful sight he'd ever seen.

"No words, Aaron. Not now."

Her terms moved him. He lowered his mouth to capture a puckered nipple. She pressed herself closer, making him growl. He fed, like a newborn babe. Her whimpers drove him mad with longing. He kissed and caressed and finally moved to her other breast, giving it the same attention.

She was heaven in his arms. Delicious, and delectable, and her passion sent his blood roaring in his ears. His hands made quick work of her gown, letting it drop to the floor.

He raised his head to look at her. His gaze took in every beautiful inch, every enchanting curve. Then he met her sparkling eyes.

"I'm asking this time. Do I have your permission to go further?"

For her answer, she pulled his lips to hers. He kissed her with deliberate slowness, building her desire, feeding his own hunger.

Suddenly, he broke free.

"I'll have your answer, wife. There will be no misunderstanding between us."

She dropped her head to his chest. Her eyes begged, but he wanted her to say she wanted him. He had no idea he could feel this way. Feel such passion it bordered on rage. He tightened his arms around her. Rebekah was his wife, by God. *His wife.* Desperation pierced his soul. He would keep her.

No matter what—come hell or heaven—she belonged to him.

The pain in his heart grew larger with every second that passed. He wanted to crush her to him, never let her go. He held her snugly. Lovingly.

"Do you want me, Rebekah?"

When she lifted her head, the emotion in her eyes rocked him. "Yes."

Good enough for him.

He swept her feet from under her, lifting her high into his arms and charged from the library. He took the stairs two at a time, protecting the bundle snuggled against his chest, and pounded down to his bedchamber. He crossed to the bed and held Rebekah's gaze before gently placing her upon the counterpane.

He quickly lay down beside her and pressed his nose in her hair. "I've got you where I want you, and I'm as clear-headed as a man can be."

Rebekah clutched his neck. He rose slightly, so he could see her eyes.

"Tell me, Rebekah. Tell me you are the woman in my dreams."

"Make love to me, Aaron. The way you did that night."

He growled his joy, and then captured her mouth in a fiery kiss. She kissed him with a fierceness he'd not experienced with another woman. His hands caressed every inch, every enticing curve, as he removed the rest of her clothing.

His lips followed, and before long, she was completely naked.

"Aaron, please."

"I can't help looking at you. You're beautiful."

"I want to feel you, too."

He tore the shirt over his head, then tugged off his boots and breeches. When he turned back to her, she held up her arms. The only invitation he needed to make love to his wife.

He kissed his way, learning her fabulous body. So tempting, so sinfully tantalizing, he finally moved from her glorious breasts, making a slow trek downward. He laved a path to her smooth belly where he greedily licked the area around her navel. His hand dipped to her center. She rotated her hips letting him know she wanted this.

She was slick with passion, and he grinned, feeling immense satisfaction.

My darling, there is so much more to come.

He kissed and licked as he crawled between her legs. His kisses trailed deeper, then he covered her center with his open mouth. When he flicked his tongue across her bud, she cried out.

Rebekah was so passionate. So responsive. He gloried in every moan, every whine she uttered. He pierced her hot, wet, heat with his tongue again and again, loving her taste, loving her jerking motion. He held her thighs with his hands, angling her so his tongue could thrust deeper. She latched onto his head, holding him where she wanted.

He dove into her, playing with her bud, and then he feasted. She moaned and suddenly her hips jerked off the bed as she screamed her release. He couldn't keep the grin from his face as he kissed and soothed her, giving her time to calm.

His name fell from her lips. He sighed in amazement at how much he liked it.

He glanced up to see the exquisite pleasure on her face. "Are you ready, my love?"

Good God. Had he called her his love?

Yes. He had. He'd deal with that later. Right now, he needed to be inside Rebekah.

Her eyes opened, and she gave a little nod.

His erection throbbed violently as he pressed to her opening, and then plunged.

Christ.

He gritted his teeth, overwhelmed at the astonishing sensation. Her heat surrounded him. Her muscles clenched him so ardently. He had to move.

He twisted his hips, and she grasped his shoulders. His wife was a bit possessive. He slowly pulled back and the need to surge inside her was strong. He submitted to his yearning and abandoned his struggle to go slow. Desire had him in its thrall and he was a driven man. Rebekah's sweetness enveloped him, her tremors urged him on.

Her body shifted, welcoming his thrusts. Each stroke swept him higher until he could not hold back. In wild abandonment, he filled her, the blood rushing through his veins. His heart pounded and his head was ready to explode.

And then ...

He rumbled a growl of satisfaction as his body stiffened, and mind-numbing ecstasy tore through his frame.

Aaron ran his fingers from her shoulder to her wrist and back up again, creating a tingling that shot clear to her toes.

Good heavens. She'd just had a pinnacle and he was setting off sensations of craving again.

Aaron. Lying beside her. Rebekah could scarcely believe this was real.

She wanted to pinch herself to see if she was dreaming. Instead, she snuggled deeper into him, enjoying the comfort of his touch.

Her belly still quivered from their heated lovemaking.

Aaron had made love to her. He was here, holding her now.

"I didn't exactly keep my promise, did I?"

Confusion had her sitting up. "What do you mean?"

He smirked. "I did not keep my distance."

It took her a moment to remember. In the library he promised not to hurt her. He had promised to keep his distance. She smiled, and rested her head back on his shoulder.

"I'm glad you didn't."

"Are you?"

She raised up again? Searching his eyes for his meaning. Was it possible her husband was not as sure of himself as she'd thought?

She smiled. "Am I the woman in your dreams?"

He sighed. "There is no doubt."

"None?"

Aaron lifted her hand and toyed with her fingers. "None at all. You've fulfilled every dream I've ever had. You're perfect."

"Aaron, I am not perfect. Earlier this evening, or this morning, whatever, you crashed the bedchamber door I was hiding behind."

"Not my finest moment. Are you glad?"

"Hindsight," she said. It was difficult to concentrate when he played with her fingers as he did. It was intimate. She had to look at him again to convince herself that Aaron was with her. "At the time I was terrified."

"I'm sorry. I would never have hurt you." He raised her hand to his lips and brushed a kiss over her knuckles.

She could hardly believe this was the same man.

"I wasn't so much afraid of you, as, I don't know how to explain it. I just ran, without thinking. I didn't know how you would feel about me. If you would hate me, or—"

"Have you figured out by now that I obviously do not hate you?"

She smiled. "I think so."

"Rebekah," he began—

"Uh, oh. That doesn't sound promising."

He hiked a brow. "On the contrary. I want to ask you something."

She pulled the cover about her and settled next to his side. Then realized he was still holding her hand.

"Okay. What is it?"

He stared into her eyes for the longest time. "Will you stay with me? Will you allow us to begin again?"

She was in shock. That was the last thing she'd expected.

"Yes, it's a bit surprising to me, too. But I don't want to lose you. I want you with me. As my wife in truth."

"You mean, you want this to be a real marriage?"

"I was hoping for a little less terror on your part."

"I'm ... it's not terror. I'm just surprised. Why would you ... I mean ..."

He released a short chuckle. "Why, indeed." He shifted on the bed. "Look. We started off shaky, well more than shaky. But we are married, so why not give this a chance? Give us a chance?"

A tear slipped onto her cheek, and she brushed it away.

"Now I've gone from terrifying you to wounding you. My only defense is I've been caught completely off guard, and I'm a mad man. Is there no hope for me?"

She cupped his cheek, and then the tears came in earnest. She gulped and tried to speak. "Aaron, just hold me. Please," she sniffed. "I'm a blubbering mess."

"Come here." He gathered her close, his strong arms securely around her. Once the waterworks started, she had trouble controlling them. She'd been on such an emotional whirlwind for weeks; everything was now catching up with her.

I love you.

I think I've loved you ever since that night.

When she finally got herself together, she leaned back. "Aaron. I want more than anything to be your wife."

His grin stretched from ear to ear. "At least we got the legal part out of the way."

She smiled, her heart filling with joy.

His eyes glazed over.

Then he brought his mouth to her lips—and took her breath away

Chapter 27

In the dead of night, a gentle wind scuffed over the waves cresting against the empty docks. Many ships had gone out with the tide, leaving few berths housing a ship. Non a single man was lurking about the waterfront. The scapegallows had gone on shore, leaving the bulk to be unloaded tomorrow morning. After a night of taverns and women, the captain would be lucky to get any of the crew back to the ship.

The captain was a nice enough sort, but the crew was an entirely different matter. Not one could be trusted. Ya might even get a blade for your troubles if you were dumb enough to turn yer back.

Blade hadn't had a choice. The ship's captain took him on at the last port, allowing him to work the fare off on the way to Brighton. Wasn't the first time he'd worked on a ship. Doubt it would be the last. Securing the heavy rope around the water-pillar, he took a glance in both directions. With no one in sight, he dashed across the muddy street and flattened himself against the tavern wall.

He was lucky to be alive. Thanks be to his maker and thanks to the ship that found him floating in the sea. Course he'd been unconscious at the time, is how he got so far away.

The last he remembered was sailing overboard like a seagull in flight. He'd swallowed half the sea before his mind kicked in to survival mode. Then the ship blew. Debris had landed all around hm, nearly knocking him out. He latched on to a floating piece of the ship before he passed out. He must have drifted, until another ship found him. And an angel nursed him back to life.

He'd been gone a long time. Finally found his way back, but he had to keep out of sight.

Now came the decision—to enter, or remain outside, where it was safe. Safe in the shadows. Safe in the dark.

Some might recognize him; the only one he feared was Bellingham. That Bastard had him thrown overboard with a knife sticking in his belly. Then again, Blade supposed it had been luck. When the ship blew apart, Blade was damn glad he hadn't been on it. He just hoped Bellingham was.

No guarantee. That snake had a way of showing up when ya least expected it. Blade saw the ship explode, so Bone had done the job. But he had no proof that Bellingham had met his demise.

A cloaked figure emerged from the tavern. The one Blade had been waiting for.

He trailed along behind, keeping a good distance between them. When Bone slipped around a corner, Blade knew the man would be waiting for him. Blade crept to the corner and whispered, "I know you're there. It's me."

A head with big eyes poked out. Hard to see, but then he reckoned the man couldn't see him neither.

"That you?" whispered a voice.

"Yeah," Blade replied, then hurried around the corner of the warehouse.

"Ye're a sight for sore eyes. Gads. I thought ye were a gonner."

"Seadog's men threw me overboard."

"Ya didna' jump?"

"No. I didn't have time. Besides. I was trying to keep you from gettin' noticed. They found me behind a pile of crates." Blade shrugged, then realized no one could see him. "Nothing I could do."

"At least ya got off afor' it blew."

Blade slapped a hand on Bone's shoulder. "Looks like you did too."

"They never saw me. I put enough powder on that ship to blow it to smithereens."

"I saw. Trouble was, I got hit on the head. Piece of ship come flying at me and slammed me good, and that was after Bellingham stabbed me."

"Gor, Blade. I didna' see that."

"I crawled on top of a plank of wood before I passed out. Guess I floated out to sea."

"How'd ya get back?"

"Another ship found me. I been hidin' in case Bellingham didn't go down with the ship."

"He's still skulking round. That damn Seadog too."

Blade swore under his breath. "Too bad. Those two are as ornery as the bunch I sailed in with."

Bone breathed a grunt. "If that's the case, yer lucky to still be alive."

"I am anyway." Blade poked his head around the wall to see if anyone was walking down the street. Black as night in some spots. Still, he didn't see anything. "Ya seen Bellingham around here?"

"Yeah. And he's got a whole new crew with a ship to match."

"Blimey." Blade said, shaking his head. "What happened to their captain?"

"Dead, most like." Bone spit a wad of juice to the ground. "I know a gent gonna be real glad to see ya."

"Who?"

"Aaron Greystoke."

"He's just the man I need to see. Got any passage going up north? I might could tag along?"

"Got some horses. We never quit looking fer ya. Come on."

———ele———

Shadows lingered in every corner. Bellingham pressed up to the planked wall as he peered around the sharp corner. Waves lapped against the hull of several ships lining the docks. He only needed to find one.

He'd handed over one hundred pounds for the information. A bloody fortune when his resources had dwindled after the explosion. A costly mistake. One that all the brothers would regret.

Damn Greystoke. Damn them all to hell. Dumb luck he'd gotten off that ship.

Bellingham slipped behind a storehouse, blending in with the other ruffians that frequented the dockside taverns. Not a savory lot. Just like the new crew he commanded. A fight most every night broke out between the men. These cutthroats would sooner slit a man's gullet for one blimey coin.

Since the brothers were looking for him, he had stuck mostly to the ship. For the trek to London, he'd traveled by land, using the dense woods for cover. While keeping to the shadows, he happened upon another of Greystoke's men, and now he stalked the man like a thief after a rich purse. How ironic—spies spying on spies.

Aaron, the youngest brother of the three, was in cahoots with the lower life of London. Men for hire, whatever the job might be, until the bloody morals got in the way. Bellingham had no such qualms. He didn't give a tinker's damn what a bloke had to do, as long as the job got done. But for the Greystoke brothers, Bellingham wanted the pleasure of destroying those three himself.

The man he followed was slipping in and out of shadows, making sure not to be followed. That meant he was headed to a secret meeting. *With Aaron?* Bellingham hoped so. He'd like to take the brother out with one thrust of his blade.

On to the next phase of his plan. He had to restore his capital. Luck had a way of getting him through most any situation. And his wit. He could talk his way into and out of about any circumstance. If one plan failed, he made another. What better motivator than greed. An emotion all too familiar.

The man came to a sudden halt. Bellingham jumped out of sight just in the nick of time. The hairs stood on the back of his neck. He tugged the cap low over his brow and did not dare move. He'd hoped to find one of the Greystoke brothers. If he had brought men with him, he'd be prepared for all three. Since he was alone—

Bloody hell.

The man was nowhere in sight. Bellingham looked left, then right. No one on the street. Not one shadow moved. He hurried several steps to the last place he'd seen the man. A dark figure jumped at him, grabbing his arm and shoulder in a hold, with a thick blade stretching his neck.

"I knew I was being followed, but I didn't knowd it was you."

"You have the wrong man. I mean you no harm. I was minding my own business."

"Is that a fact?" The man chuckled. "Imagine the reward I'm gonna get for you."

"No one will pay for me. I'm nobody."

The man loosened his hold. Before Bellingham could make a move, he was spinning around and pinned with a hard wall at his back. The man had the strength of five burly seagoers. But his eyes. His eyes gleamed with an icy chill that sent shivers down Bellingham's back.

"I knowd who you be. I also knowd the gent I give you to will pay. I'm meeting me friends down there." The man gave a jerk of his head. "Now get walking. And don't try nothin'."

Bellingham counted the seconds until the long, thick blade was moved. He released his breath and staggered as he was pushed.

Bloody fucking hell.

<hr />

"Where's Bellingham?"

"I aint' his keeper."

Samuel locked his jaw to keep from losing his temper. These cutthroats were the worst lot he'd ever commanded. Since he was their new captain, and he was clearly outnumbered, he chose his words carefully.

"Have you seen him?"

"Yesterdee. Dressed in old clothes, like the rest of us."

"You haven't seen him since yesterday?"

"That's what I said."

Samuel wanted to sock the man in the jaw, but the cur took his big knife out and rubbed his thumb along its edge. A drop of blood slid down the ten inch, razor-sharp blade.

He got the message, but Samuel hadn't lived this long by being timid.

"Any idea where he is now?"

"Said something about payback. Figure he's after an old debt."

Bollocks.

Bellingham couldn't be dumb enough to go after the Greystoke brothers alone. The man wasn't stupid, but he wasn't invisible, either. Even dressed like the riffraff on the waterfront, he could still be noticed.

Where the bloody hell had he gone?

"Let's get something straight. I'm yer captain. If ya want to see another coin, you'll get off your arse and help me find 'em." Samuel glared at the man, eye to eye, not backing down.

"I heered tell Bellingham has pretty big pockets," the cur said, sheathing his knife. "That's good enough for me."

By the time Samuel left the tavern, he'd rounded up three more. The five of them set out to find their boss.

Chapter 28

"Good afternoon, Aunt." Aaron bent down to kiss her cheek.

"Where have you been?"

He raised a brow in question. "Last time I checked, Aunt, I wasn't required to account for my comings and goings."

"Do not be impertinent."

Aaron grinned like a well-tupped fool.

"Forgive me, Aunt. You seem tense. Is there some emergency?"

"No emergency. I've been waiting." She placed her teacup on the center table.

"I had no idea you expected me for tea."

"Are you going to continue as though nothing happened? I must admit, Aaron, if I had not seen you, I would never have believed you were capable of such a maddening display. Is Rebekah all right?"

"She is more than all right, Aunt. She is wonderful."

Every enticing inch.

Penelope's shock was expected. But then, he loved being obscure.

"Why don't you come see for yourself?"

"I trust you got control of your temper and set things to right."

"I did. Aunt, you will be glad to know that Rebekah and I have come to an understanding. Our marriage will not be annulled."

"You've killed the poor girl and hidden her body."

"What's that?" Nathaniel said as he came into the drawing room.

"Aunt is feeling quite herself," Aaron said, tongue in cheek.

"Where is Rebekah?"

"As I told Aunt, Rebekah is fine. In fact, we both are."

"You have no idea how hard it was to leave her there with you. I don't see any cuts or bruises on you. Start talking before I plant you on the floor."

"No need to get your britches in a twist, brother. All is well in my household."

"I'll believe that when I see for myself."

"Aaron seems in rather a chipper mood, don't you agree Nathaniel?"

Serena came running into the room. "Oh. I thought. Where is Rebekah?"

"For you, Serena, I shall repeat myself. Rebekah is fine. I am fine. I came over to let Aunt know the house is still in one piece and she can come home. As for Rebekah, she is resting. Our discussion took longer than either one of us expected."

There. Stew on that. He was not about to inform them that most of their *conversation* had been in bed.

He couldn't keep the grin from his lips. Rebekah was truly his wife in every way that mattered.

Serena looked to her husband, then Aunt, and back to him.

"Do you not believe me, Serena?"

"Of, of course."

"You're being evasive, Aaron."

He released a heavy sigh as he sat down across from his aunt. "Are you taking me to task, Aunt?"

"Should I?"

"Now who's being sassy?"

He lifted the teapot and found it empty. "I guess you were not expecting me." He rose and went to the sideboard, then poured himself a brandy. He swallowed it whole, then poured another. When he turned, three pairs of eyes were fixed on him.

"Do you really think I would hurt her?"

"Throwing a chair through a locked door would make anyone suspicious," Nathaniel replied.

"Then why did you leave her there alone with me? You know I would never harm a woman." He turned to his aunt. "You, my dear Aunt, understand me quite well. It was you who chose to leave, and convinced this donkey's butt to go with you."

"Pour me a sherry."

Aaron glanced up at his brother. Nathaniel went to the sideboard and filled a tiny crystal wine glass, then gave it to Penelope.

"Now. Tell us the all of it."

"Forgive me, Aunt. But you don't need to know everything. Rest assured that Rebekah and I have worked out our differences."

"Why didn't she come with you?"

Aaron recalled the sleeping beauty stretched out on his bed. He took his seat, then asked, "What did I do to earn your discourse?"

"You left the ball amiable, so I thought. What happened that made you so furious?

"She locked the door." At his aunt's raised brow, he held up a hand. "I know. I was wrong to do so. I cannot explain exactly why, but I thought she was lying to me. And I wanted answers.

She knew some very important information that she had not shared with me."

"What information?"

Aaron took a swallow of brandy. "She knew everything that happened that night. I regained a flash of memory, and when I questioned her about it, she ran. When I found the door locked, I lost my temper. I wanted her to fill in the blanks, and I was not about to let her keep secrets from me."

"I must say, I was shocked when I heard you yelling. When I heard the crashing of the door, I thought you'd gone mad."

Aaron scrubbed a hand through the hair he'd left unbound. "I, uh, surprised myself. I was angry, and I do appreciate you trusting me enough to get out and let me finish what I'd started."

Aunt glared, and Serena gasped.

"Oh, don't look so panicked. "I told her there would be no locked doors between us and to please meet me in the library to finish our discussion. She did. We sorted everything out."

Nathaniel crossed his arms over his chest. "There's definitely something you're leaving out."

"You are my brother, Nathaniel. Not my counsellor."

"I've always had a soft spot for you, Aaron. With Nathaniel taking off, you've burdened yourself with responsibilities you did not need to carry. You see this as another responsibility. Can you not accept it for what it is?"

"And what is that?"

"You have a wife now. A chance for happiness."

He was happy. He was *very* happy. However, Aunt did not need to know the intimate details.

"I have given you free rein over my house, and most of my public life. I have done your bidding, even when it went against my will. I suggest you leave my personal business to me."

"You cannot manipulate Rebekah."

"Oh? And what about your recent demands. Is that not manipulation? Good God, I had no idea Rebekah was in London. You ambushed me quite well."

His aunt stiffened. "For pity sakes, Aaron. I had to do something."

"She has your mark upon her. The woman I left in Surrey was no educated miss. No debutante. Certainly not a socialite. You laid me low, Aunt."

"Aaron, that was not my intention. You needed to be with your wife."

For once, he was glad for Aunt's interference. *Rebekah.* He breathed in and out, willing his anxiousness not to show. Rebekah was elegant perfection in every aspect. Beautiful. Desirable. He could hardly wait to get home.

Serena approached him. "Rebekah is truly all right?"

"My dear sister-in-law. I would never hurt a woman. Rebekah is fine."

She studied his eyes. "I believe you."

"Thank goodness someone does."

"I never said—"

"Leave it Nathaniel. Thank you for bringing Aunt to your home. As I said, it is safe for her to return."

His aunt's expression was puzzled. "I'm not sure why I'm hesitating. Perhaps, since the two of you are newlywed, and still have much to learn about each other, perhaps I should stay here for a while."

"Your home is with me. I shall not move you out because I'm moving Rebekah in."

"Penelope, I think that's a wonderful idea," Serena cried. "The baby will be here soon. I would love to have your company."

"Then it's settled," Nathaniel said. "I've been at my wits end worrying about the baby's arrival. I would feel much better if you were here with Serena," he told Aunt.

Aaron could not have planned this better himself. Not that he wanted Aunt out of his house, but now that he and Rebekah had settled their differences, it would be nice having his wife all to himself.

"It would seem I've lost a house guest. Aunt, know that you may return home, any time you like."

"I like the idea of being with Serena during her last month. I'll go back with you, to see Rebekah for myself. Then Anna can help me pack. I will bring her with me."

"As you wish, Aunt."

Serena bubbled with her glee. "I'm so excited. Aunt Penelope, it will be grand having you here. Maybe you can help me make some booties for the baby."

"I've already made a blanket."

"How do you know which color to use?" Nathaniel asked.

"A son of yours would be in nothing but blue. I chose blue. A girl can like blue."

"Of course she can." Serena's hand covered Aunt's.

As his family droned on about the baby that wasn't here yet, Aaron couldn't help counting the minutes until he could get home to Rebekah.

Alone in the house.

Just the two of them.

———ele———

Pure luck the dumb bastard fell into their hands. Pauly and Basil knew right off who the man was. Bellingham hadn't covered his tracks well enough to outsmart them. Basil could spot an interloper with his eyes closed.

The man tried to be someone else, but Pauly knew Bellingham. Too much scuttlebutt about the man. His name was on every tongue from here to Brighton. It was only a matter of time. Now they had him.

"How about tethering my hands in front of me so I can hold on?"

"If'n ya fall off, we'll let the horse drag your carcass. Don't matter to us none."

Suddenly a wild yell echoed from the trees, sounding much like an animal screaming. The horses spooked, and before Pauly knew it, a rider was bearing down on them. More came from the forest. By the time he calmed his horse, they were surrounded.

Pauly didn't recognize any of the night riders. But he was familiar with the Seadog.

"Throw down your weapons!"

Basil and Pauly didn't have a chance. Seadog walked his horse up to Bellingham, and cut the rope binding his hands.

"You all right?"

"They were taking me to Greystoke. Kill the fools."

Basil and Pauly looked at each other. Neither one was ready to meet their maker.

Seadog gave the order to his men.

The band just sat their horses. Nary a one moved. They looked like the scum of the earth, and didn't cotton to following orders blindly.

Basil kicked his horse, and Pauly did the same. They got the hell out of there. He shot into the trees and thanked the cover of darkness.

He heard no riders coming after them.

Pauly rode fast and furious, Basil at his side. They did not slow or stop until he saw the house of the younger Greystoke. He and Basil leaped to the ground and rushed the steps up to the back door. He pounded with his fist.

"Hold your horses. I'm coming."

The door opened and a woman stood there with a frying pan in her hand. Pauly had important business, he wasn't worried about a woman, even if she welded and iron skillet.

"Where's Greystoke? It's urgent." A man hurriedly stepped behind her. "May I help you?"

"Get Greystoke. Bellingham is here."

Chapter 29

B *ellingham was back.*

Aaron had known the bastard was too mean to die.

His first thought—protect his family. As he wrote a missive to his brothers, his thoughts were on Rebekah. He would kill any man that dared to harm her. He needed to alert her of the danger. He rushed to the parlor and found a maid. "Where is my wife?"

The startled maid clutched her chest. "Uh, she went outside."

He was off and down the staircase in a flash. He ran to the back of the house and headed to the stables. He found Rebekah in the flower garden.

"Rebekah," he sighed in relief.

"Aaron? What is the matter?"

He calmed his racing heart. It would not do at all to scare her. "I need to speak with you."

She stood and brushed the dirt from her day dress. "Of course. Has something happened? Is Penelope—"

"Aunt is fine." She was at Nathaniel's, she had to be fine. He took his wife's hands in his. Good God. *His wife.* Would he ever get used to the term?

Her worried gaze searched his.

He took a deep breath and spoke slowly. "I have to tell you about someone from my very recent past, who is no longer in my past. He's a dangerous man. His name is Bellingham. Thaddeus Bellingham. 'Tis a long story, so I think we should sit down for this."

"Would you like to go back inside?"

Did he? It didn't matter.

"Yes, let's go to the drawing room." He escorted her back to the house. Thank God, Rebekah was a woman who knew when to keep quiet. He could imagine another woman, or even his aunt spouting a million questions.

Cook was in the kitchen.

"Would you have Susanna bring tea to the drawing room, please." Rebekah was preparing for the afternoon. She must have suspected this would take a while.

Cook had seen his mad dash out the kitchen door. Her expression was one of confusion, but she made no comment.

Aaron took Rebekah's elbow and steered her down the long hallway. Once they were in the drawing room, he led her to the sofa. "This isn't secret information, so I'll close the door after Susanna leaves." He sat down beside his wife.

"'Tis a long story. I'll go back a few years. When our father died, Nathaniel left, no one knew where. Edmund was running the estate as though he was the heir. He didn't want the title; he was simply doing what needed to be done until Nathaniel's return."

Lifting his hand, he used a finger to point at his ear. "Edmund had a bone pressing on a nerve that caused him severe headaches. The idiot tried to hide his megrims from everyone. He was a bear. Took quite a while for us to find out there was a problem. I wrote to Nathaniel and told him he had to come home. I thought Edmund would never forgive me for sending for our brother. But that's another story."

Unable to stay seated, he stood and started pacing.

"You'll have to get Joyanna to tell you her story with Edmund."

"She has already told me some."

Aaron stopped, and turned to look at Rebekah? "She has? Well, that's good." He took another look at his wife's face and could kick his own arse. His wife was terrified. He went back to the sofa and sat down.

"I'm sorry, darling. I didn't mean to scare you." He rubbed the back of her hands with his thumbs. "I'm so glad to have you for my wife. I mean that."

She smiled. "I am glad I married you, my husband."

He kissed her fingers, then lowered her hand to his lap. "Bellingham is a swindler, to put it kindly. He carries illegal goods on his ship, and tried to get his hands on Greystoke Manor. Along the coast there are caves. Perfect for his smuggling operation. At the time Edmund was having his headaches, Bellingham took advantage and used the caves to hide his cargo. When Nathaniel came back, everything came out in the open." Aaron rubbed a hand through his hair. "Including the kind of man Bellingham truly was."

"There is so much I have to learn. What happened?"

"Nathaniel was shot, for one."

Rebekah gasped. "He what?"

"Nathaniel, Edmund and I went to the caves, the smugglers caught us, and Nathaniel was shot."

"Good Lord, Aaron. I mean, I don't know what to say first. Were you okay? Are you all right. Obviously, Nathaniel is alive, but how bad was it? I can't believe you are telling me this so calmly."

"The idea was not to upset you. I have failed, miserably."

"No, you did a good job of keeping yourself calm. Surely you did expect some reaction from me. I mean, Good heavens!"

"Yes, Rebekah. We all are fine. It was touch and go there for a while with Nathaniel. That's a story for Serena to enlighten you."

"We did a lot of talking. She and Joyanna both said they had long stories, but my heavens, I had no idea.

"Aaron, are you truly all right. You seem physically fine ..."

"Darling, I'm good."

"You promise?"

He lifted her fingers to his mouth for a lingering kiss. Then for good measure, he leaned in and took her mouth in a heated one. When he pulled back, he and Rebekah both were breathing heavily.

"If you want to hear the rest, we have to stop that." Damn, he'd rather take her to bed.

"Postpone." Rebekah grinned.

"Yes, postpone." It amazed him how much he cared for his wife. Every day, every moment with her was astonishing. Now that they had been honest with each other, the hours they spent together were perfect.

He hated that those moments were about to change.

"Rebekah," he sighed, and could not continue. Her eyes dug a hole all the way to his soul. He wanted to say the words. Hell, why couldn't he say the words.

"I know, Aaron." She placed her palm to his cheek, with her love shining in her eyes.

"When you look at me that way, I can't think," he whispered.

He shook his head to break the spell he was falling into.

"We tried to get rid of Bellingham." Aaron ran a hand through his hair. He seemed to be doing that a lot. "I thought he was gone, but he's back. I just found out he's in London."

"What does that mean? Should we leave? Are you safe?"

"I'm sorry, Rebekah. We need to be careful, but I will protect you with my life. You have no reason to worry. I won't let him near you."

"What about you?"

He was dumbfounded for a moment. "Me?"

"Aaron, I trust you. But who will protect you from him?"

He grinned a satisfied, gratifying grin. He placed his hands on both sides of her face.

This was the moment.

He felt more for this woman than he knew was possible. She held his heart. He wanted Rebekah forever. Now that he finally admitted his love, he needed to tell her.

"Do you have any idea how much I love you?"

She gasped. She stared at him as tears filled her eyes. "Oh, Aaron. I love you. So much. For so long."

What? So long?

"I've been an absolute cad." He brought her to his chest, wrapping his arms around her. "I had no idea what I was feeling. I suppose I've been in love with you for a while, too."

She cried in earnest. He felt her tears soaking his shirt.

"I hope those are happy tears."

She balled her fist as she leaned back. "You know they are." She wacked him on the shoulder. "I am happy. I'm so happy. Oh, Aaron, I love you."

When she leaned in, he gathered her as close as he could, kissing her with everything he felt, everything he had been feeling.

It was bliss.

Chapter 30

Seemed like old times. Aaron and his brothers were chasing Bellingham again. And his good friend, Blade, was home at last. The reunion had been brief, since Blade was not one for sentiment. Besides, he'd been ready to get his own payback.

"We feared you were dead."

"Too ornery to die. Sides, I have a score to settle with Seadog."

"I never gave up on you, old friend."

"I'm glad for that. Had a rough go for a few days. Could'a bled out. Lucky a mate was in the crow's nest and spotted me. Not sure how long I'd been a sea a'for they found me."

Aaron slapped Blade on the back. "You're here now. What news do you have for us?" Blade glanced to Pauly. "Pauly had the bastard in his clutches, and Seadog showed up with men."

"An unsavory lot. No loyalty among them," Pauly said. "Seadog got Bellingham, but the men with him had no interest in us. We got away. Rode here as fast as we could."

Thank God Aaron had been home to receive them.

"Two of our men found Bellingham's trail." Blade stated. "The men he hired don't care about covering their tracks."

"They be for coin only." Basil filled in the rest. "The higher bidder gets their services. Only a few men went with Seadog. If they don't get paid, they'll leave soon enough."

Aaron spoke up. "The plan is to find Bellingham and Seadog before he gets back with his band."

Blade introduced the man standing beside him. "This here is Kitsune, another name for Moon Fox. He got his name for his unique hunting method. Some believe he is a spirit, cause he finds things and most time people can't see him.

The man gave a nod. "He is holed up in a cabin."

Aaron had heard the name Kitsune in relation to Japanese folklore. He didn't care if the man was a ghost, as long as he found Bellingham.

Bellingham had become an obsession. Closer to a sore that wouldn't go away. Kept festering up. Aaron and his brothers were determined to get rid of the man permanently.

"He's too dangerous. If he's back in the area, he's out for blood." Nathaniel looked to Edmund and then Aaron. "He's here for us."

Edmund's mouth turned up in a wrathful sneer. "He's targeted each of us in one way or another. Are we in agreement we will do whatever it takes to protect our family?"

The question was a momentous one. Nathaniel had Serena. Edmund had Joyanna. Thank the saints, he'd found Rebekah. And they all had Aunt Penelope. Nothing was more important than their family.

Aaron spoke up quickly. "Agreed."

So did Nathaniel.

—ele—

"You know Serena is going to kill me if I get shot a second time."

"If you're already dead, how is she going to kill you? That's an unnecessary fear, brother," Edmund goaded. "If you're truly worried, blame Aaron."

Aaron paused to look over his shoulder. "Why me?"

"Because, you're the one who told us the bastard was back."

Edmund had an answer for everything.

"Wait a minute, Bellingham came after the manor, and you are the earl," Aaron told Nathaniel. "He originally came after you."

Nathaniel didn't miss a step. He continued through the thick brushwood. "That's right. But he left."

"We blew him up," Edmund corrected.

"He wasn't on the ship," Nathaniel shot back.

Edmund shrugged. "Didn't know that now, did we?"

Aaron scowled. He didn't even know Bellingham existed until the gossip reached him—the man was living at the manor. "We should blame Edmund. He's the one who introduced the man to Greystoke Manor."

"Are you two going to play footsies, or get on with this carnival." Edmund may have felt guilty, but he wanted Bellingham out of their lives just as badly.

Nathaniel came to a halt. "Still got that dagger in your boot?"

Edmund's dagger was more a machete than a knife. It was a wonder he didn't cut his bloody foot off with a blade that big.

"I got it. But if my aim is true with this pistol, I won't be needing it."

Blade motioned them forward. He said little, but his steps were determined.

After hours of tramping through heavy overgrowth, Kitsune brought them to a sudden halt. "Just beyond those trees is his shelter. That's where we'll find him, if he's still there."

Kitsune turned out to be as skilled as Blade had said.

"I don't know how you found him, Blade, but I'm glad he's on our side," Aaron told Blade.

"Last count, he has four men with him," Kitsune said.

"To our seven, hopefully this won't take long."

Blade signaled to the men to circle the small dwelling. Aaron took a quick glance at his brothers to see if they were ready. Each one gave a nod.

Blade crept through the grass to the open clearing. No one stood guard. Most likely, Bellingham wasn't expecting anyone to find him.

Kitsune scurried across the open space and made it to the corner of the little house. When nothing happened, he signaled for the others to follow. Blade took one step, and a shot was fired.

Aaron cursed. Thank God it missed.

Nathaniel strode to the front. "You're surrounded, Bellingham. You won't get away this time. Come on out."

"You're crazy, Greystoke. There's no way I'm coming out. I've got plenty of men in here with me."

"There's more out here. Like I said, you're surrounded."

Several minutes passed.

"How about a truce? Look." The door opened a little and a white cloth waved through the doorway. "I'm waving a flag. I'm not surrendering. I want to talk."

"All right, talk," Nathaniel yelled back.

"You gonna shoot me?"

"I should," Nathaniel said where only Aaron could hear.

"He's not going to give up, Nathaniel. He'll always be a threat to us."

"I know that." He shouted to Bellingham, "No, I won't shoot."

"In that case, I'm coming out." Bellingham stepped through the doorway, onto the blocked porch.

"You have a lot of bollocks, Bellingham."

"You said you wouldn't shoot. You're a man of your word, Greystoke."

Nathaniel took a step and Edmund grabbed his arm. "No."

"He wants to talk."

"So he says. You shouldn't expose yourself."

"He trusted me."

Edmund gave a grunt. "You cannot trust him."

Nathaniel shook his head.

"No brother," Aaron said, agreeing with Edmund.

Nathaniel ignored them both and walked into the clearing. "Here I am Bellingham. What do you propose?"

"Well now. All I ever wanted was access to the caves on the coast. I wouldn't be hurting your property."

"I don't want you on my property."

A shot rang out. Nathaniel hit the ground.

Aaron felt a pain tear through his chest and wanted to scream. Shoot the devil, or see if his brother was still alive.

Several shots were fired.

He couldn't keep still. He ran to Nathaniel's side.

"Get down, you fool." Nathaniel grabbed Aaron's shirt and face planted him into the dirt.

Thank Christ, his brother was alive.

"You playing faux?"

"You will too, if you want to stay alive."

Silence.

"We got 'em." Blade called.

Edmund came stomping up to them. "You two want to get up now?"

Aaron raised his head and saw several bodies on the ground. Bellingham on the stone porch. Aaron jumped to his feet. "Is he dead?"

"He's dead," Pauly said. "He was keeping yer brother busy talking, while his friend here, pointed his pistol right at his heart. I got him. One of the others got yer man."

"I did," Edmund admitted. "I owed the bastard. He had a pistol hid behind his back. When the first shot went off, he brought up his gun. Didn't know if you were alive, brother, but I knew the bastard responsible was going to hell."

Nathaniel clasped Edmund on the back. "Thanks, Edmund." Then he looked at Aaron. "Good thing, or Aaron might have been shot too. Idiot came to me. His gun still in his hand."

"So, I checked on our brother instead of killing a man. Big deal. I knew the dumbass was faking."

"No, you didn't."

Aaron tuned his brothers out as they continued to taunt him. Was it really over? He strode to the stones where Bellingham lie, to see for himself. He had two bullet holes in him, so one of the other men had shot him, too. Good. Edmund didn't need that encumbrance solely on him.

Two men lay dead on the floor inside.

"We got two more over here," another man called out. "Wouldn't surrender. Rather have a bullet, I guess."

Basil came walking around the side. Blood covered his clothes and hands.

"Are you all right?"

"Seadog. Had a lot of fight left in 'em. I got 'em." Basil pointed. "Over there."

Good God.

Aaron shook his head.

"I wasn't expecting this." Nathaniel sighed.

"What were you expecting, brother?" Edmund asked.

"I don't know, but not death. Not like this. All of them."

"You go on, Lord Greystoke," Blade said. "I'll take care of this."

Aaron stepped next to Blade. "I'll stay with Blade. I'll be here if any legal questions need answering."

Someone would have to answer to this mess. Nathaniel might be the earl, and he could speak to authorities later, if need be. Blade was Aaron's friend. He would stay and make sure his friend was all right.

Epilogue

Travis Alexander Blackburn Greystoke was the center of attention. He'd come into the world kicking and screaming, telling the world the newest Greystoke had arrived. Of course, the brothers had to meet their nephew, and celebrate the new heir of Greystoke.

While the men drank brandy, the women cooed over the newborn babe. Aunt cried. She would deny it, but the dear woman held that little infant and gazed on him like he was the only baby in the world. The proud Papa would most likely agree with her.

"To the new heir of Greystoke." Nathaniel raised his glass.

"Here. Here." Edmund echoed.

"I can think of no better reason to celebrate," Aaron added. It would seem the Greystoke line would continue.

"A few more toasts and you will need to open another bottle, Nathaniel."

The proud father grinned from ear to ear. "I bought a case just for the occasion."

"Good show." Edmund emptied his glass and held it out for more.

"I suppose the ton will be wondering what the Greystoke Brothers will do next." The ton spent too much time gossiping about Aaron and his brothers. With the three of them off the market, as Aunt would put it, the gossipmongers would need to find a new scapegoat to sink their teeth into. He could care less. All of his focus was on his wife.

He glanced over to Rebekah, and his breath caught in his throat. It was hard to believe the beautiful woman belonged to him. From this day forward, he vowed to treasure the gift he'd been given.

"With all three of us married and off the market, the ton will need to find a new clan to wager on."

"An indiscretion is bound to make itself known." All eyes turned to Aunt Penelope. The woman was above reproach, but she had her secrets. And the woman was a master at hiding them.

He laughed.

"And the lord or lady will be fodder for the gossip mill," Nathaniel added.

"I care not for the wagers. I have a wedding to attend." Edmund gazed at Joyanna adoringly.

Good God. The brothers had become saps.

"That will definitely be in White's book."

"We are not here to place wagers. We are toasting my son."

"Here. Here."

Aaron rebuked his brother. "You might want to wait for the toast, Edmund."

"Whatever it is, I'm for opening another bottle." Edmund turned his focus to Nathaniel. "This is excellent brandy, brother. Did you perhaps, find it in the caves?"

"Thank God, that bounder is gone," Nathaniel said with a shake of his head.

"Here. Here." Edmund took a swallow from his topped off glass. "You didn't answer my question."

"No, Edmund. I did not find a case of brandy in the caves."

"Where'd you get it?" Aaron asked.

"Let's say I found a new merchant."

Edmund chuckled. "I knew this was bloody good stuff."

"Nathaniel, as much as I enjoy our refreshment, don't get so imbibed that you won't be able to help your wife tend to the baby this evening." What were brothers for, if they couldn't gibe each other?

"That's what nannies are for," Edmund replied.

"Good God, don't let your wife hear you say that?"

"Why? It's not my wife who just had a baby."

"I believe, brother, you are on your way to being tanked."

"You always could drink me under the table."

Aaron grinned, proud of that statement. "I must congratulate you, Nathaniel, on a job well done."

"Thank you, brother." Nathaniel clinked his glass with Aaron, then turned it bottoms up.

As much as Aaron liked to imbibe his wife might not be too happy with him, either, if he got sloshed. But then, he'd never had a problem with whisky. Until…

Aaron glanced over to the women, and singled out his wife. However it had come about, he thanked the saints again that he was married to the love of his life.

The baby cooed, and the women sighed.

Aaron could not believe a living being could be so small. "Surely we were never that tiny."

Edmund gave him a look. "You do know where babies come from?"

Aaron's brows screwed up on his forehead. "What the devil kind of questions is that?"

"A woman can only bare a baby so big."

Now he felt like an ass. "No need to get specific, brother."

"Then don't act like a dunce."

Aaron tried to explain. "I just meant, look how big we are now."

"It's called growing up."

Smart mouth.

Aaron shot right back. "Too bad you never did."

Nathaniel spoke up, interrupting. "One day, Travis will be as tall as me."

"Or me," Aaron couldn't help but antagonize his brother.

Nathaniel glared. "A quarter inch, brother?"

Aaron laughed. "Can't stand it, can you?"

"I believe I'll go speak with someone who actually possesses some intelligence." Nathaniel sauntered off to go look at his offspring.

He was a cute little bugger, all red and wrinkled. The way he was wrapped up, his face was the only thing showing. But Serena assured them he had all of his fingers and toes. And a mass of curly hair.

The clencher was how something so small could have such a big impact. Everyone in the room was focused on the tiny bundle. Every person in that room was ready to do battle for him. Travis had their love and their loyalty. With so much love for one little creature, the baby was bound to grow up happy.

He would have a very different upbringing than Aaron and his brothers.

The room had grown quiet. He supposed the baby had gone to sleep. Little stirrings of babies and children danced about in Aaron's mind.

"Good God, it was not that long ago I didn't want a wife. Now I'm thinking about children."

Edmund slapped Aaron on the back. "Welcome to married life, brother."

"You have two more weeks before the noose goes around your neck."

"And never has a man so willingly went to the gallows." Edmund laughed.

"You two behave. You don't want to scare little Travis."

Aaron looked over his shoulder as his wife stepped next to his side. "He's asleep," Aaron told her.

"And Serena would like to keep him that way."

"That's my cue to go to my fiancée. Two more weeks, brother. I can hardly wait."

Aaron pulled Rebekah into his arms. "Is it me, or is that baby making everyone in this room maudlin?"

"Babies can do that. They are so sweet. So innocent."

"Before I met you, I didn't even think of having a wife or a family. You've humbled me, Rebekah. I am nothing without you."

"I love you, darling."

"And I love you, wife." He gave a slight shake of his head. "I don't know if I will ever get used to saying *my wife*. It seems so surreal."

He enfolded her in a warm embrace, enjoying the feel of Rebekah in his arms. "My brother looks happy."

"He is a proud father."

"He has a wife who loves him, and now a son. Gives a man ideas."

"Oh? What kind of ideas?"

Aaron looked down at his wife. God, he loved this woman.

"I am who I am, Rebekah. I married you, and every day I'm glad of it. I want you with me for always. I wouldn't have it any other way."

"Neither would I. I love you, Aaron."

"Every time you look at me, I feel loved. I think it would be nice to have a little one with your eyes. I can hardly imagine a little girl looking at me the way you do."

Rebekah smiled the most beautiful, most rewarding smile a woman could give a man. His heart was ready to burst.

Before he could stop himself, he was lowering his mouth to hers.

THE END

Thank You

Thank you for reading my story. I hope you enjoyed reading it as much as I loved writing it.
And, if you did, would you consider leaving a review online? It really would mean the world to me.

Thank you!
Samanthya

The Right One For Me

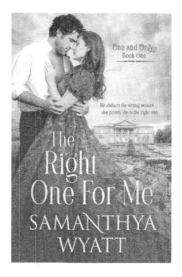

In a sizzling case of mistaken identity, the feisty and stubbornly unwed Katherine finds herself the captive of the swoon-worthy Morgan, Earl of Whetherford. She may not be the woman he intended to take, but she could be exactly the woman he needs...

Order your copy of *The Right One For Me*,
Scan the QR code below!

About the Author

S amanthya Wyatt writes sizzling hot romance with suspense. Intensely emotional characters with a deep passionate love for friends, family, and most importantly—between the hero and heroine. Although her first love is historical romance, this award-winning author also writes contemporary romance under the pen name S. R. Wyatt. Additionally, she has written a book of one family's struggle based on true life events.

Samanthya left her accounting career and married a military man traveling and making her home in the United States and abroad. She now lives in the Shenandoah Valley. On a sunny day, you can find her and her husband driving on the Blue Ridge Parkway or going to car shows in their 1969 Mustang convertible. She loves long walks, and a book to read on a sandy beach. Starbucks is her favorite drink and she likes hearing from her fans.

She invites you to lay the worries of the world off your shoulders and get lost in the pages of a romance, where you embark on a journey with the hero and heroine, become involved in a dream, plunge into a world of fantasy, and live an adventure your heart can share.

To find out more about Samanthya Wyatt and her books, please visit her website: https://samanthyawyattauthor.com/

Made in United States
North Haven, CT
17 September 2024